An Unexpected Roomie

Laura Langa

AN UNEXPECTED ROOMIE
Copyright © 2024 by Laura Langa

All rights reserved.

No part of this publication may be reproduced, stored or transmitted in any form or by any means, electronic, mechanical, photocopying, recording, scanning, or otherwise without written permission from the publisher. It is illegal to copy this book, post it to a website, or distribute it by any other means without permission.

This novel is entirely a work of fiction. The names, characters and incidents portrayed in it are the work of the author's imagination. Any resemblance to actual persons, living or dead, events or localities is entirely coincidental.

ISBN-13: 979-8-9878301-1-6

Cover design by: Enni Tuomisalo

By Laura Langa

<u>*LOVE TUCSON*</u>
Haley and the Yeti
Date the Alphabet
An Unexpected Roomie

My Heart Before You

A Guarded Heart

Between Our Hearts

For those who think they aren't enough.
You ARE enough.
Whoever told you that you weren't was wrong—
even if that person was you.

Chapter 1

"I'd do literally anything for you." Meg rolled the windows down, allowing the early summer air to infiltrate the car. True to her word, her best friend hadn't blinked at the request to pick Claire up from a swanky resort on the outskirts of Tucson first thing in the morning.

"Samesies," Claire said through a smile, letting her hand surf the desert breeze.

"I'd do one of those crazy bridge jumps. I'd get a snake massage with you." Meg shuddered, her long, auburn-brown hair bouncing. "If you were ever in a coma, I'd break into the hospital just to pluck that one stubborn chin hair that grows alarmingly fast."

Since becoming each other's *person* at the pivotal age of twelve, there'd been an invisible tether between them that'd tenaciously persisted even through living in different cities over the last nine years.

"But I can't take you back to my townhouse because"—Meg sucked in a ginormous breath—"I moved out and didn't tell anyone. My boyfriend has an Airstream, and as of tomorrow, we're going on a month-long tour up the coast, and then, I'm moving in with him." Her shoulders climbed toward her ears. "I thought you'd be here in July. You were going to be our first house guest. I'm sorry. Don't be mad."

Claire's brows knitted above her heart-shaped aviators. "Why would I be mad? That sounds like a blast."

That niggling worry over her own ability to travel again rose like heartburn, but Claire pushed it down—just like she'd been doing for the last three months when unwanted medical symptoms kept popping up like chiggers.

"But I'll miss you. Right?" The way Meg huffed almost made her laugh. "You haven't been home in what? Forever? And now I'm going to miss you."

Claire bit her lip. "You won't miss me. I plan to stay a while."

Meg skidded her Jeep Rubicon onto the side of the road, almost toppling the row of colorful rubber ducks on her dashboard. "Shut up! For how long?" She pushed her oversized sunglasses onto her head as displaced dust snuck into the open window.

"It's past time to highlight Tucson on my account," Claire said as casually as possible.

Her immensely popular solo-travel OnlyApp account—@CtheUSwithClaire—focused on finding the best outdoor places to visit in each state. Having tens of thousands of people following her verified, orange-checkboxed account still felt surreal even after all these years. The transition from recreational traveler to social media influencer had been as unexpected as it'd been swift. So much of her early adventures had been supported by part-time bartending. Now, product partners made her traveling sustainable.

"I want to feature Sabino Canyon, Douglas Springs, and Picacho Peak before heading slightly out of town to Chiricahua National Monument. HikeNPack is based in Marana, so I know they'd love for me to show their packs on Arizonan trails."

Claire wasn't about to share the real reason she was home—even with her most beloved and trusted friend—until she had answers.

"I've missed Tucson," she continued.

Though she'd slept in nearly every contiguous state, eaten countless local cuisines, and hiked more trails than she'd ever thought possible, the arid Sonoran Desert still held residence in Claire's heart. Most people complained about Arizonan summers, but there was nothing Claire loved more than monsoon season.

Nothing—absolutely nothing—smelled better than rain-soaked creosote bushes mingled with damp desert soil. After mentioning it once on a phone call, Meg sent Claire a dried bag of creosote leaves every year on her birthday. Often, Claire would sleep with the small pouch beside her pillow—the scent of the only place she'd ever considered *home* inundating her dreams.

"And I've missed *you*." She let a smile lift her lips.

"But you'll keep missing me because I'm leaving!" Meg collapsed over the steering wheel. "I feel terrible."

Meg's older sister, Erin, often labeled Meg as dramatic, but Claire viewed her friend as passionate. Better to be that than the alternative—to be so closed off that you let each day pass you by, wasted.

It was simply that, like herself, Meg encompassed a wild spirit. Double Trouble—as Meg's stepfather, Augie, had playfully deemed them as kids—could be found sneaking a smashed ghost pepper into the chili pot, tying Erin's shoelaces to the bathroom drain stub out, or sneaking to the neighborhood park to swing in the moonlight. Though they both had live-out-loud personalities, they usually—scorched tongues notwithstanding—didn't cause harm to themselves or others.

She placed her hand on Meg's forearm, giving her a squeeze. "Don't feel bad. I gave you no warning. I literally called you an hour ago."

Claire had spent yesterday in a poorly air-conditioned auto shop, receiving confirmation that, yep, the only car she'd ever owned was kaput. Yet another expensive item she needed to figure out how to pay for.

Discouraged, Claire had taken a rideshare to the nearest hotel and charmed her way into an overnight stay by agreeing to post a picture of herself in their luxurious pool. Though she usually only worked with small or family-owned accommodations that delivered unique experiences next to hiking destinations—tucked-away snowy chalets, yurts on hundreds of acres of big-sky country, or refurbished vintage Volkswagen Camper Vans parked beachside—Claire had wanted one night to decompress.

Just as she'd been about to post the pool photo, a fully clothed toddler jumped in the deep end. After diving to retrieve the unruly flower girl, Claire had received a thank-you invitation to the elaborate wedding being held on-site. The reception had been a blast until the exhaustion that seemed to sneak up unannounced had Claire running back to her room's soaker tub moments after leading the Electric Slide.

"You'll see me when you get back," Claire said. "But do you think I could stay with your parents for a few days? Just until I get settled. I don't want to have to showcase a travel accommodation while I'm home, so I plan on getting a temporary apartment."

That, and Claire wanted her solitude while she sorted this medical stuff out.

"*No.*" The word was pained. "Mom and Dad are in a hotel because they're finally renovating the bathrooms. And you can't stay with Erin." They both vehemently shook their heads at the thought. "So that leaves Rowan's. He doesn't have a spare room, but you don't mind couch surfing, right? It'll be like the good ol' days before you got all fancy," Meg teased.

"Sure. That'll work."

For her.

She could crash anywhere, but Claire wasn't sure if Meg's younger brother would want her as an unexpected roomie, especially with how things were left between them.

Throughout the years, the memory of that night would resurface like a pinching side cramp. She'd understood what Rowan's "I love you" had meant when she'd hugged him goodbye. She'd felt the shift in the way he'd looked at her in the preceding months, but Claire couldn't have processed his declaration in the wake of her grandmother's unexpected death. Not when the one person who'd chosen her was gone. Not when she'd been so utterly lost.

Claire had felt like a garbage human, ruffling Rowan's hair and parroting the sentiment back like a sister would do with her brother, but she hadn't seen another alternative. Everything had been packed and ready for her to leave the following morning. Without Gram there, without her loving steady presence tethering her to Tucson, Claire had done the thing her mother had taught her early on—she'd run.

"Oooh!" Meg swung the Jeep back onto the road. "I'll tell Knox that we need to delay a day so I can sleep over too."

The idea of Meg there as a physical barrier between her and Rowan seemed like a good idea, but . . . it'd been nine years. Surely, whatever feelings he'd had back then no longer existed.

"We can put sour gummy worms in our popcorn and watch a *Scream* marathon like we did when we were kids!"

Claire laughed, allowing Meg's excitement to ease the tension in her spine. "You might want to check with your brother to make sure he's cool with hosting an impromptu slumber party."

"Nah." She waved a hand. "Rowan loves hosting. It's become his thing ever since he bought his house. Oh! You haven't seen it. He redid the backyard with help from his college friends and fully remodeled the kitchen. This'll be great," Meg said before launching into her and Knox's full itinerary and how excited she was to escape the Arizona heat for a while.

When Rowan's gravel driveway crunched under the Jeep's tires a few minutes later, Claire's initial trepidation had been obliterated by Meg's abundant enthusiasm. Her best friend was right. This temporary stay will allow her to catch up with Rowan and the rest of the Bellamy family.

Besides, she'd only be on his couch for a week—tops—before she found a temporary apartment. Claire simply needed to connect with Heather, Gram's former business partner, who was holding the money Gram had left Claire when she'd passed.

Meg punched the faded doorbell a few times, her mouth twisting comically. "He's probably in the backyard."

Her friend strode down a gravel walkway that wound around the side of the house. A second door with a sign that read *Please knock* sat just around the corner. Beyond, a decorative wrought-iron fence with sun design separated them from an expansive backyard.

Once they'd passed through the gate, a short stucco barrier tapered down after forty feet, leaving nothing between the outdoor living space and the desert beyond. There was a fully furnished outdoor kitchen area, complete with a stone pizza oven. A large dining table stretched beneath a pergola swathed in shade-providing Cat's Claw vine. The paver patio flowed seamlessly into the desert with stepping-stones leading to a firepit area and a second pergola. Beneath it, a suspended daybed begged to be occupied.

"Wow," Claire said, pushing her sunglasses atop her head.

She could take six shots in this backyard alone, probably more. Her mind was already thinking about where to set up her tripod to capture herself stretched out on that daybed with the mountains aglow with waning sunlight.

Meg elbowed her. "I know, right. I salivate over the potential in this yard. I keep telling Rowan he needs to rent it out. Put an altar over there and, boom, instant venue."

A chuckle left Claire's lips. Her best friend *always* had weddings on the brain. Four years ago, Meg had transitioned from the unofficial photographer of her family's outdoor supply business to a sought-out wedding photographer. Peak wedding season in Tucson ran October through May, leaving Meg free to take summers off. Often, she'd fly to whatever corner of the country Claire was in, and they'd spend a few weeks together.

They sighed in unison for very different reasons before turning toward the small house.

Overlapping terra-cotta tiles covered the back patio. Usually, this would have been the place where an average homeowner would put their table and chairs, but it was empty with the exception of a large, reinforced crossbeam covered in various, colorful rock-climbing holds.

And Rowan.

A swallow squeezed down Claire's tight throat as her brain tried to reconcile her last memory of Rowan and the man whose chalked fingers held him suspended above the cement patio. Rowan's tan, muscled back narrowed to where a loose pair of gym shorts hung on for dear life. One tensed bicep kept him hovered above the ground as he brushed back a wry strand of hair falling from his bun.

As much as everything about the man in front of her looked foreign, Claire recognized that hair. It was the same auburn-brown shade every Bellamy family member possessed. But . . . his had always been short. At one time—during a brief, rebellious, preteen period—it'd been buzzed because Rowan had refused to comb it. Meg had sported a short bob most of her childhood for the same reason.

Rowan's large hand continued to another hold, completely oblivious to their presence. While Claire marveled at his effortless glide down the beam, Meg strode beside him and tapped her brother on the shoulder.

"Meg? What the heck?" Rowan dropped, tugging out an earbud. "Are you trying to scare the crap out of me?"

"I rang the doorbell." Meg gestured to the house. "Three times."

His gaze briefly bounced to the closed sliding-glass door. "I was listening to a continuing-education podcast."

"Ugh. You're such a *nerd*."

Rowan rolled his eyes, rubbing a chalked hand over his beard scruff. "Some of us have to be responsible members of society."

"Don't say that. You sound more and more like Erin every day. It pains me." Meg stabbed her chest with a clenched fist.

Part of Claire wanted to smile at their predictable back-and-forth. Though Rowan had always been the quietest of the Bellamy children, he'd learned to hold his own through his early teen years—particularly against Meg, who teased him the most. But Claire's eyes were too busy cataloging the differences between *this* Rowan and the one from her memory.

The Rowan in front of her didn't look like the boy she remembered. He looked like he should walk slowly out of the ocean while being photographed, water trickling down the impressive hills and valleys of his abs. Claire hadn't known there were so many distinct muscles over the ribs, but Rowan's were popping and straining as he argued with his sister. Her fingers twitched at her sides, already wondering what it would feel like to smooth over those subtle ripples.

No, stop that.

Claire's blood didn't seem to care that her mind was feebly shouting, *This is Rowan! Your childhood friend!* It kept rushing to every inch of her skin, flushing everything.

When Rowan's familiar hazel eyes scanned the rest of the patio and settled on her, the relief cascading through her veins was as unexpected as it was overwhelming—because she'd found something that was the same, that hadn't changed. Rowan's eyes held the slightest creases at the edges, but they were still the same as she remembered—compassionate and wreathed in thick brown lashes.

A nervous chuckle bubbled up in her chest. How many years had Claire wished for those luscious lashes? No mascara could ever compare.

When Rowan's expression twitched with confusion, Claire thought maybe he didn't recognize her. The last time Rowan had seen her, she'd had long, rainbow-dyed hair. Now, her light-brown hair was cropped just above the shoulders for minimal maintenance.

The impulse to step forward and slide her fingers over his jaw to displace the remaining white chalk buzzed through her, but Claire cleared her throat instead. "Hey, Rowan. It's been a while."

It was impossible not to notice the way those massive shoulders rose with an inhale, how his eyes widened. But then his expression shuttered, and cool evenness replaced it.

"Hey," he answered before looking at his sister with furrowed brows. "What are you doing here?"

Meg's full-wattage smile blasted her brother, the one that tipped into mischief at the corners if you were really paying attention. "Claire needs a place to stay."

Chapter 2

In the two seconds Rowan spent staring at his sister, his timer went off. The little hen egg timer—obviously named Henrietta—prevented him from getting distracted during his daily climbing session. If he didn't twist Henrietta's red body from her matching base to the twenty-minute time slot, he'd often get lost thinking. His ability to hyperfocus was incredibly helpful on challenging climbing routes or when he'd had to study for his psychology licensure test, but it also made him late for appointments.

Claire's smile as he silenced the timer punched the air from him. It'd been so long since that radiant grin had been directed at him.

He wasn't prepared.

Claire showing up at his house unannounced, her windblown hair haloing her face in the most breathtaking way, was in complete opposition to his plan to avoid her as much as possible.

"Still using timers to keep on track?" Claire's smile widened, and the agony intensified, radiating down his back in scraping tendrils.

It was unfair how well Claire knew him . . . how well he knew her.

Rowan glanced at Meg for help before recognizing its futility. Meg had no idea that she'd just hand-delivered the one person who could systematically rearrange his insides. As far as his sister knew, they'd all been childhood playmates turned allies through the tumultuous teen and young-adult years. No one in his family was aware that, somewhere on the pimply precipice of fourteen, Rowan's feelings for Claire had morphed into something more.

Meg stretched to hang from the crossbeam, rambling about his "rigid habits" and how she's always trying to "break him out of his shell."

"But what are you gonna do?" his sister asked.

Claire shrugged in agreement. "Brothers."

There it was.

The painful reminder that Claire only saw him as her best friend's brother.

"Right?" Meg's laugh bounced around the patio as she gripped different handholds to swing herself facing the desert landscape.

Henrietta made a measly shield against the excruciating sensation ripping through his chest, but Rowan held the little chicken in front of his heart, nonetheless.

And then . . .

The strangest thing happened.

Claire's gaze followed the motion, but instead of her eyes flicking back to his face as he'd expected, her lips slacked. Softly. Slowly. Almost as if she'd forgotten she was supposed to be joking along with Meg, not blatantly staring. Then, her gaze dragged down his chest as her teeth bit her lower lip.

It was comical, the two impulses running opposite directions through his body. One was to cover himself while pointing to his face with a scolding, "I'm up here!" The other was to preen like the pretty, pretty peacock he apparently was.

The last time Claire had seen him, he'd been a skinny twenty-one-year-old. Though he and his family had always been active hikers, Rowan hadn't grown into his body until he'd begun rock climbing in his mid-twenties. Muscles came naturally as he'd focused on gaining the strength and agility to make him a better climber, using calisthenics to cross-train.

The way Claire scanned his exposed skin made some caveman part of him fire off, pulverizing his well-checked ego. Reflexively, Rowan stood taller, shifting his shoulders until the left one popped. Her gaze flittered over the pulse point in his neck, his jawline, until it stalled on his hair, her right fingers curling slightly like she wanted to touch it.

When Meg dropped to the ground, they both startled.

"We should get you settled." Rowan used the excuse of being a good host to turn his back to both women, opening the sliding-glass door. "Come on in."

Meg went to her Jeep to get Claire's bags as he escaped to his bedroom to grab a shirt and take a few purposeful breaths. Justifications came swiftly and easily, preventing his mind from racing three hundred miles per minute. Claire had just had a physiological response to an attractive member of the opposite sex. It was almost an involuntary action, like your leg kicking up when a doctor hits your knee with a mallet. Reflexive. Instinctive. Not meaningful.

When Rowan returned to the main room, Meg was rummaging through his tea cabinet.

"Mint. Chamomile. Jade Green. Ginger Lemon. Lavender Honey. Hibiscus. Rose . . ."

"Mint's fine," Claire said, setting her faded green hiking pack and a canvas duffel bag beside his oversized Pottery Barn couch.

Meg had teased him when he'd brought the fluffy, cream couch home, but it was undeniably comfortable. Rowan rejected the notion that just because he had a Y-chromosome, he had to decorate his house in black, leather, and tortuous furniture. His childhood home was almost always covered in half-emptied hiking packs, dog fur from their rambunctious German shepherds, and potted vegetables parading as house plants.

Home had been like a favorite jacket—comforting, well-used, and filled with love. That was what Rowan wanted this house to feel like. He wanted it to welcome everyone—even the last person he'd *ever* expected to be dropped on his doorstep.

Claire's gaze stalled on the couch as she began rubbing the inside of her left wrist—her tell for when she was uncomfortable or anxious.

The first time he'd noticed it was a few days before school started, the year she'd been fourteen and he'd been ten. Meg had been throwing outfit choices around her room and babbling about how exciting it was to finally be a high schooler, and

Claire had been staring off, rubbing her wrist raw. He'd leaned over and tapped Claire's fidgety thumb with his, smiling. Claire had frozen for a few seconds before taking a deep breath, calming almost instantly. Then she'd wrapped him in a side hug and ruffled his hair.

Rowan's response was automatic—something he'd done hundreds of times before. Four large steps was all it took for him to wrap his fingers around Claire's wrist, stilling her thumb.

This time, instead of Claire's bunched shoulders relaxing, her breath hitched. It was audible over the impending rumble of his copper tea kettle and Meg pulling mugs down from the open shelves.

Regret smashed him in the sternum as everything came flooding back. It was like living innumerable memories at once, experiencing infinite versions of themselves in various locations. Just like this. Him steadying her, always there for her.

Rowan had foolishly thought he could keep his feelings for Claire boxed up, set aside, but there was no escaping the perfection of her skin. Though this slight contact was innocent, it was nearly enough to undo the last nine years of trying to get over her. Claire's gaze lifted, giving him a showcase of the golden flecks that scattered through her left iris. He'd almost forgotten how that made her eyes uneven since the right one was as still as a glass of whiskey.

To keep himself from doing something tremendously stupid, like framing her cheek with his other palm, Rowan glanced at his hand over hers. An upside-down, black heart outline stretched the width of her left wrist.

"It's new," she whispered.

Rowan's mind flew through his catalog of Claire's tattoos. The mermaid on her right hip from the high school swim team. The watercolor chrysanthemum in between her shoulder blades. The tiny cartoon stegosaurus on her left ankle, matching Meg's. The finely lined bay leaves delicately gracing her collarbones to remember her beloved late grandmother.

What else had Claire added over the years? His gaze unconsciously swept the skin not covered by her ribbed tank top and hiking shorts.

"Row? Want anything?" Meg asked.

Rowan dropped Claire's wrist and stepped back, clearing his throat. "Green. Thanks."

Boundaries defined every aspect of his life, and this one needed to stay uncrossed if he was going to survive however long Claire was to stay here. Even if they'd casually touched each other throughout their lives—like this, high fives, sitting next to each other on the couch—they were different people now. They wanted different things.

Rowan needed to remember that.

"I'll get you some sheets," he said, putting more distance between them. "There's not much I can do about the light, though." He gestured to the unadorned floor-to-ceiling windows that ran along the living room.

"It's fine. Really. I'm just grateful for a place to crash."

"I forgot to tell you the best part about staying here," Meg said from the kitchen. "RowRow, could you please, pretty please with Tajín on top, make us your green chili omelets for breakfast? I'm starving."

"Now I see why you're here so early. You need me to feed you." He huffed even as gratitude for the distraction wisped over his temples. "Typical."

There wasn't a formal dining space inside his home. It was too small. Outside of the open-concept living/kitchen space, there was a tiny half bath, his bedroom with en suite bathroom, and a second bedroom he'd turned into a home office to meet with his therapy clients. The four stools at the countertop sufficed for day-to-day. If he was hosting, everyone ate outside. Rowan preferred to be out there anyway.

Meg snorted. "You love feeding people almost as much as Dad."

Rowan continued to grumble but tied his striped half-apron around his gym shorts and pulled fresh eggs from the fridge. His friend Kyle kept chickens in his midtown backyard. Rowan would have loved to have chickens of his own, but since his property contained four acres of wild land, any sweet hens he brought home would be picked off by desert predators.

"How's Augie surviving without a kitchen?" Claire sat on one of the stools as Meg handed her a steaming cup of tea.

When his sister positioned herself beside Claire and dove into the nitty-gritty details of their parents' remodel, Rowan could almost believe it was fifteen years ago. He'd be in the kitchen, cooking with his stepfather, Augie, while the women in his family set the table and chatted. Though he was pretty sure neither of his sisters starved while living on their own, they only *ate well* when he or Dad were cooking.

Rowan lost himself in the simplicity of food prep, grounding himself in every movement. The sensation of the eggs cracking.

The sound the fork made against the glass bowl as he beat them into oblivion. The scent of cilantro as he pinched a sprig from his window box full of viridescent herbs. The ease of flipping the halfway-cooked egg mixture with a simple flick of his wrist.

"Are you going to get that? Your phone is blowing up like the Fourth of July," Meg's voice broke into his moving meditation.

Rowan plucked the sprouted multigrain bread from the toaster and put it on the awaiting plates. He'd asked to have these mismatched ones from his father's kitchen when Mom gifted Dad a new, artisan-made set two years ago. After setting the steaming breakfasts in front of Claire and Meg, Rowan scooped up his phone.

The vibrating text messages were coming from the 'dorm bros' group chat. His friend Kevin had come up with the moniker for their group of five after how they'd all met freshman year of college. The University of Arizona had undergone an on-campus housing crunch, squishing five twin beds into a dorm study room turned temporary living space. They'd all gotten along so well that they'd moved off campus the following year into a bachelor house until they'd graduated and had been close ever since.

Rowan quickly scanned the rapid-fire stream of messages.

Kevin: *Not a drill. Repeat. Not a drill. I just saw Meg's latest OnlyApp post, and it's of her and Claire with saguaros in the background. She's back in Tucson now.*

Ethan: *To borrow from Haley, holy crap.*

Zane: *Oh *%#@, this is totally on me. I saw her at Rene's wedding last night and meant to text out a warning. I'm sorry. I got distracted. Rowan, you okay?*

Kevin: *You knew?!?*

Zane: *Seriously, man. I'm so sorry.*

Ethan: *Is this what it feels like to NOT be the group troublemaker? It's nice. Cozy, even.*

Zane: *I'm going to throw up my flapjacks.*

Ethan: *Zane, take a breath. It's okay. Accidents happen.*

Kevin: *Where's Kyle? He needs to be here. This is an all-hands-on-deck situation!*

Ethan: *You know he likes to sleep in.*

Zane: *Rowan? How can I make it up to you?*

Kevin: *On that note, where IS Rowan?*

Ethan: *?*

His thumb hovered over the screen, prepared to respond, when Claire took a bite from her omelet and let out a guttural, satisfied groan. The sound radiated through his chest like a livewire, short-circuiting his organs in its wake. Rowan's eyes pressed closed, fighting against his body's response.

"This is . . . wow."

"I know, right?" Meg mumbled over a full mouth.

"Glad you like it." Rowan couldn't help the roughness of his voice.

Kevin: *That's it. I'm calling him.*

The phone lit up with Kevin's call, but Rowan refused it. There was no way he was having this conversation within earshot of Claire.

Kevin: *Color me offended. He just rejected my call.*

Rowan: *It's fine. Everything is fine. You're all overreacting.*

Nothing about his message was even a fraction of the truth, but Rowan wasn't about to hash this out now. He needed to get his footing with Claire being in his house, with the fact that she was going to sleep within forty feet of him tonight. Once he'd had time to process everything, Rowan would explain the situation to his friends.

Kevin: *I beg your pardon. I don't overreact.*

A scoff escaped his nose. Kevin was always one hundred percent over the top.

Zane: *Can you call me later? I'd feel better if we got together or something.*

Rowan: *Zane, I've got plans with my parents today, but everything's okay. Everyone else, shush. You're freaking out about nothing.*

Ethan: *Did he just shush us?*

Kyle: *Why are you all this awake at eight in the morning? It's inhuman.*

Kevin: *DID YOU NOT SEE THAT IT WAS AN EMERGENCY?!?*

A calculated breath filled Rowan's lungs before he held and then released it even more slowly. Rowan loved his friends. He couldn't imagine his life without this incredible support system, but sometimes, they were a lot.

Rowan: *All is well. Return to your normally scheduled activities.*

Kevin: *Cheeky.*

The corner of his mouth kicked up.

Zane: *I'm sorry again.*

Rowan: *It's okay. I'll talk to you later.*

The best thing to do now was separate himself from Claire. Otherwise, he'd make a fool of himself again, like he'd done before she'd left Tucson. Resisting the urge to tuck away the disobedient strand of hair that kept falling in her eyes was already difficult.

"I've got to get going. There's an event at the store today." More than anything, Rowan needed the stability of his oldest sister. If Meg had been his sparring partner growing up, Erin had been his safe haven. Rowan rummaged around his junk drawer to find a spare key and placed it on the counter next to Claire. "Make yourself at home."

"Oh, yeah." Meg turned to Claire. "There's this Wholistic Health Fair we're hosting that starts at ten today. I managed to get out of it, but you should go with Rowan. Mom and Dad will be there, and you can see the changes to the store. It doesn't even look like the same place."

"You could come too, you know," Rowan clipped at his sister while leaning against his industrial-sized refrigerator. "It's *our* family business."

"Nah. I need to head back and let Knox know about tonight's sleepover." Meg winked.

"Tonight's what?"

"You'll see." Meg's smile was wicked as she hopped off the stool to put away her dishes. Claire was only three bites in, but Meg always ate like a famished wolverine.

Sensing she wasn't done making his life miserable, Rowan said, "Put it away properly, Meg-a-tron."

"What fun is that?" His sister didn't break eye contact as she laid her plate horizontally over the top drawer of his dishwasher. *Dirty side up.*

His growl was instinctual.

Rowan wasn't a neat freak. Things would often pile up before he'd go on a necessary cleaning bender, but even a five-year-old knew how to load a dishwasher.

Claire's pearlescent laugh only made the situation worse, especially when it was accented with that adorable snort. Her laugh always sent light streaking through his muscles. *Everything* about Claire was lightning—bright and beautiful with the power to awe. But that also made her dangerous. She could spark a flame that could burn a parched mountainside, destroying thousands of acres. If Rowan let himself absorb her energy, he wouldn't escape this unscathed.

Boundaries.

He just needed to keep his boundaries.

Mental ones because evidently the physical boundary that he'd been hoping for was non-existent now that Claire was going to be sleeping on his couch.

"Let me grab a shower, and we'll head out." Rowan tossed the words over his shoulder as casually as he could, though his heart was doing its best to demolish his breastbone.

Chapter 3

Most of the single-story shopping complex's parking lot was covered by pop-up tents—vegan co-ops were next to beekeepers next to Reiki healers. As Rowan pulled into one of the remaining spots, Claire kept her gaze locked on the right side of the building.

"Meg wasn't kidding. The store looks great."

Canyon Outdoor Supply Company—or "the store" as every Bellamy referred to it—stretched over what otherwise would have been three individual storefronts. A new sign and shade-providing overhang shadowed the large glass doors. Huge pane windows held floor-to-ceiling photographs of athletic people doing various outdoor activities—hiking, rock climbing, camping—next to window displays showcasing the supplies needed for those activities.

Claire's eyes were immediately drawn to the back of a shirtless man suspended on an orange-banded, sandstone rockface. His muscles flexed as his chalked hands reached for another hold. Climbing pants were splattered with dust and rolled to mid-calf as the harness highlighted his very firm backside.

Rowan's backside.

Heat surged over Claire's collarbones before she could stop it. What was going on with her? Maybe this was another side effect of whatever was going on with her medically? That would be a logical explanation for her inability to regulate her body temperature around someone she'd known her whole life.

"When did you get into modeling?" she teased, because that was something normal Claire would have done.

Rowan shifted his thirteen-year-old Jeep Wrangler into park with a disgruntled sound. "*That* is the result of two years of Meg's incessant badgering."

"Sedona?" she guessed, focusing on the impressive rock formation instead of the rock-hard body of the man clinging to it.

"Yeah."

On closer inspection of the other photos, she recognized Augie's hairy calves on the close-up photo of two sets of boots ascending a saguaro-laden trail. The pant-covered legs next to him must have belonged to Rowan's mother, Kelly. And it was unmistakably the shadow of Erin's jaunty, high ponytail inside the tent surrounded by towering ponderosa pine trees—clearly a campsite on Mount Lemmon at dusk.

"It's all of you! That's such a great idea. Your family is the epitome of outdoor adventure."

Rowan chuckled, and the low sound made a strange vibration zip through her. "Except Meg."

Meg had always been the disgruntled square peg in a family of outdoorsy circle ones. She had shirked her family's hikes as often as she could by staying over at Claire and Gram's tiny historic casita. Much to Meg's chagrin, Claire had begun joining the Bellamys on hikes in her late teens. Though she hadn't meant to disrupt her friend's avoidance of all things nature, Claire had found a peace from pounding one step over the next through the dusty dirt. That calm could never be attained otherwise. No matter how many of Gram's yoga classes she attended.

Reflexively, Claire's gaze swung left. Blissful Desert Yoga was nestled into the last storefront of the complex. The soothing lilac-and-tan mandala Gram had painted over the stucco exterior had obviously been touched up throughout the years.

Claire briefly wondered if Heather, Gram's business partner, had made any changes to the studio. Would the tiny brass disks still rattle when the front door opened? Would the scents of eucalyptus and mint still greet you as you stepped inside? Did they still teach the classes in Sanskrit, encouraging their members to learn the names of each pose? Would Gram's favorite wooden bowl still hold beaded bracelets for sale, proceeds going to a local women's shelter?

Her short, painful exhale made an audible sound in the quiet car.

Rowan's hand moved as if to cover hers before he cut the engine and collected his keys. "Come on. Mom and Dad will be excited to see you."

"We're not parking in the back?" In the past, they'd always come through the business entrances of their respective stores. Canyon Outdoor Supply Company's nondescript beige doors had 17b, 17c, and 17d on them. Gram had painted a purple Om symbol above the peephole to 17a.

Rowan shook his head. "Not today. I'll repark in a minute, but I want you to get the full effect."

Not four steps toward the building, Claire was hip-checked by a wayward goat. Not a little goat, like the ones used at petting zoos, but a large Nubian one.

Claire was accustomed to unexpected animal encounters. She'd shared a meadow with a black bear (gratefully from a great distance away), had a family of skunks rub against her tent (blessedly keeping their scents to themselves), and had to turn around mid-hike due to a stubborn and unmoving water moccasin. But nearly being head-butted by a bleating Bovidae in central Tucson was new.

That starburst of excitement cascaded through her veins. *Nothing* was better than something unexpected.

A quick pivot and Claire was after the galloping goat. The shopping complex sat on Speedway—one of the busiest roads in Tucson. Great for customer foot traffic; not so great for runaway goats who wanted to remain breathing. Her fingers caught the dragging woven lead a few feet before the goat collided with Sunday-morning traffic. Thankfully, the misbehaving mammal only tugged twice before surrendering with a resigned head bow.

A chuckle left Claire's lips. "You need to be careful," she gently chided the now docile animal. When it pressed its soft head into her ribs, Claire affectionately scratched its large velvety ears. "Cars are bigger than you, and they will *knock you down*."

Rowan's voice synchronized the "knock you down" part of that sentence. He apparently also remembered the slogan that their wacky summer camp counselor had said ad nauseam. To be fair, it had helped remind them to look both ways before crossing the road from the soccer fields to the community pool.

When their gazes met, all was right with the world. Rowan was just Rowan. She was herself. Their shared memories were wholesome and sweet.

See.

She didn't need to worry about that overwhelming flicker of attraction and a sense of belonging that had surged through her when Rowan's fingers had encircled her wrist earlier. Whatever *that* had been was clearly a fluke.

They were friends.

Same as always.

"Angelina Goatlie! What were you thinking?" A woman with gorgeous ringlet curls arrived beside Claire, taking the proffered lead and crouching to examine the goat's flank, shoulders, hooves. "Thank you. I'm so sorry she ran into you. I'm not usually this unorganized. Really. I genuinely thought she was secured, but then—" The woman's scattered, breathless explanation halted when her gaze lifted to notice Rowan. "Oh . . . hi."

"Hey, Emmy."

A spike of jealousy pistoned through Claire's spine at the warmth infused in Rowan's greeting. A very unwanted spike. *You're friends, essentially family*, she reminded herself, shifting her shoulders to dissipate the sensation.

"Hi." Emmy waved, dropping the lead.

Both Rowan and Claire stooped to pick it up, their hands brushing before she jolted upright and offered hers to Emmy. She was clearly *imagining* the spark that just shot up her forearm. The static electricity in the air must have been high today. Maybe monsoon season was starting early this year.

"I'm Claire. I love your goat's name." She gave her brightest smile. "It's very punny."

Emmy tucked away a blonde curl, the bridge of her nose flushing. "Thanks. All the girls are named after celebrities."

"Girls?"

"Our dairy goats," Emmy said, tugging on her sky-blue Monroe Dairy Farm t-shirt. "There's also Meryl Bleat, Goaty Hawn, and Lady Baa Baa."

"Emmy and her cousin made the goat cheese that was in your omelet," Rowan offered. "It's the best in the city."

Claire wondered if the unwanted emotion she'd felt seconds ago had been as transparent as the displeasure staining Emmy's otherwise beautiful cheeks.

"That's high praise." Emmy glanced at her well-worn boots for a beat. "It was good to see you, but I've got to get back to helping Amelia set up."

"Sure thing. I'll see you later."

Claire waited a few seconds before asking with a goofy eyebrow lift, "Now that we *goat* that out of the way, am I still getting the grand tour?"

Rowan suppressed an eye roll, his lip twitching as he stepped toward the building.

The inside of Canyon Outdoor Supply Company was even more transformative than the façade. Gone were the linoleum floors, old-fashioned clothing racks, and seizure-triggering fluorescent lighting. The polished concrete floors complemented well-coordinated displays, highlighting each outdoor activity.

A purple tent was set up with full accoutrement, including an adorable teddy bear nestled atop the unrolled sleeping bag. The rock-climbing wall on the far side of the store allowed patrons to test harnesses before buying. Three different kinds of hammocks hung in another corner, ready for relaxing.

All throughout, various forms of gear, clothes, and supplies hung from wrought-iron racks or sturdy, welcoming shelves. There was even a couch with Southwestern-fabric pillows next to the wall of hiking boots. It felt like a hangout spot, not just a place for purchasing titanium cutlery, trekking poles, and a portable stove.

"This is . . ." She blew out a breath.

"I know. Erin did a great job. She has this ability to see things that aren't there." The blatant pride in Rowan's voice warmed something in Claire.

Though Meg and Rowan now had careers of their own, leaving an eager Erin to run the business, every member of the Bellamy family played a part in their store's success. As kids, they'd stocked shelves, worked the register, swept floors, and assisted customers even before they could legally work. And once they'd turned eighteen, each sibling became an equal-part owner.

Claire's mind flashed briefly to a moonlit night in April when she'd been twenty-two. She'd been complaining to Meg about her disastrous boyfriend when Rowan had uncharacteristically piped up.

"That's not how a man should behave. Men should protect and cherish the ones they love. Like Dad. He made us each part of the business he spent years building before he even knew us. When he and Mom got married, he changed his last name to match ours instead of making the four of us change. You should—" Rowan cut off his words with a clenched fist before excusing himself.

"Oh my goodness." Kelly's voice brought Claire back to the present. "Look who's here!"

Claire barely had time to respond before Kelly rushed over and wrapped her in a maternal hug.

"Is that our Clairebear?" Augie's deep voice asked before joining the embrace, making her the meat in a parental Bellamy sandwich.

"Make sure she can breathe," Erin piped up from somewhere.

When Augie's deep rumbly laugh soaked into her skin, unexpected moisture sprung to the corners of her eyes. Claire took a steadying breath as Augie and Kelly let go of her.

"I like the beard," she said through a growing smile.

Augie's black hair was peppered with gray, complementing the slight gray in his thick beard.

"It's distinguished, is it not?" He stroked his facial hair as if posing for an Elizabethan portrait.

Claire laughed. Everyone looked older, creases more firm at the corners of their mouths or around their eyes, but they were simultaneously the same.

"I love what you did with the store."

"That's all Erin's doing." Augie wrapped his eldest under his shoulder. "I knew there was a reason we sent her to business school and put her in charge."

"So you're retired, then?" Claire teased.

Augie and Kelly would be fixtures in this store until they could no longer walk, and then they'd happily rest in camp chairs to answer customer questions.

"Don't give Kelly any ideas," Augie stage-whispered. "She's trying to get me on a cruise ship. Can you imagine? Walking around and not being on land?" He laughed heartily again. "It's absurd."

Rowan turned to Erin, asking what still needed to be done to prepare for the fair. It was then that Claire noticed that each Bellamy was wearing the same company-logoed, moisture-wicking polo. That feeling of *other* pinched her neck. It'd been a sensation she'd experienced often growing up. The Bellamys were undeniably a team, stitched together both by blood and choice. No matter how much they made sure she was included in their activities, Claire was still an outsider.

"Can you put me to work?"

It was the only way to combat the loneliness of not belonging. When she could wash the dinner dishes, or push the vacuum around Meg's room after a sleepover, or help Augie tend to his indoor garden, it made the gnawing sensation of never being an honest part of this family diminish.

"Absolutely!" Kelly beamed.

It was only after Augie motioned her to follow him toward the storage rooms that Claire caught the deep downturn of Rowan's lips.

Chapter 4

"**Y**ou're seriously going to deny me delicious ice cream after your family benefited from my free labor all day?" Claire had her leg tucked up, partially turned toward him in his Jeep. "I need a reward. No, I *deserve* a reward."

"Dad fed you dinner," he quipped.

"And I thanked him sincerely, but *come on*." When Claire shoved his shoulder, Rowan had to forcibly stop his body from responding. "It's been a long day. Let's get a treat."

Statement of the millennium.

It'd been a long, *tortuous* day of trying to avoid Claire and failing miserably. When he'd brought her to the store this morning, he'd expected her to say hi to everyone and then head home with his Jeep, giving him the respite he desperately needed.

But she'd been everywhere. Leaning over the counter whenever he came back inside to replenish the company-labeled giveaways he'd been passing out at their tent. Sneaking up

"

behind him with an icy bottle to the back of the neck while refilling the outside cooler. Laughing with his parents while sitting cross-legged on the ground in their shoe department, eating the tacos Dad had ordered for everyone to celebrate a successful day.

With her knowledge of camping and backpacking gear, Claire had been inundated with curious customers. Her effortless, personable nature had probably doubled their overall sales—something Erin would be ecstatic about. At one point, Claire had sat in the tent setup with a drooling baby in her lap, giving an impromptu storytime to a gaggle of rapt children so their parents could shop without distraction.

He, on the other hand, had been as pleasant as a thoroughly poked bear. His mother had thrice reminded him to tuck his scowl away, probably attributing his resting grump face to the fact that she had him out of his element. His mom knew he'd rather do inventory than field questions, but the fair had required him to chat up potential customers. Rowan preferred one-on-one, in-depth conversations, like those he had with close friends or his therapy clients. Small talk made his stomach curdle.

All Rowan wanted was the peace of his backyard and four states' distance from Claire. Since neither of those was going to happen, he needed to reframe this situation so the tempest churning in his chest would simmer down, because the sight of a goofy-faced Claire surrounded by the sound of toddler giggles had done something irreparable to his heart.

Intentionally loosening his grip on the steering wheel, Rowan took a slow breath.

It was time to regard Claire the same way she thought of him—like family.

Just think of Claire like you think of Meg.

Annoying older sisters he could handle. He had a lifetime of experience.

"If I take you to Coneheads will you quit your fussing?" Rowan asked.

"Maybe." The defiant smile in her answer made the corner of his mouth tip up reflexively.

Being a thorn in his side was classic Meg behavior. This was going to be easier than he thought.

Rowan sighed dramatically but flipped on his blinker to drive toward Coneheads Ice Cream.

A computerized foghorn sounded as they passed through the shop door, and Rowan shook his head with a derisive snort. This place was so chaotic—which was exactly why Claire loved it. Every inch of the walls was covered with stickers. As long as they were family friendly, the owners encouraged patrons to bring their own from home and go nuts. In fact, there was an animated squirrel hovering over a pile of acorns with that sentiment right above the light switch.

The ice cream was also served in a hectic way. Your chosen flavor would be scooped into a cone and then smashed upside down into a clear plastic bowl, thus giving the ice cream ball a "cone head." If you selected toppings, they ended up in the bottom of the bowl, like it or not. In the history of Rowan's patronage of the quirky small business, he'd never seen them deviate in their serving style—unswayed even by the oversized tears of a few distraught children.

"What are you going to get?" Claire rocked back and forth, joy evident as she surveyed the myriad choices.

"Vanilla."

The look she swung at him was the dictionary definition of 'disturbed.'

"Vanilla," she said flatly. "You're still ordering vanilla. When you have all this?" Her arm swept over the two dozen crazy concoctions behind tilted glass.

Though Rowan hadn't ordered vanilla in years, he kept up the teasing repartee. After all, that's what he'd do with Meg. "I know what vanilla will taste like."

When Claire pinched the bridge of her nose, Rowan tried not to chuckle. But then his forehead creased when all the fight went out of her. Claire had always been boundless energy, an immutable spark. All day, she'd been a beacon during the Wholistic Health Fair, drawing potential customers to her like a blazing lighthouse, listening intently as they told her their life stories.

Now she just looked . . . exhausted.

Rowan understood his weariness, but Claire had always powered up in the presence of people.

"What'll it be, captain?" The teenage girl behind the counter beamed at Rowan. That was another thing about this crazy store, they gave silly nicknames to their customers.

"Pickle banana cream with rainbow sprinkles," he answered, gaze still trained on Claire.

Picking up on minute facial expressions had been a skill he'd learned in early childhood and honed through hours of practice as a psychologist. When Claire glanced up and locked eyes with him, the tightness around her mouth slacked, and her brows relaxed. It was almost like she mouthed, "Yeah?" before her lips broke into that blinding, dimpled smile.

That was another intimate seed of knowledge Rowan held about Claire—the levels of her smiles. Her left dimple would pop with a false smile, but the right only emerged with genuine happiness. Whatever she'd been struggling with, he'd annihilated it by ordering pickle banana cream with rainbow sprinkles. The Bo Burnham song from the store speakers was efficiently replaced by the blood rushing in his ears.

"And for you, sugarplum?"

Claire held his gaze as she answered, the spark returning to her whiskey eyes. "Peanut butter topped with chocolate chips."

His focus dropped to those ever-rising lips before Rowan remembered the decision he'd made in the car.

"Peanut butter?" He ripped his gaze away, faking a disappointed grimace. "How basic."

Paying for ice cream had never been so engrossing. Rowan ran the pad of his thumb over his embossed initials of the leather wallet Erin had gotten him for his last birthday. He forced himself to calculate the tip in decimals before rounding up and then adding a dollar. He'd almost—*almost*—settled the prickly sensation scratching over his shoulders before he heard a woman's voice behind him.

"Hey, everything alright?" A woman in her mid-forties had Claire by the elbow, like she'd steadied Claire from falling.

"I'm fine." Claire's fake smile lifted her cheeks as she freed herself from the woman's grasp. "My shoes just got stuck to the floor."

"If you're sure." The woman's concerned expression didn't soothe.

"I am."

"Just take it easy." The woman double-checked Claire twice before joining her friend waiting through the doorway.

Claire's eyes flicked to his before lifting that fake smile higher to receive her ice cream with a murmured, "Thank you."

Rowan followed her toward a high-top table with no chairs.

"Claire." He couldn't help that her name was breathed over her hair. That instead of standing across the table, he'd instinctively moved closer—almost bracketing her in case she became unsteady again. "Are you okay?"

She'd always been as nimble as the goat that had tried to plow through her at the fair earlier. Her natural athleticism had made her an easy addition to his family's weekend hikes—much to his teenage torture.

"Just a little tired," Claire said, avoiding eye contact as she scooped up a spoonful. Her shrugging shoulder bounced into his chest before she let it settle lightly against him.

Rowan wasn't sure if she was leaning into him for comfort or because she physically had to, but his body didn't care. Gratification cascaded through him like monsoon floodwaters deluging the mountainside. He wanted to set his ridiculous bowl on the table and properly wrap her in his arms. He wanted to kiss that stubborn cowlick on her forehead that always sent a strand of hair over her eyes.

So much for thinking of Claire as his sister.

That had lasted a whopping twenty minutes.

If there was an award for worst-laid plans, Rowan should hang it in his home office next to his diplomas.

"You know what time it is!" A cowbell rang from behind the register.

Claire set her spoon in her cup in preparation, that elated spark spreading over her again. "I wonder which song it'll be."

Coneheads had a list of eight songs they rotated through every hour, on the hour.

"If you're happy and you know it, clap your feet," the staff began.

"Toot sweet!" Claire shouted while bracing the table with both hands to slap her feet together.

Rowan's brows wrinkled. In the past, she'd always jump-clapped her feet like a jubilant leprechaun.

"If you're happy and you know it, slap that meat."

"To the beat!" Along with the rest of the restaurant, Claire beat her belly with open palms.

"If you're happy and you know it, and you really want to show it. If you're happy and you know it, scream yippee!"

"Yippee!" chorused around him.

Claire chuckled to herself, picking up her bowl and taking a huge bite from the bottom of her cone. "I freaking love this place."

"Yeah, it's fun," he said flatly.

Claire laughed again. "Convincing."

He was about to explain that crazypants-anything wasn't really his scene, but since it was fruitless, Rowan took a bite of ice cream instead.

The choked, gagging sound escaping him was unavoidable. This flavor was terrible. Truly horrendous. There was no other way to describe it. The only people who could want this flavor combination were pregnant women craving these *specific* ingredients. Perhaps that was why it was on the menu in the first place.

"I thought you liked disgusting things?" Claire's lips curved up around her spoon.

Rowan managed to swallow the melting monstrosity and chase it with a bite of unadulterated cone.

"Just because I enjoyed taking your and Meg's money growing up, didn't mean I enjoyed ingesting the things you two created."

Meg had gone through an *I'll-give-you-twenty-bucks-to-eat-this* phase wherein she'd mix most of the fridge's condiments into a concoction or add opposing spices to scrambled eggs before presenting them to Rowan.

Claire narrowed her eyes playfully. "You loved it."

No, Claire. I loved you. There's a difference.

The emotion he didn't want to feel sat right under the surface. Knowing that if he dipped his fingers into it, it would follow him all evening, Rowan slapped his abs and played along instead.

"Teenage boys' stomachs are impenetrable. It's a well-known fact. I was simply profiting from your ignorance."

"Nice." She scrunched her face. "Way to take advantage of us."

"First"—he held up a finger—"I was younger and therefore more likely to be taken advantage of. Need I remind you of the sock scandal of 2008?"

Claire pressed her lips into a line, fighting a grin.

"Second, you would never allow someone to take advantage of you. You're one of the strongest people I know."

Something solemn flitted across Claire's face, quick as a flicker from the obnoxious overhead lights, before she looked into her cup. "What do you think about me sleeping on the outdoor daybed instead of the couch tonight?"

Rowan shrugged, still unsure what he'd seen a second ago. "You could . . ." Her being outside would actually be a best-case scenario. He'd finally get some space. "But Herbert Nenninger has been by a lot lately."

The glint in her eyes was going to be the end of him. "Did you just say Herbert Nenninger?"

Claire was losing the battle with her smile, her lips all trembly and uneven. It was the most adorable thing. A woman shouldn't be allowed to be cute and captivating at the same time. It was wholly unfair.

"May I ask who Herbert Nenninger is? An unruly coyote? Kangaroo rat?" Any second now that teasing tone would peel into laughter, and then his straining heart would have to contend with that snort.

"Bobcat." He cut her off.

"Really?" Those gorgeous eyes brightened even more. "Now, I'm absolutely sleeping outside."

Rowan shrugged even as a protective pulse beat in his chest. Which was ridiculous. Claire had been sleeping outside, alone, for the last nine years.

"He won't hurt you. He doesn't get closer than a hundred feet—or at least I think it's a *he*. I've never been close enough to see for sure, but based on his size, I'm assuming."

Claire finished her cone in a single bite. "You named your neighborhood bobcat after Bill's bunny from *Curious George?*"

As a kid, Rowan had held onto childhood things a little longer than his sisters. He'd learned in his professional studies that it was a result of his turbulent early childhood before his mother left his biological father and moved them to Tucson. Even after Mom had remarried and they'd settled into his stepfather's cozy house, Rowan still clung to specific comfort items. One of those had been watching *Curious George* on PBS. Something that Claire, despite being twelve at the time, had occasionally joined him in.

Rowan shifted his shoulders, not answering.

"I missed you."

The wistful sigh that accompanied those words felt like poison slowly infiltrating his bloodstream. Claire shouldn't be allowed to utter words like that. Didn't she know the devastating impact that simple sentence had on his psyche?

Obviously not.

For Claire, her stating that she missed him was the equivalent to her telling Meg or his parents that same sentiment. It didn't mean what he wanted it to mean.

Rowan checked his phone as if it'd buzzed just to give himself something to focus on. By some saving grace, Meg texted him a photo that very second. It was of his kitchen counter—covered in various bags of candy and a box of microwave popcorn.

"Looks like Meg's ready for the movie marathon." Rowan turned his phone toward Claire, keeping his attention away from her face. "We should get going."

"You're not going to finish your ice cream?"

Rowan ignored the teasing lilt in her question as he tossed his dessert in the trash. "That's a big no."

If only he could say no to Claire inundating his home and his heart.

Chapter 5

Rising with the sun was a usual part of Claire's routine—a holdover from when she used to exclusively sleep outside. So when her phone yanked her out of her gummy-worm sugar coma at the indulgent hour of nine in the morning, she was more than a little rattled. Her left eye insisted on remaining closed as she squinted at Meg's tongue-out photo dominating her screen.

"Whatever happened to letting me sleep in?" Her voice was some combination of garbled sewer water and a rusted-out engine.

Meg had left around three this morning, promising she'd check in later, but *also* promising that it'd be well into the afternoon when she called.

"I know, but it's really boring driving for hours. How do you put up with it?"

Claire flung the blanket that'd been shielding her eyes away, suddenly too warm. "Talk to Knox."

"I did, but he's listening to some history podcast, and I'd already cried enough saying goodbye to you that I don't want to further deplete my blood sodium by also being bored to tears."

Even with exhaustion wracking over her body, Claire's lip twitched upward. "This morning was one of our better goodbyes."

Meg always ugly-cried when they left each other, often prompting concerned stares from other travelers at the airport. Claire—who *never* cried—would hug Meg and fend off nosy looky-loos with a different excuse each time:

"I've got two hours to live."

"I'm moving to the Arctic Circle for the next seventeen years."

"Do you know who this woman is?"

Each explanation would only make Meg laugh and then blubber about missing her even more.

"But I think the one in Dallas, where you couldn't stop sneezing between sobs, is still number one." Claire flipped, letting her head dangle off the edge of the couch and her legs fold over the back.

"It's not my fault that I was allergic to the TSA agent's perfume."

Claire allowed a beat of silence to pass before asking, "What do you want to talk about since Knox has blocked you out?"

"It's not like that. We're going to be together nonstop for a month. He just needed a break. I can be a lot."

She spun upright. "You are not *a lot*. You're perfect. If Knox doesn't see that, if he makes you feel—"

Meg cut her off. "Easy there, killer. Knox doesn't make me feel anything other than happy. For this road trip, we set up a plan—three hours of together time, then one hour of solo time. I couldn't find a podcast I liked, and this crocheting thing isn't as easy as Rowan makes it look." An annoyed huff sailed over the phone.

"Rowan crochets?"

The defensive anger swirling in her stomach abated as confusion overtook it.

Meg always kept Claire updated about everything happening with the Bellamy family. Claire had heard about Erin's unfortunate attempt at stand-up comedy—something scandalously out of character. She'd known every detail of Augie's disastrous decision to try frosted tips. How Kelly had taken up landscape painting and was shockingly good at it. That Rowan had graduated with the highest honors, ranking first in his psychology PhD program. She'd even heard about a woman named Bethany whom he'd dated for over a year.

"Bethany had come home one night after a long shift and complained that there had been no caps for the newborns she'd delivered," Meg said. "The next day, Rowan had picked up supplies at a craft store and taught himself during his lunch break by watching videos online. Even though they're no longer together, he still makes them and takes them to Tucson General once a month."

"Of course he does," Claire muttered. *Right after he singlehandedly bottle-feeds all the lost kittens in a five-mile radius, reads three storybooks—with the voices—to a preschool class, and rescues four elderly ladies from being pummeled by oncoming traffic.*

His inherent goodness was just another way that Rowan was her complete opposite. For him, it came naturally. Claire had to strive to be a good person.

That, and Rowan always accomplished his goals. He judiciously set aside distraction and went for what he'd wanted. She lacked the kind of dogged dedication to know that *this one thing* was what she wanted to do with her life. Instead, she'd fallen haphazardly into her current profession. Most days, Claire felt like she'd hoodwinked people into caring about her travels, and at any moment, they'd figure out that there wasn't any substance beneath her one-sentence captions.

Claire cleared her throat. "So Rowan taught you to crochet?"

Meg's laugh burst over the phone. "He tried. I assumed he was a bad teacher, so I told him I'd watch videos instead. But I've been at it for thirty minutes with no success. That's when I decided to phone a friend."

"I don't know anything about crocheting."

"No, not with crocheting. Just to chat."

"Got it," Claire said, standing to fold the sheets and noticing the crocheting basket stowed beneath the end table.

Her fingers itched to graze over each fluffy skein of awaiting yarn. She'd always had the need for tactile exploration. It was like her brain wasn't happy until it knew what something felt like—fern fronds, beaded jewelry, the rough edges of a bottle cap, *any* form of fringe. Growing up, there'd been a specialty grocery store Gram liked that sold dried beans in barrels, and it'd been impossible for Claire not to dive up to her forearms in pinto beans.

Claire allowed her fingertips to trail over the rolled yarn ball connected to the metal crochet hooks. The attached, half-completed blue cap sent a tug deep in her abdomen. A startled inhale sucked into her lungs before Claire expertly repressed that particular desire with movement. Striding toward the kitchen, she transferred the phone to her other ear.

Each cabinet was open wide before Claire realized Meg was still talking. "Sorry. What?"

"I said you need to help me get him out more. All he does at the end of the day is crochet those darn baby hats. He's never going to meet anyone else if he's squirreled away every night. It's been almost a year since he broke things off with Bethany." Meg sighed. "Poor thing. She was crushed. So nice too. We all liked her."

The stabbing sensation piercing between her ribs was likely hunger related. Claire grabbed a Clif bar and tore the package open with her teeth. "Wing-woman. I can do that."

"Thank you. I know it's silly, but I worry about him. Erin will never date and happily lives by herself like some self-sustaining microbe, but Rowan is too tender to be left alone. I know I mess with him a lot, but I want him to have what Knox and I have."

The rumble of Knox's reflexive, "Love you too, baby," efficiently decimated Claire's previous reservations. Though Claire hadn't spent any time with Meg's new beau, her best friend was crazy about him, sending Meg on a match-making kick. Claire should just be grateful that *she* wasn't in Meg's crosshairs.

Her nomadic lifestyle made *serious* dating nearly impossible.

At least that was the line she fed herself and everyone else.

Meg monopolized the conversation as Claire rummaged around the kitchen, finding the freshly squeezed orange juice and indulging in two glasses.

"I'm going to the studio to see Heather," Claire replied to Meg's question about her plans.

"You ready for that?"

"No." She left out the real reason why she needed to talk to Gram's former business partner about the money Gram had left her. As far as Meg knew, Claire was getting that money to buy another car. "But it's got to happen."

"Virtual hugs." Meg made a humming, squeezing sound like she always did when they chatted but couldn't wrap their arms around each other.

"Thanks."

"You know my hugs beat the pants off anyone else's hugs."

Claire huffed out a laugh. "This is true."

Though, honestly, Claire longed for one more hug from her grandmother.

"Um." She pushed that thought away. "I should get going, but look up *Stuff You Should Know*. I usually listen to that podcast when I'm driving long, boring stretches of highway."

"I knew I kept you around for a reason."

Her smile was reflexive. "Yeah. Yeah."

◊◊◊

Despite the simmering heat, Claire drove with the windows down. Rowan had told her to use his Jeep since he'd be busy seeing clients all day. A few regal saguaros still held onto their last blooms, their white petaled flowers preening in the blistering sunshine. The light was almost sharp, like a razor cutting your retina. In other places, it could be subdued or even playful, but here, the sunlight burned bright.

Gone was the brief green of spring. The browning greens of the creosote and mesquite trees provided the only break from the dusty, tan soil dominating the landscape. Even with every living thing—including the people—protecting themselves from Tucson's harshest season, the desert was still undeniably beautiful to Claire.

The hot sting from the asphalt parking lot crept into the windows once Claire arrived beside Blissful Desert Yoga. A deep breath accompanied her fingertips slowly tracing the black upside-down heart on her left wrist. The tattooed image was a reminder. One she'd intentionally placed after she'd finished the Pacific Crest Trail. During the several-months'-long hike, she'd proven to herself that she didn't need anyone else to love her.

She'd never had a father, her mother had carelessly abandoned her at twelve, and though the loss of the one person who'd truly cared about her still stung, Claire could love herself.

You can do this. You can handle all of this on your own.

Claire swallowed over the cactus spines pricking her throat and followed a couple through the studio door. She had to close her eyes firmly when Gram's tiny brass disks chimed at the door's movement.

The couple held their phone-screen barcode to a scanner on the counter before placing their shoes and belongings in the cubbies beneath the benches lining the entry. The main practice room was still through a door to the left, the wood floor covered with mats and yogis in various states of repose. Gram's paper signup sheet had been replaced by technology, but most of the walls still contained art and thriving plants.

Claire's fingers traveled the uneven edge of Gram's wooden bowl before picking up a beaded bracelet.

"Hi, did you need—" Heather stood stunned in the doorway to the practice room for a few seconds before regaining her composure. "Claire. Hey. It's good to see you."

Gram's long time yoga instructor employee turned business partner had barely aged in the near decade Claire had been absent. Her short, dark hair was still swooped in an effortless but incredibly trendy style, bangs nearly kissing her dark, arched brows. High-waisted, boho-style pants flowed beneath her snug, cropped tank. The same hammered gold pendant rested in the dip between her tanned collarbones. How Heather had managed to be nearly wrinkle free at forty-five was some kind of wellness-enthusiast magic.

"Hey." Her greeting came out tinged with dust. "You too." Claire moved to the side when a trio of yogis came up behind her to check in. "Are you teaching this class?"

"I was." Heather hesitated. "But just give me a minute. One of our teachers was attending, and I'll ask them to sub for me."

"That's fine," Claire said as she took a step back. "I'll come back."

"Will you?"

Claire hated the trapped sensation that surged through her stomach but forced herself not to move. "You're right. Maybe we should do this now."

In the time it took for Heather to disappear and return, Claire had fought three never-ending battles within herself. It was a character flaw, her urge to run. Claire knew that. But it was also as instinctive as one's desire to take a breath after being under water.

"Come on."

The hallway to the small office/storage room was largely the same. They passed the bathroom and the massage treatment room before Heather moved to close the door and then paused, leaving it open instead.

Apparently, her need to bolt was transparent.

Though she'd initially wished the studio to be unchanged, it being nearly identical to her memory sent an unanticipated and painful sensation scorching through her muscles.

A few beats of silence hovered before Heather's Ujjayi exhale audibly filled the small space. "I assume you're here to collect your money."

"Yes," Claire said, emotionless.

After Gram had died, Claire had arranged the celebration of life ceremony Gram had detailed wanting in her will. She'd felt broken but stood with dry eyes, accepting stories from so many in the community who'd cherished her grandmother. Afterward, Claire had been an overused and wrung-out sponge.

Blissful Desert Yoga had fully transferred to Heather, as expected, and Claire had asked her to hold the ten grand that Gram had left her. Logically, she could have transferred that money to her own bank account, but Claire couldn't do it.

She hadn't wanted numbers in some electronic file somewhere.

Claire had wanted her Gram.

She'd wanted her patchouli-scented arms to wrap around her. She'd wanted her cackling laugh surrounding them as they ate in their tiny, rented casita. She wanted the one person who didn't make Claire feel like a massive disappointment.

Now, though, Claire needed the money. Her nomadic lifestyle didn't come with health insurance, and the internet was crap when estimating how much it would cost to get basic bloodwork or see a doctor. Hopefully, choosing a low-rent apartment would leave enough money to solve her medical mystery and find another cheap car to get her to her next destination.

Wherever that will be.

"I have it. I set it aside in the business savings account and haven't touched it. You've accrued a little over two thousand in interest too." The maternal compassion in Heather's eyes was systematically unraveling Claire's insides.

"Thank you for looking after it all these years," she managed to scrape out.

A sad smile swept Heather's lips. "I hadn't thought about it in forever, but I felt the need to check it the other day. Almost like Ann Marie had been letting me know you'd be coming."

Claire swallowed, fighting like crazy not to rub her wrist.

Throughout the years, there were moments when the light filtered between the trees, and Claire could have sworn Gram was there, admiring the view beside her. Surrounded by the studio's familiar sights and sounds, Gram's presence felt palpable. It should have been reassuring. Instead, Claire thought she might stain the polished floors with vomit.

Heather surveyed her for several seconds. "It'd be nice to see you in a class sometime."

"Yeah, maybe."

Disappointment splashed over Heather's blue irises before they swept to her computer. "Why don't you give me your bank information, and I'll set up a transfer."

Chapter 6

"Oh good, you're done," Claire said as Rowan shut the door to his home office. She pushed back from the kitchen counter and held up something black and sparkly. "Put this on. We're going out."

The last of the sun's embers lit the black-sequined, collared shirt Claire held between pinched fingers. Monday nights, Rowan saw clients until eight p.m., providing slots for those who couldn't come either in person or virtual during normal business hours. It also allowed him to schedule his Friday afternoon's off.

"See? We'll match." She dropped one side of the shirt to wave a hand over the strappy, belted romper hugging her frame. Just like the shirt, it was black and sequined.

How Claire's legs looked longer beneath those tiny shorts must have been some bizarre, sequin-induced optical illusion. She wasn't a particularly tall woman. Rowan knew for a fact that Claire was five foot five and a half inches tall. Her heights over time were marked on the same plank board in his parents' house that held his and his sisters' growth measurements.

He forced his gaze to the ground to keep himself from staring, finding green hiking socks and boots covering her feet. "Are we going on a super-secret glitter mission?" Rowan asked, nodding to the functional choice of footwear.

"No," she said through a blazing smile, both dimples prominent. "We're going to a silent disco in the desert. So . . . party up top, practical on the bottom."

"Ah. The distant cousin of the mullet."

Claire was pure energy, sparking and crackling the air between them. Nothing he could say would dampen her excitement now—not that Rowan was aiming to.

"And when does this magic disco start?"

"Eleven, but I thought we'd get dinner first."

"Hmm." He tapped his thumb on the counter twice, standing entirely too close but unable to keep his distance when Claire was lit from within like this. "Why don't I cook for us?"

His suggestion was two-fold. One, Rowan wanted Claire's blissful food groan to only result from something *he'd* made. And two, if Claire wanted him to be sociable, he needed an hour or two to recharge first.

After finishing with his last client, Rowan had written his notes and allowed himself to mentally debrief. Helping others solve—sometimes truly tragic—problems was draining.

At least half of his clients were parolees assigned to him for anger-management therapy. Unlike the private clients who sought him out, it took longer to establish a therapeutic alliance with a parolee. Generally, their only experience with a psychologist had been from their sentencing period when they'd been mentally evaluated to be judged by the law. It took time, but eventually, each of his parole clients understood that Rowan was there *for them*. He was only interested in helping them become better versions of themselves, helping them control the rageful impulses that had landed them in jail.

"Thank you for the offer, but I have it all set up." Claire picked up her phone.

Reading over her shoulder, the scent of *his* sage body wash accosted him. It smelled tormentingly incredible on her.

"I know you're a foodie," she continued, oblivious to the war zone raging within him. "So I picked all these different eclectic places to do a food crawl. Appetizers here. Main dish there. Dessert at another. It'll be fun. I promise. A thank-you for letting me crash."

Claire spun away, doing a strange little waggle dance. "I didn't tell you the good news. I went apartment hunting this afternoon and found a place in midtown. Tomorrow, I just need to sign paperwork and make a deposit." That fake smile replaced the real one that'd been there a minute ago. "I'll be out of your hair in the morning, so I thought this could be a fun last hurrah."

"It's not like you won't see me again." Even as Rowan sent those joking words forward, twin emotions braided down his spine: relief at having his sanctuary back and an aching loss at the idea of her absence.

This morning, he'd spent much longer than he'd ever admit watching her sleep. Claire had been belly down, one arm dragging on the floor, toes escaping the blanket. The pillow had been discarded to the ground. That stubborn single tendril of hair had crossed her eyes, and it had taken everything in him not to lightly brush it away. Claire regaining consciousness with him hovering would have decimated the delicate balance he'd barely managed since she'd arrived.

"I know." She took a swig of a mostly melted iced coffee. "Because we are going to have lots of fun adventures since Meg designated me to be your wing-woman for the next month."

Rowan barely trapped a groan behind his teeth.

This wasn't the first time he'd found himself at the blunt end of Meg's matchmaking schemes. A month ago, she'd said they'd meet for dinner and then abandoned him and her *very single friend*—Meg had used that phrase at least four times—before ordering. Before that, she'd arrived at the store while he'd been helping Erin, toting another friend. The breaking point had been two weeks ago when she'd brought yet another single woman to his climbing gym. Blessedly, Zane's presence had kept the overly flirtatious woman from giving Rowan a migraine.

Not taking the bait, Rowan nodded to Claire's drink. The plastic cup held Ground Street Coffee's name and logo—the coffee shop his friend Kevin's wife co-owned. "You stopped by Ground Street?"

"When in Tucson…" Claire held the cup up as if to toast before downing another gulp. "I needed a few extra shots of espresso to keep me going today."

Rowan had cut out halfway through the second *Scream* movie, but Meg probably kept Claire up most of the night.

"You sure you want to rave in the desert?" he asked, noting the dark shadows beneath her eyes.

"Yes." Her head dipped in a decisive nod. "I need this." She set the cup down with over-exuberant force. "And you do too. Meg says all you do is hide from the world."

He leaned against the counter, crossing his arms. "I'm happy with my life." Claire knew he was an introvert, that he preferred to surround himself with a select few rather than giant groups of strangers. "I don't need to change to appease the subtle-as-a-freight-train meddling of my middle sister."

The shocked fluttering of Claire's lashes would have led you to believe that he'd spat at her rather than simply stood up for himself.

"You need to *live*, Rowan," she continued, the delicate skin of her neck flushing. "You never know when what you think is stable will change, when something outside your control will force your hand."

Rowan wanted to laugh at the irony of her words. Her very presence was upending all his routines.

"You've always held back. You can't deny that. You've always kept a part of yourself reserved. What if you completely let loose? No timers. No schedule. No regimen." Claire's hands found her hips. "It's not like the world would fall apart."

A muscle in his jaw tweaked at the idea of what exactly would happen if he let his diligent guard down. Not just the wall that kept him from telling Claire how he really felt.

The part that made him dangerous.

The part of himself he had to continuously override.

The part that was built in.

Rowan mentally settled himself before swiping the shirt off the counter. "Dancing is life. Got it. Any preference on what I wear with this? Keep in mind, I left my glowstick-lined pants at Erin's last week."

He'd anticipated a shoulder smack or an eyeroll, but her face pinched, clearly not done with what she'd started.

"Don't." Her tone was colder than the remaining ice rattling in her coffee cup. "Don't do that. Don't agree with me to change the subject. Don't deflect."

"I thought psychoanalyzing was my territory?"

A nasally breath blew between them. "So, what? I'm still the dumb girl who barely made it through high school, and therefore I couldn't have—I don't know—read a book or two over the last nine years?"

Her response was so unexpected it took Rowan a beat to respond. "I never meant—"

"Save it." She spun away, her boots making a slight squeak on his tile floor. Stopping at the sink, she pressed her back against it.

A measured breath drew into his lungs. Rowan recognized *he* wasn't the reason for Claire's rising irritation, just an easy target to release her frustration. Being yelled at wasn't uncommon for Rowan. Anger was one of the emotions his male clients could freely express without ridicule, so it was often the one that came up first. Eventually, when they trusted him, others would make it into their sessions—the emotions that really needed to be addressed.

"Did something happen today?" Rowan asked in his gentlest voice.

Claire shook her head at the floor. "What if I want to Dutch braid your hair before we leave?"

"I guess," he said slowly. This conversation was more erratic than a pinball in a machine.

Claire pinched the bridge of her nose. "Don't just agree with me." Her gaze rose and snagged his, eyes almost pleading. "Fight with me."

His eyebrows rushed together. "Why?"

"You never fight with anyone. You're like the cinnamoniest cinnamon roll. The gentlest giant. An agreeable Adonis. Don't things irritate you? Don't you get fed up with life? Because I'm fed up with life."

Ah. Here we are. Claire finally getting to what was bothering her made it easier to ignore that she'd offhandedly called him an Adonis.

"What are you fed up with?"

"Ugh." She began pacing the short kitchen rug beneath the sink. "I don't want you to therapize me."

He didn't like having to be Therapist Rowan with his friends and family. The physical door that divided his home office from the rest of his house was always closed for a reason. Separation between work life and home life was imperative. But right now, he was at a loss.

"You want me to fight with you," Rowan repeated back.

"*Yes.*" The word was elongated as her arms flopped to her sides, almost instantly looking as tired as she must have felt.

"Why is it important that I fight with you?"

"You're doing it again." Her hand swept her face with a heavy exhale before her head lulled to the side, her lashes fluttering.

"Claire?"

The question came a millisecond too late.

In retrospect, it was like watching the most terrifying part of a horror movie in perverse slow motion. Claire twitched, almost as if she'd been experiencing a full-body shock, before she crumpled to the floor, landing in a buckled heap on the mat beside the sink.

Chapter 7

Claire hadn't expected Rowan to throw her words back at her the very next evening. "You wanted me to fight with you. I'm fighting with you. You should be happy."

Claire wrinkled her nose. "You're being unreasonable."

"I'm not." Rowan stood like an imposing gatekeeper beside the open passenger side door to his Jeep. "If you want in the house, you'll let me carry you. The doctors said the weakness might last a few more days and that you should rest."

"So you're going to carry me around and tend to my every need?"

"Yes." She'd never seen Rowan so serious, so steadfast.

"You should probably relent," Kelly said, coming to stand beside her son. "Once he gets like this . . ." With a head tilt, she gave a *what-are-you-gonna-do* gesture.

"It's true." Augie joined his wife. "You should have seen him after my heart attack, years ago. He blew off a midterm to take care of me."

It'd been the only other time Claire had considered coming back to Tucson. When she'd regained cell service along the long stretch of the Appalachian Trail and learned what had happened weeks earlier, Meg assured her that Augie had been doing great with his recovery.

"Face it, Claire. This is happening," Meg said from her position in the backseat.

Knox just shrugged from his spot beside Meg. Not that she blamed him.

The Bellamys could be intense. Case in point, this current bombardment.

If only Erin were here. She'd talk some sense into the rest of them. But she'd had video meetings she couldn't get out of today. With the rest of her family, Erin had been at Claire's side as the doctors unraveled the cause of her little "fainting spell."

Fine. It'd been slightly more than a fainting spell.

She'd had a significant electrolyte imbalance—something that had led to the irregular heartbeat that caused her to pass out for several minutes. The imbalance coupled with the excess caffeine from the quadruple-shot iced coffee had been a recipe for disaster.

Her levels had been so out of whack that she'd been admitted after arriving via ambulance to the ER. Then Claire had undergone a gauntlet of tests to determine why an otherwise fit thirty-four-year-old would be exhibiting these symptoms.

After being put through the medical wringer, the doctors discovered she'd developed celiac disease. Her destroyed intestinal lining had been unable to absorb nutrients, resulting in looming fatigue, muscle weakness, and the electrolyte imbalance that landed her in this predicament.

Rowan's expression softened. "Piggyback ride?"

Resigned to her fate, Claire sighed and motioned for him to come closer. They needed to get out of the afternoon heat. The cool air from the AC Rowan had run at full blast during the short drive from Tucson General had vanished. A drop of sweat had already slid down her spine.

Once inside, Bellamys swarmed around her, doing various tasks, while Claire sat like a queen bee upon the sofa, accepting forms of nourishment. Knox handed Claire a smoothie Rowan had whipped up. Kelly stripped the bed and washed sheets. Meg snuggled next to her, tabbing through Netflix. Rowan and Augie took the large black trash can from the garage and began pitching anything that contained wheat, barley, rye, or oats that weren't certified gluten-free.

Ignoring Meg's question on whether they should start a Turkish or Korean drama, Claire twisted to face the kitchen. "Don't throw things away. I'll be moving out in a few days."

The kitchen was Rowan's happy place. He had four distinct ice shapes in his freezer, an entire wall dedicated to spices, and a set of open shelves for his various self-jarred foods. His burnt-orange KitchenAid stand mixer even matched his Le Creuset. Rowan shouldn't rearrange his life because she'd unexpectedly developed an autoimmune condition.

"Yeah, that's not happening." Rowan pitched a full bottle of soy sauce into the trash and crossed his arms. "You're staying here until we get this sorted out."

Where did all this bossiness come from? Had he taken overnight lessons from Erin? The entire hospital stint, he'd been immovable. On several occasions, the nursing staff mistook him for her overprotective boyfriend, and Rowan had corrected them with a gentle, "I'm her brother."

Augie cleared his throat, causing Rowan to loosen his tight shoulders.

"It would be best if you stayed here until your allergen levels are redrawn." Rowan was referring to a slew of autoimmune markers the gastroenterologist wanted retaken—*three months* from now.

"You can't be—"

"Bed's all made," Kelly said as she stepped into the living room. "Do you need anything out of your bags before I move them?"

"Wait. What?" She couldn't be taking over Rowan's bedroom in addition to his kitchen.

Claire made to stand, but Meg pulled her back down.

This was ludicrous. They were treating her like she was made of spun sugar and would disintegrate any second.

She'd done everything by herself *for years.*

She'd hiked thousands of miles, withstanding sweltering heat, bone-chilling cold, ticks, horseflies the size of your head, blisters . . .

So. Many. Blisters.

Claire could handle taking some supplements, getting her blood drawn, and avoiding the allergen that'd decimated her intestinal lining. Thanks to the nutritionist who saw her before she was discharged today and the glorious internet swathed with gluten-free recipes and tips for eating out, Claire had this. Hands down. She only needed a few days to recover from the muscle weakness. Not three months.

Kelly sat on the coffee table, gathering one of Claire's hands in both of hers. A maternal sigh left her lips before she spoke. "Last night, your heart stopped working long enough for you to pass out."

"But I woke up right after the medics arrived." Protesting was futile. Kelly was using that this-is-decided voice she'd always used when she and Meg wanted to do something beyond their years.

Kelly rubbing her hand only deepened the doomed feeling stirring in Claire's belly. "We had a family meeting about it. If my home was in working order, you'd be set up in the guest bedroom, but since we're temporarily houseless, this is what we settled on."

"But—"

"You're family, Clairebear." Augie's large hand settled on her shoulder from behind the couch. "This is what we do for family."

Claire fought the moisture pricking at her eyes like she'd fought a twenty-mile-per-hour headwind. Then she took everyone's solemn expression as she glanced from one person to the next. The only set of eyes she didn't catch were Rowan's. His shoulders hunched as he pressed his hands against the kitchen countertop, staring at the floor beside the sink.

"Okay." Her voice wobbled slightly. "That's—" An overwhelmed exhale escaped her lips.

Augie's hand gave her two hearty pats, Meg stated that a Turkish drama was the way to go, and Kelly squeezed Claire's fingers before asking Rowan for the white vinegar to scour the shower tiles.

Dinner was held under the stars once everything had been settled within the house, and Meg and Knox's shiny Airstream was set up in Rowan's driveway. The fact that her best friend had barely started her summer vacation before having to drive back overnight from San Diego made bile flick at the back of her throat, but each time Claire brought it up, Meg dismissed her with a cheeky, "I'd do literally anything for you."

Kelly and Augie had given hugs and gone home, but Meg and Knox still kept Claire company on the couch while Rowan washed the dishes. Even though the male lead was distractingly handsome enough that even Knox commented on it when he'd joined them, Claire couldn't focus on anything other than how much disruption she was causing.

Her goal had been to come to Tucson, collect her money, and discreetly figure out why she was having mystery muscle weakness. Now the entire Bellamy clan had seen her in a hospital gown with a nasal cannula up her nose. For someone who rarely even asked fellow hikers for a strip of Leukotape when she'd run out, leaning on her best friend's family this much felt like an army of fire ants was traipsing up her legs.

The second her phone rang, Claire flashed the Tucson General caller ID at Meg. "I've got to get this. It might be important."

After edging around Knox's legs, Claire slipped into Rowan's therapy office and clicked on a floor lamp.

"Hello?" Claire answered, looking over the room.

The space was warm and inviting, yet masculine. Burnt-orange curtains framed the main window facing the driveway, now showcasing Knox's camper. A caramel leather armchair sat opposing a structured loveseat. Beside the couch was a reclaimed wood end table with a box of tissues, a pad of paper, a small dish filled with mint Life Savers, and four different fidget devices. Kelly's desert landscapes were placed on two walls, and the third held a squat desk with a closed laptop, above which Rowan's degrees hung in simple frames.

"Claire Winesett? I'm Dr. Connolly. I'm calling about the samples they took during this morning's procedure."

"Right, um. The . . ." What was it called again? "The EFG?"

The man on the phone laughed. "EGD. Short for Esophagogastroduodenoscopy. Anyway, yes. I'm calling because as Dr. Reyes probably explained that your intestinal villi had the telltale signs of celiac disease . . ."

The kind, young doctor had compared her villi to grass, explaining how they're supposed to be tall and healthy, but hers were short and stubby. Not the best analogy for desert dwellers, but Claire got the gist.

". . . and she likely mentioned that she took some tissue samples during the procedure."

"Yes." Claire remembered Dr. Reyes mentioned that. *Just a routine part of the procedure,* she'd said.

"Unfortunately, we had a bit of a situation."

"Situation?"

The man sighed heavily. "Yes. Um, not to divulge all the details, but I was in the middle of reading your slide when . . . well, I lost the sample."

Throbbing in Claire's skull prompted her to put the call on speaker and set it on the end table. She rubbed her temples as a voice next to the man urged him to continue, but Claire only caught parts of it. Something like, "Tell her how you screwed up if you want a chance at keeping your job."

"What should I tell her? That my girlfriend trashed my workstation while we were fighting?" Dr. Connolly asked the voice.

"What?" Claire asked.

He groaned this time, still speaking to the person next to him. "Yes, I know. I shouldn't have let Stacey into the lab. I didn't know she was going to freak out and throw medical samples."

Claire's brows crashed together, the pain in her head intensifying.

"Ma'am," a stern woman's voice overtook the line. "We apologize for this egregious error, but my *colleague*"—the word was spat with the utmost disdain—"had mentioned that prior to . . . the incident, your cells looked questionable. Of course, there's no way to verify his observation without a viable slide."

The heavy silence hovering on the line was promptly overshadowed by the blood rushing in her ears. "What does that mean?"

"Unfortunately, we'll need to obtain another sample, which means you'll need another endoscopy. We've notified Dr. Reyes's office, and a scheduler should be calling you tomorrow to set it up. The pathology department apologizes for the mistake and assures you that you will not be charged for it."

Claire sat hard on the chair, staring out the window.

"So I won't have to pay for the next endoscope?"

That inhale-through-teeth sound slipped over the line. "We will waive our portion of processing any future samples and the physician time evaluating them for irregularities, but unfortunately, I don't have the authority to waive the cost of the procedure."

The heels of her hands met her eyes. The cost of last night's overnight stay—complete with multiple blood draws, imaging, and this morning's endoscopy—would probably decimate what Gram had left for her. There was no way that money would also cover the electrolyte blood draw she was supposed to have done Monday, the allergen markers in three months, the DEXA bone scan Dr. Reyes wanted, *and* another endoscopy.

"I apologize again, ma'am. Please know that Dr. Connolly will be held accountable for his poor judgment."

"Yeah. Sure." Those words took what was left of her energy as the call ended.

Lost in her thoughts, Claire failed to notice Rowan knocking and entering until his shoes appeared in her downcast gaze. She remained hunched over, fingertips to forehead, pretending she didn't know he was there.

When Rowan knelt in front of her, Claire was forced to look up.

"What is it?" The worry pinging in his eyes only made his face seem more rugged. This deep groove folded directly between his brows that Claire swore hadn't been there when he'd been younger. "Are you okay?"

Claire tilted her head back with a sigh just to give herself respite from Rowan's gaze. "Yeah. I'm fine. They made a mistake with the samples and need me to have another endoscopy."

"Oh."

At his relieved tone, Claire hazarded a glance in his direction. He was still kneeling in front of her, but that forehead notch was gone. Somehow, its absence made a calm brush over her cheeks as well.

Rowan tilted his head, thinking. "Just let me know when they set it up, and I'll rearrange my clients so I can take you."

The groan coming from her throat was far too loud. Claire was used to being on a trail—often alone—so when she got frustrated at a broken pack strap or an ankle-twisting rock, she could fuss as loud as she wanted to.

"What?" Rowan's warm hands settled on her knees before he pulled them back like her kneecaps were molten lava. "What is it?" he asked, clearing his throat and leaning back on his haunches.

"I can't afford another procedure." Once the first bit came tumbling out, it was like the first loose stones of an avalanche before the entire mountainside came crashing down. "I don't have health insurance. I haven't had insurance or seen a doctor since I left Tucson. Gram left me some money, but I'm not sure it will cover everything that has happened in the last twenty—" Claire glanced around for a clock. "However many hours I was at the hospital." A deep breath staggered into her spent lungs. "Why isn't there a clock in here?"

"It distracts my clients," he said. "What about what you earn from traveling?"

"That only pays for the next location. Sometimes gear." Her shoulder lifted pitifully before dropping. "It looks glamorous, but it's not."

Rowan's hand lifted like he wanted to run it over her arm, but he brushed it over his jaw instead. "Okay."

When Rowan tilted his face up with a deep inhale, Claire knew he was mentally fixing things. He'd done that hundreds of times when they'd been kids. He'd get this calculating yet peaceful expression, as if doing geometry and composing a sonnet all at once. Then he'd burst forward with the answer. It never failed. Erin kept everyone in line, but Rowan was who you went to if you were already in trouble.

The corner of her mouth spontaneously lifted, waiting for the solution to her problem.

When Rowan gave her the answer, Claire choked on her own spit—her fist hitting her chest so hard she winced.

Because there was *no possible way* he'd just said, "You should marry me."

Chapter 8

A woman choking like the idea of being your wife is worse than having her eyeballs removed by a grapefruit spoon is not exactly the response a man dreams of. Of course, this wasn't a real proposal.

Though, technically, he *was* on his knees.

Rowan scrambled to stand. "For my health insurance," he added. "Obviously."

Claire's hand was now covering her mouth, eyes doubling in size.

He crossed his arms, looking out the window and leaning against the edge of the couch his clients sat on. Though he'd always been exceptional at masking his emotions, something about impulsively proposing marriage made him feel as if he was stark nude instead of wearing yesterday's work clothes.

"I've got great insurance. We all do. We never pay anything out of pocket as part of our plan. Our employees even have only a $250 deductible a year, and then everything else is covered.

That's one of the reasons our staff stays with us so long. It was something Dad was adamant about since medical debt crippled his parents' finances before they passed."

Rowan swallowed, remembering one of his first meetings with his stepfather as a boy. Augie had wept openly in front of Rowan and his sisters because he'd been grieving the recent loss of his parents—something they'd never seen a man do before.

"Crying is for sissies. You're not a sissy, are ya?" His birth father's scratchy voice seared into his mind before Rowan actively shook the memory away.

"If we get married, I can add you as a dependent, and then you could have any other medical procedures, scans, bloodwork, etc without paying. And it's not like it will mean anything. It'll just be paperwork. We won't even tell anyone. You'll stay here until you feel better, as planned, and as soon as your health sorts out, we'll get a divorce. Easy."

Nothing he'd just said was easy. First, they'd be committing insurance fraud. Second, he'd have to hide this marriage from his family and friends. Third, he'd be tethering himself to someone that, as much as he'd tried not to, he still loved.

If Rowan hadn't been sure after spending all day with her at the store, he'd known the second her body had hit the tile floor yesterday. A small woman shouldn't have been able to make such a thunderous clap. The only thing that mollified that sound was the near-silent whisper of her unconscious breath once he'd scooped her into his arms. The EMS staff had to reassure him four times that Claire would be okay before he'd relinquished his hold so they could put her on the stretcher. Ten seconds later, her eyes had fluttered open.

The drive following the ambulance had been one of bargains. He'd bargained with the universe for Claire's well-being, promising he'd do anything.

Claire made the world better just by existing. She had to be okay.

Now, it seemed the universe was asking for payment in the sum of a marriage of convenience.

"We're not going splitsies on a takeout order. We'd be committing insurance fraud." Claire's deep frown punched him in the solar plexus.

"I know that."

"*Rowan.*" Her head dipped to the side with a *come-on* expression.

"Claire," he said, tone stoic.

Rowan wasn't sure he'd blinked once since he'd begun explaining the obvious answer to this problem. He was undoubtedly being even more rigid than normal, but after watching her collapse, it was like all of his tendons had shortened a half inch. Everything in him was unyielding and tight.

A sigh floated between them. "This is too much."

"It's not too much." He couldn't help the roughness of his voice.

Claire's expression continued to pinch. "How are we supposed to keep a fake marriage from your family when it's *your family's* insurance?"

That one was easy.

"Our new broker doesn't know the family well and is less sociable than Liza was. I don't think changing my insurance will be something he'll report back to Erin."

Claire's head was shaking, her gaze unseeing. "I can't do this. I *won't* do this."

"Then what am I going to do with you?"

It was the exact phrase she'd asked him so many times growing up, usually in an affectionate way, before ruffling his hair.

Something in Claire cracked as she drew a staggered breath.

The instinct that something had been left unsaid ticked his right earlobe. If Claire had been one of his therapy clients, he would have spent a few moments debating the most effective way to help her open up.

Instead, Rowan blurted, "What?"

Her mouth popped open before it closed, firming into a tight line.

"Tell me." He'd never heard his voice so gruff before. So direct. So commanding.

It was like the dynamic between them shifted in some subtle, unseen way. Like their friendship up until now had existed as invisible Tetris cubes, and he'd just verbally rearranged the expected order.

Her gaze stalled on his tight jaw before she said, "The doctor . . . she said my cells looked 'questionable.'"

The air sucked out of the room the second Claire's uncertain eyes met his.

Rowan took a step forward before he could stop himself. "What does that mean?"

"I don't know." Claire flopped up her hands, and they fell with a smack on her bent legs. "They need more of my insides to get an answer."

His mind was already seventy-six miles down the track, calculating worst-case scenarios. "All the more reason to get on my insurance. If you need"—Rowan didn't want to say *treatment*—"anything, it'll be covered."

Claire nodded at the floor, silent for a long time while rubbing her wrist.

It was agony not being able to touch her.

"If . . ." She sucked her lower lip between her teeth. "I can't agree to this if I'm going to be a burden."

"You're not a burden." What was up with his voice? He couldn't keep that growly rasp from infiltrating all his words.

They stared at each other for a long moment before Claire blinked and shattered the tension with an animated clap.

"Like it or not, this is only going down one way." The jokiness in her words was like a hard reset, shuffling them both back into their expected roles.

The second his tight hands unfurled, Claire grinned with that wicked little twist. It was the same smile he'd seen countless times as a kid before she and Meg got into some kind of trouble. It generally showed up right before they'd ask him to play henchman or lookout or bait.

"No," he said automatically. Relief over slipping into their usual repartee smoothed over his tense muscles. "Whatever you're thinking, no."

This time, Claire gave him a dramatic pout. "When did you stop being fun? I remember you used to be fun."

He scoffed, playing along. "I was never fun."

"Are you sure about that?" Claire's brow wrinkled in the most adorable way. "I remember a boy who used to hop fences to play midnight baseball." Her brows lifted as she pointed at him. "I remember sharing Augie's cooking sherry in the garage because we were dumb teenagers and had no idea what real alcohol was."

A ghost of a smile lifted his lips.

"I remember buying each other outfits at Goodwill, and then we'd have to wear them out to dinner. No questions asked."

His unrestrained smile broke free as Rowan shook his head. "You and Meg were always trying to get me to wear something sequined—even back then."

Claire's smile mirrored his own, both dimples prominent. "I think the best outfit we found for you was the Richard Simmons wig with an old basketball jersey and plaid bell bottoms."

"I'll reluctantly admit that was one of your better combinations."

"See." Claire leaned back in his chair, folding her legs up on the seat. "Let's do stuff like that again. We'll call it a Fun Pact."

He lifted a dubious eyebrow. "A Fun Pact?"

"Yes. Two nights a week, we're going to do something fun. Meg is convinced that you've turned into some grumpy hermit."

Rowan supposed that grumbling would only prove his sister right, but it also would keep that grin on Claire's face. At this point, he'd do anything to keep Claire smiling, laughing, lighting up.

Did Claire want him to belt "Celebration" and dance in the University of Arizona fountain? Just let him grab his Bluetooth speaker.

Did she want him to eat an entire meal at his favorite restaurant with socks on his hands? Crew or ankle length?

Did she want him to tap into the skills he'd learned in the *Introduction to Acting* class Kevin and Kyle had made him take sophomore year and butcher his way through an Australian accent? No dramas, mate.

"Shoot. Meg." Claire slapped her forehead. "How can we slip down to the courthouse for some fake nuptials with Meg and Knox occupying your driveway? You saw her today. She was like a barnacle on my backside."

"Then I'll just have to take her place."

Claire laughed, that irresistible snort punctuating like an exclamation point.

"What?" he asked in mocked offense, trying to keep his heart from bursting. "I've got excellent barnacle skills. I can fixate on one task for hours, *and* I can suspend my entire body weight from these three fingers." Rowan bent his index, middle, and ring finger into a half crimp position.

Claire's gaze stalled his hand before she fixed it on one of his mother's paintings, her neck flushing. "Do you think she'll listen? Meg can be pretty stubborn."

He ignored the stifling desire to determine what exactly was causing that pink to creep toward her ears and stayed on task. "We'll convince her that you're doing well enough for her to go back on vacation, and between me, Mom, and Dad—and Erin if need be—we've got you covered. I'll also talk to Knox. I'm pretty sure he'd rather be parking his Airstream at the beach than in my driveway."

"So we convince them to leave, and then we get married." She did that distracting lip-wetting thing again. "When?"

Rowan pulled his phone from his pocket. "I'll check the details and try to schedule a courthouse appointment later this week. The sooner the better. That way we can get you on my insurance and find out"—he forced a breath into his tight lungs—"everything."

"Right." She nodded at his mother's springtime rendition of Picacho Peak.

As he passed in front of her on his way toward the door, Claire's left fingers circled his wrist like a ball python. "Rowan, wait."

His name came out cracked, and it took everything in him not to pull her into his arms like he'd done the night before.

"Thank you for this. And thank you for not leaving me last night." Claire swallowed. "It was hard being there. In the same place . . ."

Rowan knew she meant at the same hospital where her grandmother had been taken after her unexpected stroke, where she'd passed a few days later.

Memories of the three months after Anne Marie's death rushed forward. His whole family had jumped in to support Claire, much like they were doing now, each using their own strengths to help. Erin and Dad had worked out the legal specifics, leaving him, Mom, and Meg to provide solace.

Only . . . Claire had never cried, never broke down with sorrow. It had almost been as if someone had flipped a manic switch. She'd sold Anne Marie's belongings and gave all the money to the women's shelter. She'd severed the lease on their historic, adobe casita and temporarily moved in with Meg. Though, she often would stay out late, not answering her phone. She'd quit her job bartending at a local cowboy bar and then prepared to leave for the several-months' trek of the Pacific Crest Trail, claiming she needed to walk off her grief.

"Of course." He brushed the thumb of his free hand over her heart tattoo. "I'll always be here for you."

When Claire shivered at his touch, Rowan pulled his free hand back, adding, "*We'll* always be here for you. Like Dad said earlier, you're family."

She slowly uncurled her fingers, releasing him. "I appreciate it. Just let me pull my weight over the next few months, okay?" Claire looked up with an inhale, determination settling in the slight hollows of her cheekbones.

"You better," he said, setting his lips in a dubious smirk. "I expect a barrel of laughs from each of these 'fun excursions.'"

Rowan knew he was in trouble the second her eyes flashed with mischief. "You just wait and see."

Chapter 9

It'd only taken some mild cajoling from both of them, and a few displays of strength on Claire's part, to convince Meg to resume her vacation. Every morning, Rowan made Claire a nutritious, gluten-free breakfast before heading to his home office to meet with therapy clients, virtually or in person. The low murmur of Rowan's voice snuck under his office door, and though Claire couldn't hear what he or the other male voice was saying, their conversation filled the room with peaceful white noise.

Meg was usually a late riser, but she'd begun coming into the house early to enjoy Rowan's surprisingly diverse portfolio of omelets, frittatas, and egg souffles. Claire had helped with the dishes, not only to mollify that ache that sat right at the base of her chest but to show Meg she was strong enough to be left without supervision. Also, working with Meg over a soap-filled sink had wrapped her in the sweet memories of her childhood, tidying up after Augie had made everyone a weekend brunch.

Meg and Knox eventually agreed to leave today, Friday, since their next campsite reservation in Laguna Beach started tonight, which meant this morning had been another epic sobfest. But then, after waving so hard her arm hurt, Claire was left with the daunting reality of today's big task.

She was marrying Rowan Bellamy.

On paper only, she quickly reminded herself.

And keeping the whole thing from the person you love most.

That thought brought the roasted red peppers from this morning's breakfast racing up her throat.

Firmly placing both her hands on her belly, Claire swallowed. No part of this felt right. Lying to Meg was like fracturing her foot and having to tough it out another few miles. Taking advantage of Rowan's overabundant generosity was as appealing as licking the handrails in a bathroom stall.

Though she could suppress that weird ribbon of attraction that flared at odd times, Rowan worrying about whether she liked the gluten-free naan he'd made from scratch or if she'd been getting enough sleep in his ridiculously comfortable bed made it harder to deny how nice it was to be taken care of.

Self-sufficiency is the name of the game when backpacking. Sure, you could hope for a trail magic moment like a tin of cookies appearing around the next bend, but most of the time, you had to rely on yourself.

Being nurtured like this brought her too close to a desire she'd long suppressed. The idea that had seemed so far-fetched after watching her mother barrel through one damaged, unstable relationship to the next. Even Gram had never dated again after losing her husband when Claire's mother had been a child. But after witnessing Kelly and Augie's love, Claire wondered if what had seemed impossible was actually achievable.

A stable home. A picket fence. Two point five kids. A friendly family companion.

The whole shebang.

Claire had always felt that such a life, with its permanence, would never be for her. But sometimes, particularly when she'd been a wistful teen, she'd fantasize.

Of course, her vision had always been based in Arizona, so it went like this: a little beige stucco-walled house, a sternly tempered firstborn followed by rambunctious twins, and maybe a labradoodle or a border collie or . . .

A friendly neighborhood bobcat.

When Herbert Nenninger popped into her mind, Claire straightened so fast her spine popped.

No.

No. No. No.

This is not your future.

A hundred or so miles into the Pacific Crest Trail, Claire had finally figured out why she couldn't accept Rowan's last words to her. At that time, she'd *needed* his "I love you" to be given in a brother-sister way because there'd been a wrongness in his words.

Someone like Rowan—so kind, compassionate, and *good*—shouldn't love someone as messed up as her. Someone who couldn't process grief without shutting down and running away. Someone who had the emotional maturity of a toddler. Someone who had thousands of acquaintances but only one true friend because though she loved the company of others, she hated them *knowing* her.

Claire had made a lot of mistakes in her life—wearing cotton clothing on her first through-hike, staying at that questionable hostel in Montana, *bangs*—but there'd be no coming back from crossing the line with Rowan. She was not going to hurt him nor jeopardize her relationship with Meg. Doing so would be as reckless as intentionally chopping off one of her toes with a hatchet.

Firmly pinching her thigh, Claire forced herself to focus. This was about discovering if anything else was medically amiss and getting out of town as quickly as possible. Rowan was simply allowing her to do that while not going into debt.

This was all pretend.

◇◇◇

A little after noon, Rowan opened the door to his home office. His mouth opened as if to say something before his gaze focused on her—that worried notch settling between his brows.

Claire nervously ran a hand down her years-old, black, high-neck shift dress. Everything else she owned was some form of trail or lounge clothes. This garment usually sufficed for the random night in town but made for a very sad wedding dress. To combat the fact that the only other nice-ish outfit she had was a sequined jumper, Claire had taken her time double-Dutch braiding her hair into a pretty updo, finishing with a small chignon at the nape of her neck. She'd even tucked a handful of yellow brittlebush flowers into the style and found some months'-old mascara, applying three coats.

She hardly wore makeup anymore. It just wasn't a priority when you were alone outdoors most of the time. Sunscreen . . . now that's a priority. But the way Rowan grimaced at her made Claire feel like she was covered in mud and sticks.

"I'm sorry," she blurted, resisting the urge to squirm beneath this scrutiny. "This is all I have. I didn't want to tip off Meg by asking her to take me shopping for something nicer."

Rowan's gaze flowed over her attire before stalling on her tan Teva sandals. "What you wear doesn't matter. It's just a formality, remember? A means to an end."

"Right. Okay." Though queasiness surged through her stomach, Claire tipped her chin toward the garage. "In that case, shall we?"

Twenty-five minutes later, they were weaving through the one-way streets of downtown Tucson on their way to the courthouse. Claire had tried several times to engage Rowan in a conversation about his day, or the impending monsoon season, or—shoot, she would've been happy if he'd simply recited the alphabet. Anything other than the looming silence that sat between them.

As the tires hummed against the pavement, Claire's mind fixated on a single thought.

She was the only one benefiting from this arrangement.

Claire knew he didn't need her to chauffeur him around to various activities twice a week. Rowan had thriving relationships with his college friends and his family. He had hobbies. He loved his work. He even contributed to his community by crocheting baby hats, for goodness' sake.

She was the one that was lacking. The one that had to be charismatic and entertaining because she had nothing else to offer. Claire tried to shut out the grating sound of her mother's voice reminding a younger version of herself what an inconvenience she was, what a burden it was to take care of her.

The stabbing knowledge that she didn't have anything to give Rowan ate at her heart like corrosive acid. Claire had to do something to make this situation better. She had to pull her own weight, even in some small way. So when she spotted a store just ahead that could *slightly* improve the situation, Claire couldn't help shouting.

"Stop! Pull over!"

Rowan swerved his Jeep into a parallel parking spot. "You don't have to yell. I can take you home." He was already looking in his side mirror to pull back into traffic.

"No." She gripped his forearm, the heat of him searing her fingertips.

Rowan had worn his usual work outfit today: slacks and a button-down shirt, collar open and sleeves rolled. Though, this morning, his shirt was a stark white—something a groom would wear.

Claire swallowed over the knot growing in her throat. "I know this isn't a real marriage, but I feel like if I show up in a black dress, the court security officers will know this is a hoax and drag us straight to jail." She tilted her head toward the small, eclectic boutique just beyond the curb. "We're a little early. Just let me get another dress. I'll be quick. I promise."

Rowan nodded, and she let herself out into the oppressive midday heat. "I'll be back in two licks of a cricket."

Her nerves over this whole day were now apparently dismantling her ability to put sensical words together.

"Two licks of a cricket? Who says that?" she muttered to herself after she'd shut the car door.

A cheery saleswoman called to her while cashing out another customer. Claire managed a halfway friendly, "Hey," before barreling toward the dress rack. This store catered more to the Bohemian than bridal clientele, but surely there was a sundress in here that was more suitable than what she had on.

Claire ended up grabbing a quilted multicolor one, a green striped maxi dress, and a yellow midi with a tiered skirt and straps that tied at the top of the shoulders.

The green dress was halfway back over her head—having already nixed it since it firmly resembled a circus tent—when the gentle rumble of Rowan speaking to the saleswoman whispered below the psychedelic mood music piping from the speakers.

Rushing, Claire tugged on the yellow sundress. She tied the straps into bows before noticing that her sports bra completely ruined the look. Fortunately, the smocked bodice held everything in place once the gray bra joined her black dress on the floor.

Claire twisted and stooped, trying to catch the whole dress in the tiny mirror before giving up and looking for the full-length one she'd seen on the sales floor. Rowan was seated in the velvet chair beside the mirror, practically man-spreading, that grumpy expression still pinned to his face.

Claire expected that deep frown to lessen now that she was wearing something other than her overworn dress, but if anything, the sight of her only deepened his scowl. She took one retreating step, intending on trying on contestant number three, when Rowan's voice halted her progression.

"Stop." He was using that commanding tone again. The one he'd used the other night. The one that sent unwanted goosebumps pricking her skin.

Claire wasn't one to click her heels and murmur, "Yes, sir," when being barked at. She'd met way too many obnoxious alpha types who thought they knew better than her. Even before her life as a solo-traveler, bartending had taught her how to handle entitled and bossy men. But Rowan was none of those things. If anything, he was respectful to a fault. So when that no-nonsense tone came from him, it felt like a flick of electricity weaving between her ribs.

"Come here."

Darned if her feet didn't just float her right over, facing the mirror.

Traitors.

Rowan rose, coming to stand behind her, his gaze fixed on her bare upper back. Claire's brain had just begun working again, and she was a millisecond from coming up with a quip about how she was a strong, independent woman who wouldn't respond to commands, when his knuckles brushed the nape of her neck.

A startled gasp slipped between her lips, but Rowan didn't pull away or apologize. He kept his eyes trained on his hand as his knuckles slowly slid down the center of her upper back.

"This dress is fine."

The gruff words somehow rumbled *into* her body. She felt them behind her eyelids, over her waist, and curling her toes in her hiking sandals.

With a swift motion, Rowan pulled the sales tag from the back of the dress, tore it off, and headed to the register.

"Come on. We're going to be late."

The last time she'd been this thrown had been when she'd misstepped during a creek crossing and ended up doused in freezing ice melt. When Claire had collected herself enough to snatch up her black dress and bra from the dressing room, Rowan had paid and was already exiting the shop.

Chapter 10

Rowan fiddled with the gray silicone rings in his pocket to keep himself from recklessly running his hand over Claire's skin again. He hadn't meant to touch her earlier, but she'd stepped out in that sunbeam of a dress, and all logic had seeped from his brain. It was just that the soft yellow was a near perfect match to the flowers she'd woven into her hair.

That little touch had arrowed straight through him.

He knew this was all pretend, that none of it mattered, but the fact that Claire cared enough to worry about her appearance set a low frequency humming in his spine. She'd been beautiful in her black dress, but she was almost indescribable now.

Unfortunately, her sweet gesture wasn't enough to pull him from his grumpy mood. The charade of today had been ticking at his temple all morning. He'd barely slept last night, thinking about how this whole situation was completely wrong.

He'd only wanted to do this *once*—preferably with the woman he loved.

The woman was here, her toes wiggling in her sandals as she chatted with the other awaiting couples with Friday afternoon appointments, but the circumstances were all wrong.

And it was his fault.

That knowledge was like a sucker punch to the kidneys, leaving irritation in its wake. Because next to these happy couples, he and Claire were frauds. His parents had set an exceptional example of what a happy marriage looked like, and marrying Claire like this was spitting on their love.

Claire laughed while playing with the flower girl of the couple two appointments ahead of them. The girl smiled, running her chubby hands over Claire's braids. The girl's mother gasped, apologizing and helping Claire tuck most of the wayward pieces back into place.

"It's okay." Claire beamed. "It probably looks better this way. More natural."

The mother—who was also a bride—simply hugged Claire in response. Then she held Claire at arm's length with a surveying look before loosening that single rebellious strand that always sprung from Claire's cowlick. "Beautiful."

"Excuse me." Rowan rose from the bench. "I'm going to use the bathroom."

The effort it took to keep his hands from fisting or punching one of them through the shabby hallway walls was gargantuan. His ever-present anger, as much a part of his body as his lungs, was bubbling over. Boundaries and rules usually kept it in check, but Rowan was barely subduing it. Only one thing would happen if he couldn't stop the infernal rage that zipped through his body regardless of how many hours he spent trying to extinguish it—someone would get hurt.

Claire would get hurt.

One look at his haggard expression in the bathroom mirror and Rowan slammed his eyes shut. When dragging breath after deep breath didn't help, he began a five-senses grounding technique, starting with five things he could see: *Black-and-white-checkered tile. Dirty walls. Almost empty paper towel dispenser. Dripping sink.* Rowan averted his gaze from his reflection. *Hard-water stain on the porcelain.*

Four things he could feel: *The sweat dripping down his spine. The cool dampness of the sink basin. The stretch of his shirt over his shoulders. The tightness in his chest.*

His pulse racketed, moving in opposition of the intention of the exercise.

Three . . . Rowan forced himself to think. Sounds. *Water running. People talking. The whoosh of the barely there AC.*

Two: The omnipresent scent of urine and body odor.

One: The remnant staleness of his mid-morning peppermint LifeSaver on his tongue.

Rowan returned to the queue to see the judge once he felt mostly composed.

"Darling." Claire entwined her arm in his. "Steve and April have agreed to stay after their wedding and be our witnesses since"—she frowned theatrically—"our families disapprove of our union."

"Oh. Great." He extended his hand to Steve, efficiently dislodging Claire. Rowan was struggling enough without having her warmth encircling him. "Thank you."

"That's tough that both families are against you two," the blond man said, shaking hands.

"Such a shame that they won't acknowledge your marriage unless you both agree to wed at their nudist colony." April nodded with solemn eyes.

Rowan nearly choked on his spit. "Uh. Yes. It's . . . upsetting."

"What can we do?" Claire flung her hands in the air. "We prefer clothes. Being naked all the time is *so* problematic, especially with all the cactus spines."

The overwhelming pressure in Rowan's chest was now due to the effort of trying *not* to laugh.

"Oh, I can only imagine." April looked horrified.

"It's worse than you think." Claire nodded. "And cholla spines . . ."—she hooked her finger—"they have that little backward barb, so it's a mess getting those out of your—"

"Let's just say the nude life wasn't for us," Rowan interrupted before Claire could further scandalize the couple and their small wedding party.

Someone's grandma was clutching at her thick turquoise necklace as if it were pearls while an uncle ran a leering gaze over Claire's body. Rowan's right forearm tensed a second before the clerk called for the couple, keeping him from doing something reckless. Once everyone had left, Claire gestured to the open bench with that playful twist on her lips.

"Nudists, huh?" he said, trying to get some control over his heart rate.

"Both sets." She tilted her chin, rueful. "And we're the rebels that ran away from the compound, spurning everything we've ever known."

His head shook on its own. "What am I going to do with you?"

"Today?" That full-wattage smile knocked the air out of him. "Today you're marrying me."

Claire clocked his painful inhale, her eyes darting from his jaw to his shoulders to his tense hands on his knees.

"Rowan, it's not too late. We can walk away from all of this. In fact"—she rose, grabbing his hand—"let's get out of here."

He gripped her fingers and tensed a bicep, halting her movement. "No. We need to know you're okay."

I need to know you're okay.

"Not if it's going to upset you this much." Her free hand rose as if to caress his cheek before tucking it to her side. Antsy fingertips flitted with the fabric of her dress.

Rowan shook his head. Didn't this woman understand she was worth everything? There wasn't a single thing he wouldn't do if it would ensure her safety, her happiness.

They remained like that for a long moment, hands and gazes entwined. Rowan couldn't let go, couldn't convince his rigid muscles to relinquish. It wasn't until the clerk called their names that he even noticed how tightly Claire's fingers were gripping his.

"Let's run," Claire whispered.

"No." Her gaze followed his face as he stood, her chin tilting up to keep their eye contact.

The clerk called for them a second time before Claire relinquished with a small nod and a smaller, "If you're sure."

Rowan barely heard the judge throughout the ceremony, barely recognized his own voice repeating the standard vows. It was like he was outside himself, uncharacteristically uninterested in the fact that he was marrying the woman he'd loved half his life.

He kept thinking about how Claire never wore jewelry, but now a ring covered her left finger. How the four-year age difference had felt like a potential obstacle at twenty-one but now felt like a sidewalk crack. How her twitchy hands felt flawless between his, her shoulders visibly relaxing when he pressed his thumb into the center of her palm.

Rowan had kept himself so removed he could almost convince himself that the whole thing had been play, like when Meg used to make them marry their stuffed animals as kids. It wasn't until the end when reality blasted him like a fire hose.

"You may kiss your bride."

He had to, of course. To keep up appearances. Not doing so would raise suspicion.

But something about the word *your* made a transitional shift in Rowan's bones.

Claire was *his* wife.

It was unimaginable, yet completely true.

Rowan blinked, his mind working too hard over the sudden change as his fingers brushed the side of Claire's face, tucking away that wayward strand. A satisfying hum vibrated in his chest as his thumb skirted over her ear. Days. He'd been wanting to do that for days. Ever since she plopped down on his kitchen stool, and he'd made her that first breakfast.

And Rowan was about to do something he'd dreamt about for *years*.

Claire's wide eyes darted to his before they drifted to his mouth. It took every ounce of restraint to take his time, to elongate every second to its full potential, to memorize everything. Because Rowan used to fall asleep imagining what it would be like to cradle Claire's face between his rough palms, to feel her shaky exhale skip over his mouth, to see her lashes drunkenly flutter closed in anticipation.

By the time Rowan gently pressed his mouth to hers, his heart was rioting, threatening to explode and drop him to the floor.

Claire made the slightest, sweetest sound before lightning coated every nerve ending in his body, deadening all but those in his lips. For all his dreaming, he couldn't imagine a kiss like this. Rowan wasn't prepared for the all-encompassing knowledge that this was where he belonged.

With her.

It had always been that way. No matter how much his brain tried to logic itself out of loving Claire, it never succeeded. It was as predictable as the rise and fall of the sun, as steady as the mountain ranges surrounding Tucson. Rowan would love Claire.

Always.

When Claire's hands fisted the fabric of his shirt, dragging him closer, something fundamental in Rowan shattered. His fingers burrowed in her hair, knocking a few flowers loose while deepening the kiss.

Only the sharp whistle coming from Steve reminded Rowan that they were standing in the too-warm chambers of Judge Hernandez. That the man himself was a mere three feet from them, witnessing everything.

"Let me tell you. I can always predict which couples will last." The judge chuckled. "You two have staying power."

Claire's lips slowly dropped from his, eyes closed, her breathing as scattered and irregular as his own. Rowan stared, simultaneously doubting his reality while committing the perfect flush of her skin to memory.

The puzzled astonishment when those lovely lashes fluttered open was almost as jarring as the judge shouting, "Next!" over their heads. Because Claire wasn't looking at him like he was her best friend's brother, her childhood playmate, or her friend. Raw desire blinked over those whiskey irises.

"Betcha they'll get naked after this." Steve snorted.

April swatted at him. "Every couple gets naked after getting married."

"Congratulations again, but I have another happy couple waiting." The judge's hand on his arm startled Rowan into realizing that he and Claire were still frozen, gazes locked.

Then everything tilted sideways.

Claire's face transformed from one of rapture to absolute horror as it fell to his chest, seeing her fabric-clenched fingers. It would have been comical, the way she flung herself from him, if Rowan hadn't just experienced the most meaningful kiss of his life.

This piercing, fake laugh barked from Claire's mouth before she covered it with her fingertips. "S—sorry. So sorry."

Steve's firm hand slapping his back saved Rowan from completely losing it. "April's not one for PDA either, but it's easy to get caught up on your wedding day."

Claire recuperated quicker than Rowan—signing the marriage license like it was a restaurant check, accepting April's number and promising to get together after they returned from their honeymoon, and smiling politely at congratulatory staffers.

Meanwhile, the light that had previously occupied Rowan's bloodstream had been replaced by lead. Nothing felt right. Nothing could replicate that kiss. He knew it to the marrow of his bones. Just like he knew he'd never kiss Claire again.

She'd obviously viewed this whole thing for the mistake it was. Only he'd been stupid enough to hope that Claire might finally see him as more than a friend.

As Rowan started up his steaming-hot Jeep, two thoughts kept buzzing like annoying gnats.

Claire had wholly and completely ruined him.

And he'd let her.

Chapter 11

"Whoa. Is it the apocalypse?" Kevin leaned over Rowan's shoulder to sniff at his cup before warily eyeing the rest of their friends sitting outside Ground Street Coffee. "Rowan is drinking coffee."

Normally, he'd wordlessly grumble. Rowan was used to his friends poking at him on the rare occasion he varied from his firmly set patterns. Even through the worst days of graduate school, Rowan refused to drink coffee. The caffeine amped him up too much, making impulse control more challenging.

But yesterday, he'd systematically destroyed what was left of his heart by marrying a woman who'd been horrified by the idea of kissing him. Someone who'd regretted her decision so fiercely that she retreated to his bedroom and barely spoke to him for the rest of the night. Which meant Rowan had spent another night fixating on the exposed-beam ceiling instead of sleeping.

So yeah, he was exhausted.

Unlike his friend Zane, Rowan couldn't function without a minimum of six hours. In college, he used to pass out right in the middle of their dorm room while everyone else was studying or chatting. He'd always attributed his ability to sleep anywhere from being the youngest and having roomed with Erin and Meg until he turned six. Whether his bed was a rock or the carpet or a pillowy mattress, Rowan could sleep.

Except since he'd opened his mouth and a proposal fell out.

"Not today, Kevin. I'm not in the mood." Rowan swiped beads of sweat from his forehead.

The air was already hot, making the coffee he'd ordered barely enjoyable. Pretty soon, the oppressive summer heat would force their biweekly get-together inside the coffee shop, which was challenging due to the limited indoor seating.

"When are you ever in the mood?" Caroline, Zane's daughter, quipped. Her blonde eyebrows tweaked from over her sprinkle-topped, whipped-creamed monstrosity of a hot chocolate.

Rowan set his face in his palm with a hard exhale, jostling his aviator sunglasses. He usually didn't mind the subtle sparring match he and Caroline kept ongoing, but Rowan was barely holding it together. It took more effort than normal to keep his anger in check and not snap at those surrounding him.

Zane gently gripped his daughter's shoulder. "Honey, why don't you show Liz and Tina what's new in your sketchbook?"

Caroline made a show of rolling her eyes and huffing but moved along to the matrons' table at the edge of the outdoor patio space. The two elderly women were steady fixtures at Ground Street, almost as much as his friend group. Kevin's wife,

Becca, co-owned the shop, and Kevin, Kyle, and Zane had all worked as baristas in college. As usual, Caroline was engulfed in loving hugs and friendly licks from Liz and Tina's barking bichons. Since Caroline usually spent time with the two women, even without being asked, Rowan knew she didn't mind catching up.

"I'm assuming this is about Claire," Kyle said.

"Yeah, what's the story with that?" Kevin leaned back in his cafe chair, shaking his iced coffee over the armrest like a bored king. "You've been radio silent since Sunday. Did your parents set up a family dinner yet? How much time do we have to prep for the eventual Claire-vasion?"

Defeat hunched his shoulders. "It already happened. She needed a place to crash, and—"

Rowan didn't even get to finish that statement. His friends already filled in the blanks.

"What?" "Are you kidding me?" and "Why didn't you tell us?" clamored at him at once.

Kevin stood up, did a flustered half-spin, and then plunked back down.

"Explain." Kyle's tattooed arms propped on the metal tabletop, his chin settling on his thumbs.

The stress of the last week took the last of his strength as Rowan recounted almost everything—from her surprise arrival, to the unexpected hospitalization, and the plan for her to stay with him for the next few months.

Zane's reassuring hand gripped his shoulder. "That . . . sounds like a lot. I wish you'd reached out earlier."

It was challenging to be on the receiving end of Zane's abundant compassion. Usually, Rowan was the one helping his friends through life's various foibles, not the other way around.

"Yeah." Kevin slugged him in the other shoulder. "What the heck? We could have helped."

"It's just . . . There's more." Rowan set his elbows on his knees, exhaling.

The plan had been to keep it a secret, but Rowan had to tell *somebody*. Keeping this marriage from his family was already going to be hard enough. He didn't think he could also keep it from his friends without losing any more sleep.

"We got married."

The way his friends reacted, you'd have thought they'd just witnessed their favorite team lose the Super Bowl in double overtime due to a botched call. The only one who stayed seated after the uproar was Zane, blinking from behind his black-rimmed glasses.

"You did what?" he asked.

"This is bananas," Kevin said, drawing the attention of those remaining on the sweltering patio. "Simply bananas."

Kyle seemed to realize he was also standing and slowly lowered himself. "Please tell me you have a really good reason for doing that."

In their long friendship, Rowan had never been verbose. He'd always been quiet, more comfortable in the background. Observing allowed him to ensure that everything was as it should be, that everyone was safe. Even when Claire had left town nine years ago and he'd finally told his friends their history, Rowan had held back some.

Now every detail rushed forward like he was setting the stage to one of Kevin and Kyle's plays at the vibrant theater they co-owned. All three men winced when Rowan recounted Claire's response to their courthouse kiss.

"That's . . . that's rough, man." Kyle shook his head.

"I don't understand. You just ran down to the courthouse for a quickie marriage? You, Rowan Bellamy, Mr. Order, Mr. Always Do The Right Thing"—Kevin lowered his voice, his eyes checking the perimeter of the essentially empty patio—"are committing insurance fraud for a woman who can't stand you?"

"It's not that she can't stand him." Kyle shot Kevin a glare before focusing back on Rowan. "One person felt the stage kiss more deeply than the other."

"Like Arabella and Daniel," Kevin said with a comprehending hum. "Yikes, that was a mess. We almost had to recast the whole show."

"Focus," Kyle growled.

"Right, sorry." Kevin waved a hand over his face. "So you're . . . unexpectedly committed roommates. What now?"

Rowan shook his head. "Get her on my insurance. Make sure everything is okay with her medically. Get divorced."

"Does Ethan know?" Zane adjusted his glasses before leaning back.

His forehead fell into his fingers with a long sigh. "No. I wasn't even sure about telling you all."

"I'm glad you did." Zane's voice held that sincere warmth of his.

A hushed pause settled over the table before Zane spoke again. "How can we make this easier on you? Can you limit interactions with her? Can she manage on her own, health-wise?"

Claire hadn't shown weakness since she'd been discharged from the hospital. This morning, when he'd come out of the shower, she'd been furiously scrubbing his baseboards while listening to a podcast on her phone. Since they'd barely exchanged two words once they'd gotten home last night, Rowan had simply taken his keys and left to meet his friends.

"She seems fine." That admission came out reluctantly.

A part of him had enjoyed those moments of taking care of her. Claire had never seemed to need anyone. Even as a kid, she'd been fiercely independent. It was as certain as the summer heat that once Claire had a clean bill of health, she'd be off touring the country again. There was no reason for her to stay in Tucson long term. Getting attached to the idea of being someone Claire relied on was a dangerous knife edge to trod.

"That's good to hear." As always, Zane's words were genuine. "Since she's doing better, why don't I meet you at the climbing gym a few nights this week? Tess is picking up Caroline in an hour, so I'll be by myself."

Though he appreciated the offer, Rowan knew that Zane would otherwise be spending his evenings with his new girlfriend, Ann. As a third-grade teacher, Ann should have had the summer off, but she'd volunteered to teach full-time for a summer catch-up program for at-risk students. Rowan wasn't about to chip away at the coveted hours Zane had with her.

"Thanks, but—"

"You're welcome to sit in the theater if you don't mind a bit of construction noise." Kevin removed his Panama hat, setting it on the table. His friend was always the epitome of eclectic style. "The scenic carpenter is finishing up set designs."

Kevin and Kyle's small community theater—All World Theater—was preparing for their 90s take on *A Midsummer Night's Dream*, which explained Kevin's recent enthusiasm for high tops.

"We've got rehearsals in the evenings, but you can camp out in our office," Kyle added.

Rowan nodded. "Thank you. I think maybe I should do that."

He needed to wrap his head around the fact that this wasn't real. His marriage meant nothing. Rowan had to assume that Claire was healthy and that her second endoscopy would confirm that fact. Then his life would return to normal.

Claire was never going to love him.

It was time to abandon the fantasy that'd come bursting back the second his fingers had wrapped around her wrist in his living room.

"What about Tuesday and Thursday evening?" Zane looked at the calendar on his phone. "Ann has tutoring, so I'm free. We can grab dinner afterward."

"Okay. Yeah. That'd be great."

After ten more minutes of firming up plans, that coiled knot in his chest loosened a bit. Maybe he could make it through the next few weeks.

Bro hugs and back pats were given before Rowan began driving to the store to check on Erin before he headed back home.

At a long light, Rowan opened his center console to see their wedding rings. They'd taken them off as soon as they'd gotten in his Jeep. He'd reasoned that they only needed to wear them in front of medical personnel in the future. Claire had dipped her chin, not looking at him. She hadn't met his gaze since she'd pulled away from him in front of the judge.

His ringing phone jolted him out of the memory. Rowan grimaced at his screen before putting the call on speaker.

"Seriously? You're married?" Ethan muttered something in Spanish that was probably riddled with swear words. "Okay," he said, almost as if settling himself. "You just need to get through this. Lucky for you, I excel at surviving sucky situations."

Ethan casually referencing his burn recovery after being trapped in a house fire snapped Rowan out of his selfish lamenting. He was healthy. His family and friends were safe and happy. He could get over his first love. It was doable. Especially with help.

"Teach me the ways, oh wise one."

When Ethan's rumbly laugh filled his Jeep, Rowan knew he'd be okay.

Chapter 12

OnlyApp was *perfect* for distraction. Claire knew there were a lot of negative parts to social media. Distorted sense of reality. Cyber-bullying. Sugar daddy spammers. A chuckle bubbled up her throat. If she had a dollar for every time she'd been asked to be a sugar baby, Claire could have paid her medical bills without marrying Rowan.

Nausea contorted her stomach, and Claire double-tapped another scenic square image to keep herself firmly in the diversion zone.

Only pretty pictures of nature existed here. No looming sense of despair that she'd made a monumental mistake.

Snaps of people at parties. No reality-tilting knowledge that Rowan's kiss had been the best of her life.

Hilarious travel memes. No need to acknowledge the grounding sense of belonging that swept through her when his calloused fingers tucked that loose strand behind her ear.

This was supposed to be an arrangement. Something simple. Okay, fine, it wasn't exactly *simple*, but it shouldn't be something that caused her mind to linger on the memory of that knee-quaking kiss.

Claire took her hand away from her phone to pinch her thigh. It wasn't Rowan. She was only reacting this way because she hadn't been kissed in what? Five? Six months?

People often thought because she traveled so much that Claire didn't have relationships. She did, but they were fleeting. Men often approached her, and Claire was upfront about her short stay in each area. The last time had been when she'd occupied a cabin in Tennessee for three weeks. Justin had given her the same knowing smile dozens had before, thinking he'd be the one to change her mind, the one to make her stay.

But the tepid memory of snowy cabin kisses was nothing compared to how Rowan's hands had felt like they'd left a bioluminescent wake over her skin. The slow, focused way he'd brought his lips to hers had made her mind tailspin into what it would feel like to be the center of that single-minded attention for more than a kiss.

Claire shook her head firmly before her imagination got too carried away.

She was simply having a heightened reaction to his unbelievably soft lips, to the perfection of his beard scruff rasping her skin because . . . it'd been a while. That's all. It was like how after a grueling day of physical exertion, anything you ate tasted ten times better. Add in all the pressure not to get caught doing something illegal, and no wonder her nervous system went haywire.

That was the only reason why the kiss had been so soul satiating.

It hadn't been Rowan.

It had been the circumstances.

With her head on straight, Claire let herself out into the morning air. She needed to post something to her OnlyApp account today. Her followers were used to sporadic posting due to traveling in areas without cell service, so dropping off the radar at a moment's notice wasn't unusual and didn't need to be explained. Leaving the account dormant for several days meant that a barrage of comments awaited her. And unfortunately, there were several negative ones from her poolside post.

@suxit7694 *Wish I could take a picture of my legs in water and make money off it. Must be nice to be a girl.*

@itsyounotme *I'd die before I posted a picture of my cellulite. Gross.*

@yep_2000_gavin *Please check your DM, little mama. It'll be worth it.*

@stevelucken *So this is what young people do nowadays? Travel? I had to work every day for forty years before I got to do things like this. How do you all think you get to jump the line? Why does no one want to put in the hard work anymore? You're why America is failing.*

There were a dozen more like that and at least fifty that were multiples of the fire emoji.

Claire left the emoji ones. Though some were undoubtedly meant in a *hubba-hubba* kind of way, others were likely encouragement from fellow women. Her travel followers noticed the real feature of the photo, which was not her outstretched legs but the gorgeous pool with vista-like views of the mountains in the background.

Those comments, she liked.

As much as dealing with trolls was exhausting, it was the comments and messages from women saying they'd camped alone outside for the first time after following her account that fueled Claire. Too much of the current zeitgeist was still centered around falsehoods regarding women's capabilities. By posting photos of herself in raw wilderness areas, she was setting an example that anyone could follow.

Of course, Claire was always transparent that solo-traveling rarely meant lonely traveling. Although she planned her trips on her own and went where she wanted without consulting a travel buddy, Claire often connected with fellow travelers. The more popular trails were frequently busy, and on those, she'd complete long legs with others. Sometimes that would end in a body- and soul-nourishing post-hike meal in town or, if she'd been backpacking, a shared campsite.

The best kinds of people were in the woods. It was only when Claire had returned to civilization that she'd had trouble.

Hiking also allowed her to wander without the fear of getting lost. After feeling so untethered with Gram's sudden death, knowing that if she stayed on the trail, she'd get to her destination had been unbelievably comforting.

Before the gnats could have a field day with the sweat accumulating on her face, Claire lay on the daybed and snapped a few photos of herself with towering saguaros in the background. Their beautiful accordion-shaped exteriors were tucked in tight, ready to expand to accommodate the upcoming rain.

Generally, Claire never posted about a location until after she'd left it, but since she'd be in Tucson for a while, she wanted to give her followers something. The uncertainty of her future settled like a boulder in her stomach.

Thanks to Rowan, she didn't have to pay for any upcoming medical treatment, but Claire needed money for a new car and to cover whatever costs remained from her hospitalization. Though Claire had made brand deals with companies in the past, she'd always kept her sponsored content to a minimum, only accepting what she'd needed to pay for the next adventure. Profiting from her popularity wasn't something Claire was comfortable with.

As soon as she got back inside, however, Claire would need to sort through the ignored messages from companies and coordinate additional brand deals. She'd never used affiliate links in her posts, but that was something she could incorporate as well.

Most importantly, Claire needed to keep hiking. Tomorrow, she would try a short trail that was close to the road in case fatigue snagged her in its claws. If that was successful, Claire could work her way up to the nine-mile, 2,890 feet elevation gain of Agua Caliente Hill Trail. Fortunately, there were numerous trails to explore in Tucson.

A slight breeze kissed Claire's already damp skin as she sighed. The desert looked rose-colored through her favorite heart-shaped sunglasses. Agave blooms on their upturned pedestals appeared peach instead of their traditional yellow.

Others might see a water-starved landscape, but Claire had always appreciated the desert's unconventional beauty.

Once she retreated into the delicious air conditioning of Rowan's house, Claire perched on a kitchen stool with an apple. Yesterday's homemade gluten-free blueberry muffins sat on the counter, but Claire couldn't bring herself to eat them again. Every gluten-free baked good had a gritty texture that she'd yet to acclimate to. Though she appreciated Rowan helping with her dietary changes, Claire really, *really* missed bread products.

It took her a while to get her OnlyApp photo the way she liked it, but a second after she posted the image, Meg's call lit up her screen.

"Hey, hottie," Claire answered the call on speaker.

"Me? You! How do you manage to look breathtaking while sweating your buns off in the Arizona heat?"

She chuckled. "That's the magic of filters."

"Filters, my foot. You're gorgeous and you know it."

Her mother used to say the only thing Claire had going for her was her looks. There were times when she wondered if her OnlyApp success was solely hinged on that. Normally, she'd exclude herself from the next post to balance things out, but brands preferred her face in their sponsored product posts.

The bitterness flooding her tongue urged Claire to push aside the apple. "How's California?"

"Crowded."

An amused huff left her nose. "It's the most populated state."

"I know. I just want to have one adventure without also having to share it with half a dozen others." Meg's voice brightened. "Speaking of adventures, how's that whole getting-my-brother-back-out-there plan going?"

Claire pressed her hands on the granite countertop, closing her eyes to steady the spinning kitchen. That's right. She'd agreed to be Rowan's wing-woman. But instead of setting Meg's brother up on dates, she'd married him.

Her forced laugh sounded half-convincing. "I've been a bit busy with the whole hospital thing, but we did agree to . . ."

Do NOT say get married.

"A Fun Pact." The words rushed out in a gush.

"A Fun Pact?"

Claire swallowed. "Two nights a week we're going to do something fun together. It's a way for me to say thanks for living here."

Meg clapped once. "I love it! You can take him out, and while you're . . . wherever, you can push a kind-looking woman his way. Brilliant."

The obvious answer was as incessant as a strobe light. Of course! That's *exactly* what Claire should do. Then she could shift herself back into the friend zone she'd always occupied.

"I think I should take him to that silent disco tonight."

Claire searched for the event site on her phone. *Perfect.* The event ran nightly through the end of the week.

"He'll hate that." Meg snickered. "You should totally do it."

"And . . ." The corner of her mouth kicked up. "I think I know who I should invite to go with us."

"Oooh! I love when you get that tone in your voice. I'd tell you that my hands aren't rubbing together like a fiend, but I'd be lying."

Claire chuckled, tabbing over to OnlyApp and clicking on the search bar.

Monterey? Miller? No. What was her last name?

A sigh blew over the phone. "I wish you lived nearby so we could do our nefarious plotting together."

Occasionally Meg would say things like this, particularly during the winter, when it'd been a while since they'd seen each other.

"But," Meg added quickly, "I completely respect your career and your ambition, so this virtual scheming is just as good."

"I'll still be here in July," Claire reminded her.

"Oh, yeah!" Meg's laugh swung through the kitchen. "I'm so used to you moving from place to place. I forgot that Rowan strong-armed three months of Tucson living out of you."

The phrase 'strong-armed' brought a memory of Rowan's muscled forearms flexing while mincing spinach. Claire had never been attracted to men who cooked before—though she always appreciated and acknowledged the effort behind a prepared meal. A man knowing his way around a kitchen wasn't some giant feat. Food preparation was a basic life skill every human should possess. Even though Rowan's meals teetered on chef quality, it was the deftness with which Rowan's fingers took on a task—

"Claire?"

"Hm?"

"I asked who you are inviting."

"Oh. Um." She tugged on the collar of her t-shirt, suddenly flushed. "Emmy. She was at the Wholistic Health Fair last Sunday."

The gravity of that sentence was like getting caught in an icy deluge. Had it only been a week? It felt like four lifetimes.

"Okay, you'll have to tell me more later because Knox just got back from the coffee shop, and he's holding a donut the size of a ring light."

An impressed sound escaped her. "That man knows his way to your heart."

"Does he ever."

After ending the call, Claire closed her eyes to think. A few failed attempts finally yielded Monroe Dairy Farm with a Tucson address beneath the account name. Claire liked, followed, and sent a message. A slow smile spread over her face at seeing the almost instant reply. Having such a large account meant that people seldom ignored her.

Chapter 13

"What a great idea. Let's all get into the creepy van that's driving us to the middle of nowhere in the desert. They're not going to harvest our organs at all," Rowan deadpanned as one of the sketchier vehicles she'd seen in a while pulled up to the parking lot.

Claire softly shouldered him. "Come on. This'll be fun. Plus, this silent disco has *rave* reviews"—she emphasized the word with a bounce of her eyebrows—"with absolutely no organ removal or murdering. I promise."

"I didn't think about the murdering," he muttered, climbing in after a woman wearing a leopard bodysuit, sheer black skirt, and killer boots.

The various outfits of the rest of the five attendees waiting in their line to get shuttled to the silent disco's remote location almost made Claire wish that she'd worn her sequined jumper. But since that garment was now associated with the hospital, she'd stashed it in a grocery bag to drop off at Goodwill later.

Tonight, her most colorful shorts—a muddied mauve—and tight white tank would have to suffice. Rowan matched her in his gray canvas shorts, powder-blue t-shirt, and trail boots. They looked like two misplaced hikers rather than EDM enthusiasts ready to party until dawn. Hopefully, there'd be a vendor selling glow sticks, light-up glasses, or glow-in-the-dark fans to liven up their looks.

Since Rowan clearly wasn't in a sociable mood, Claire shifted in her seat to chat with the third person in their row. Jackson not only had an unbuttoned metallic fish-print vest topping his kilt, but he had glittered his eyebrows green.

"Why is everybody half naked? Are exposed pecs part of the dress code for this thing?" Rowan's growly words rushed over her ear.

Claire couldn't help that her eyes fluttered closed. When she opened them with a controlled inhale, trying to get a grip over her body's automatic response, Jackson winked at her. Then he leaned out over the edge of the seat bench to chat with the red-headed woman in front of them.

Two seconds was all Claire gave herself to calm the heck down before turning to Rowan. "Are you going to be Mr. Grumpy Pants this entire night?"

The van lurched to a start, jostling them even closer. It was already a tight squeeze with her between the two men, but Rowan seemed to be intentionally pressing his thigh against hers. Heat streaked down her leg, warming each and every one of her toes.

Rowan folded his arms. "You're the one who has me going out at eleven o'clock."

"It's Saturday night." She scoffed. "What are you? Eighty?"

"I crochet and prefer to get a solid night of sleep, so . . ." He shrugged. "Maybe I am."

Claire bit the inside of her cheek to keep from responding to the brush of his shoulder. "This is part of me pulling my own weight, remember? Fun Pact? Barrels of laughs? Could you at least cooperate? Crack a smile, perhaps?"

Mocking irritation was a lot easier than owning up to the fact that since yesterday's courthouse kiss, she was completely thrown by each simple touch from Rowan. Claire was not this woman—the kind who got flustered by a shoulder brush. Confidence with men had always been effortless.

"Fine." He rolled his eyes like a surly teenager. "But can our next adventure be at a reasonable time? I don't know if you've noticed, but we've got ten years on everyone in this van."

Claire pursed her lips and poked him in the ribs—*hard*—right in that spot where he was ticklish. His elbow shot up in response, knocking her in the jaw.

"Claire. I'm sorry." His fingers slid over her face, examining, soothing. "I didn't mean to . . ."

It was like they both realized at the same time that it was too similar to their kiss—his hands cradling her face, his intense gaze focused on her. Rowan's hazel eyes dipped to her mouth before the van lurched to a stop, and they both jerked forward.

Rowan plastered his massive frame against the window, and they didn't talk again until they were filing out of the van and collecting their headphones twelve minutes later.

"You've got five DJs to choose from. Use the white button on your headphones to click through each one. Each DJ's table is the corresponding color to your headphone channel. So, DJ Sound Stick at the red table is mixing on the red channel, etc. The event grounds are roped by lights, so stay within the boundaries." He chuckled. "We don't want anyone falling into cactus again."

Determined to leave the awkwardness of the van ride in their wake, Claire tugged Rowan toward the bar. "Let's get a drink to limber up our hips."

Seriously? Limber hips? That's the *last thing* she should be thinking about.

Claire shoved her headphones on, keyed into DJ Boomasta, and crossed the dance floor toward the bar. LED jellyfish hung in a thick cloud above, their crystalline tentacles barely brushing the raised hands of the people jumping along with DJ CamCan. A gibbous moon lit up the jackrabbit prickly pear, acacia trees, and creosote bushes surrounding the event area. Claire rolled her shoulders as she waited for the music to drop. Her eyes floated closed while the pulsing in her ears climbed to a pinnacle.

Rowan's hand on the small of her back made her gasp and remove her headphones.

"We need to move forward in line." His voice was soft, but it sounded like a blow horn with the absence of music.

"Right. Sorry." She kept her headphones around her neck since they were next to order. "What do you want? My treat."

Rowan looked like he was going to argue but said, "I'll have whatever comes with a flashing ice cube."

"Really?" She grinned, a deconstructed version of "Sandstorm" pounding around her neck.

"Really." The corner of his mouth tipped up.

Rowan hadn't cued anything up yet; his headphones were still on the white empty channel. As carefully as she could, Claire snatched his headphones from his shoulders. Had she attempted to change his channel with them around his neck, her hands would have been too close to that sharp, stubbly jaw. Claire knew without a doubt that if she'd done that, her itchy fingers would've ventured off course.

And then she'd be in trouble again.

Shoving one hand into her pocket, Claire switched Rowan's channel and held his headphones out with her other. "Give DJ Motles a try."

Rowan collected his headphones a second before Claire was happily distracted by the bartender asking for their order. It was nice not to have to shout at her to get their drinks. Actually, it was a little funny hearing shuffling and quiet singing without music blasting overhead. Around the dance floor, different groups were chatting in various seating vignettes. The whole thing was incredibly chill for how hard some of them were dancing to the music.

"Um. Hey, Claire." A timid voice came from her left.

"Emmy!" Claire picked up their drinks, shoving one into Rowan's hand and giving Emmy a one-armed hug. "You made it! And this must be your cousin. Amelia, right?" She engulfed a woman whose ringlet curls were a little darker than Emmy's.

"I don't want to freak you out, but I follow your account, and I am probably going to fangirl on you the whole night." Amelia barked out a nervous laugh. "You've been warned. I have so many questions."

"I love fans." Claire gave her brightest smile. "Much better than the trolls I have to deal with."

Though Rowan had slipped on his agreeable mask, Claire knew he was uncomfortable. His thumb tapped, in rhythmic duplicates, on the seam of his shorts even as he smiled and greeted both women.

Springing a date on him where he couldn't escape except via murder van was a chump move, but this weirdness between them needed to be aired out *tonight*. One easy way to fix that was to find Rowan a girlfriend. If Rowan was spoken for by a particularly shy cheesemaker, Claire would be able to keep her distance. Yesterday's kiss had nearly demolished her self-preservation skills, but her morality was *firmly* intact.

"I just hope I don't crash. I'm so used to milking the goats before sunrise," Emmy said over a yawn.

"Rowan's an early riser too. He gets a workout in before anyone else is up."

The second it was out of her mouth, Claire realized her mistake. She'd said it to point out how well suited they were, but Rowan's gaze burrowed into the side of her skull. He wasn't supposed to know that she'd seen him do a thousand pull-ups, or those crazy handstand push-ups while gripping that parallel handlebar thingy, or holding a plank for what felt like twelve minutes.

Ameila laughed again, breaking the tension. "We'd go out of business without Emmy doing all the hard stuff. I can make cheese all day, but I hate getting up early. That and math. My brain doesn't math." She twisted her lips, rueful.

"Rowan is crazy smart. He was in honors everything growing up."

"You knew each other as kids?" Emmy asked, tucking a ringlet behind her ear.

"Yup. I'm essentially his sister." Claire punched Rowan in his firm shoulder for emphasis. "I'm only visiting for a few weeks, then I'll be off to my next adventure."

Rowan's focus on her face exploded to molten lava temperatures, but Claire continued to avoid eye contact.

Emmy finally quit fussing with the puff sleeves of her stunning eyelet mini-dress. "Where will you go next?"

"I—" Her thumb went to her wrist before she could stop herself. "I haven't decided."

Normally, Claire spent downtime organizing her next trip, but uncertainty of the next few weeks had made planning feel like tempting fate. What if something *really* was wrong? Something worse than making sure everything she put in her mouth was gluten free?

When Rowan's hand flinched forward automatically, Claire realized she needed to remove herself if there was to be any chance of him hitting it off with Emmy.

"Amelia, why don't we check out that glow-in-the-dark face painter, and you can ask me those questions?" The effort to ignore Rowan almost tripped Claire, but she steadied herself by hooking her elbow with Amelia's and leading them to the other side of the dance floor.

◊◊◊

The artist had just finished painting a breathtaking feather pattern over Claire's right temple when Emmy plucked Amelia from her place in line, feigning exhaustion. Claire's head swiveled, looking for Rowan. It couldn't have been twenty minutes since they'd left. She exchanged hugs with both women before they took off toward the awaiting vans to drive people back into town.

It took another five minutes to find Rowan, nestled in a hanging egg chair. Claire snatched his phone out of his hands, checked the screen to confirm that he was indeed reading work emails, and slid it into her back pocket.

"What happened? Emmy looked like she was going to cry."

"What happened was you forced me on a date I didn't want to be on." Rowan stood, crowding her.

It took everything in her not to step back. She was still getting used to the size difference of him now versus her memory. "So you were mean to her?"

"What? No." That line between his brows deepened. "We chatted until it became obvious she had a different expectation of how this evening would end. Then I was honest with her that I wasn't interested in anything other than our existing friendship."

"But she's perfect!" Claire brought up her hands, ticking off fingers. "She's smart like you. She's a business owner like you. She's unfairly gorgeous for someone who works with livestock all day. She—"

"Claire, she isn't—" He pinched the bridge of his nose, exhaling. "Never mind." He glanced away before focusing back on her. "Let's dance. You wanted to dance, right?"

The angry ember just beneath her heart turned over into flame. "I wanted—"

What? For him to be unavailable so she wouldn't inadvertently destroy things?

"No. Let's go home. You're right. This wasn't a good idea." She shrugged, forcefully infusing playful warmth into her voice. "My next one will be off the charts. You'll see. Unless you're opposed to pits of snakes?"

Rowan chuffed, a reluctant smile tugging at his lips.

"You are?" She wrinkled her nose. "Okay, let's go with something milder. Skydiving?"

"No."

"Mt. Lemmon?"

He tilted his head to the side, considering. "Maybe."

"Water park?"

A wistful expression softened Rowan's jaw. "I haven't been to a water park since I was a kid."

"Water park it is. Should we invite Erin?" With another person there, these unruly—and unwanted—thoughts might stop pummeling her brain. "Surely she takes time off once a quarter."

Rowan snorted. "Erin doesn't like getting her hair wet."

"Oh yeah."

A memory of being nineteen lurched forward, accompanying the Bellamys on a hike to Seven Falls. After the long, sweaty hike, everyone launched themselves into the chilly mountain snow-melt flowing into the canyon. Everyone except Erin. She sat perched on a boulder while even Kelly jumped into the water.

"Time to get grandpa to bed. Murder vans here we come." Claire turned to march toward the exit, but Rowan's fingers on her wrist stopped her.

A simple yank and she nearly collided with his firm chest. "No. Let's dance."

"But you don't want to." Her pulse was trying to win against the DJ's superspeed set.

"*You do*, Claire." He tilted forward, his tone dropping.

Auto-tuned voices from opposing channels warred with each other while their gazes remained locked for several breaths.

"Why did you invite Emmy?"

She opened her mouth, and the truth fell out. "Meg's worried about you."

A grimace accompanied his hard exhale. "Can you promise me something?"

She'd already pledged to have and to hold him for better or worse. What was one more promise?

"What?"

"Don't do that again. We can go out. You can toss me in pits of snakes, but please don't set me up again."

It wasn't until that second, when Rowan released her wrist, that Claire even noticed she'd been leaning toward him. His sudden absence from her personal space was like an icy gale stinging her skin.

Her lips pressed together before Claire rasped, "I promise."

"Okay." He gazed over the hyperactive dance floor. "Then I think we can salvage this." The suspended tension disintegrated when Rowan quirked a goofy smile. "What's that saying? Dance like no one's watching?"

Slamming his headphones over his ears with a whoop, he flung himself into the dance mix like one of those wavy balloon men placed in front of used car dealerships. Two women wearing glow-in-the-dark mini-dresses cheered him on as he switched to some fancy foot move that looked straight out of an OnlyApp dance challenge.

A radiant laugh burst from Claire. Her fingers flexed automatically as that starburst sensation that came from something unexpected flooded her system. Then Rowan flung an imaginary fishing line her way, and the only option was to wiggle-jump her way over.

When they collapsed into the musty van an hour later, Claire bumped her shoulder into his. "I *knew* you were fun."

"Shhh. Don't tell anyone." Leaning his sweaty temple against the window, Rowan closed his eyes.

Claire simply shook her head, her forearms still buzzing from dancing. When Rowan began to softly whisper-snore halfway through their ride home, the warmth in her body turned over to something achy and raw. It took all of her energy to keep her hands curled in her lap when all Claire wanted was to lean Rowan's sleepy head onto her shoulder.

Chapter 14

Rowan tried to mollify his response to the sound of gravel crunching beneath his Jeep tires on the gravel driveway and the gentle rumble of the garage door opening the following Thursday. He should have been focusing fully on his client, not on the ribbon of peace that braided down his spine from knowing that Claire was home from her morning hike.

Firmly gripping and then releasing his toes within his loafers, he listened to Liam's recounting of setting successful boundaries with his overbearing boss.

"He made that face—the one that always made me cave—but this time I counted in my head and stood my ground. So tonight, this"—Liam held up his work phone—"will be turned off at six."

"I hope you took a moment to congratulate yourself on setting a healthy boundary," Rowan said with an uplifting tone.

Liam reddened slightly. "I might have done a few air pumps in the men's stall."

A genuine smile tugged at his lips. "It's great that the work you're doing here is impacting your daily life."

Unlike his clients who were assigned to work with him on their detrimental anger issues that had landed them in jail, Liam was here to work on his confidence.

Once his session finished, Rowan took a minute to make notes in Liam's chart before venturing into the kitchen. Usually, he didn't come out of his office until his lunch break, but Rowan needed to talk to Claire about the email he'd received early this morning.

"Hey, roomie," Claire called out from her head-in-the-fridge position when he closed his office door behind him.

Roomie had become his new name—ever since she'd woken him with it in the van after last weekend's disco.

This boundary had been as necessary as the one he'd helped his client set, and overall, the week had been reminiscent of their relationship before Claire had left Tucson. Now that Rowan fully understood that nothing between them would change, reverting back to these familiar familial roles hadn't been as tortuous as he'd expected.

Claire would hike early in the morning, taking his Jeep. With her leaving before first light, Rowan could workout, shower, dress for work, and prepare a breakfast for Claire to reheat later. His house had never been cleaner because Claire insisted on keeping everything spotless since he was preparing all the meals. He'd even managed not to scowl too much at the books about Badlands National Park that she'd attained using his library card. And when he'd been out with Zane Tuesday night, Claire had waited to watch the next episode of the Turkish drama he'd reluctantly become invested in.

Even though he'd adjusted surprisingly quickly to this newly established routine, Claire had been acting like a trapped animal. Her antsy restlessness was as thick as grease-fire smoke. Hiking in the morning and completing their two Fun Pact activities were the only things that seemed to settle it. Last night, they'd listened to the a capella stylings of a barbershop quartet while enjoying a milkshake since Claire was saving the water park for Saturday.

"Quiche today?" She pulled his Tuscany orange Emile Henry pie dish from the fridge.

"Caramelized onion, kale, and applewood smoked bacon. I added a pinch of xanthan gum like Becca recommended, and the crust held together better than last time." Rowan positioned himself on the stool side of the counter, setting a foot on the lowest rung.

"She's the pastry chef, right?" Claire asked, cutting herself a slice. "Kevin's wife?"

"Yeah." His thumb found the countertop, tapping it a few times as he collected his thoughts. When Rowan glanced up, Claire was smiling at him. "What?"

"Nothing." She turned away to pop her breakfast in the microwave.

Rowan drew in a breath, checking the clock over his office door. If he didn't get to it now, he'd have to wait until after his next appointment. "I received an email from the insurance company this morning."

Claire's hand froze in the silverware drawer before she reanimated with a high-pitched, *"Oh?"*

"Everything is set. I printed a copy of the digital insurance card for you to take to appointments." He pulled the folded paper from his back pocket, placing it on the cold granite. "I wanted to let you know so you could schedule your endoscopy and the DEXA scan."

Her eyes flicked to the paper. "Do you have a preferred date or time for when I call?"

"Whenever they can get you in. Like I said before, I'll rearrange my schedule."

Claire frowned. "I don't want to inconvenience you."

"You're not, but . . ." One last controlled breath filled his lungs as Rowan tried to loosen the tension between his collarbones. "I've been thinking about what my family decided on your behalf, how we forced you to stay here. You haven't had any weakness since you've changed your diet and started taking supplements."

He shoved his hands into his pockets. "And I'm sure everything will come back normal."

It didn't make sense that something nefarious was hiding around the corner. Claire was strong and healthy. Whatever the pathologist had seen had likely been a lab error.

Rowan hesitated again, stalling.

Let her go. You need to let her go. She's not yours to keep. She doesn't want to be here.

Cactus spines pricked down his forearms as he cleared his throat. "I'd still like you to keep my insurance so you can have your allergen markers drawn in a few months and if you need anything else. But once you've completed those two appointments, there's no reason you can't go back to traveling."

Nothing could have prepared Rowan for the expression on Claire's face. He'd expected Claire to be overjoyed about returning to her life and leaving Tucson behind. Earlier this week, she'd offered to split for groceries, stating that she'd secured some new product partners and was saving up for a car. But her eyelashes fluttered as if he'd knocked the air out of her. Hurt flickered over her sun-kissed cheekbones before she turned away, tugging down the brim of the hat she always wore hiking.

Rowan wanted to vault over the counter and gather her to his chest, but he gripped the edge instead.

"Um." She pulled open the beeping microwave. "I'll work on getting those appointments scheduled ASAP so I can get out of your hair."

Why had giving Claire her freedom backfired? Wasn't this what she wanted?

"Claire, I—"

A loud knock reverberated through the house. Chad, his most challenging client, was early.

"I thought—"

Another knock punched the stilted air between them.

Claire spun, cheeks pulled into that fake smile. "You thought right. I've been wanting to get a move on."

Didn't Claire know she was a terrible liar? At one point in their late teen years, Dad had interrogated Claire separately from Meg after they'd gotten home too late after a concert, because though Meg could spin you a web of lies you'd swear was your own history, Claire was terrible at keeping the truth hidden.

If she didn't want to leave, then what did she want?

He opened his mouth to ask when Chad called out, "Hey, doc. We doing this or what? I've got things to do."

"Go," she said, eyes trained on the floor. "Don't let me mess up your life more than I already have."

Every single cell in his body burned, concentrating painfully in his throat. Without thinking, Rowan moved around the counter. Claire drew in a staggered breath as his fingers framed her face, tilting her chin until their gazes met.

"We're talking about this later." Though he kept his touch gentle, his tone was an abrasive brick to the jaw.

Her lashes widened as her head bobbed with a small nod.

Everything was too much all at once. Her quick agreement set off some cascade in him that he didn't fully understand, but Rowan knew he was back in dangerous territory. Claire smelled of clay and wind, and her skin was impossibly hot beneath his palms. Those soft lips hadn't closed since she'd sucked in that startled breath, as if waiting.

"Doc!"

Claire flinched, lifting her hands to push against the center of his chest. "Go answer him before he breaks your door down."

After a few seconds of hesitation, Rowan left the kitchen, locking his office door behind him before letting Chad in.

"Chad." Rowan stood back with an even expression, allowing his client to stomp his way to the couch.

He kept his movements casual as he settled into his chair, folding one ankle over the other.

"What took so long?" Chad mirrored his stance, crossing his arms.

"I was using the bathroom."

An agitated snort shot between them as Chad stared out the window. His jaw was set tight, the foot over his ankle wiggling aggressively.

When he'd first started working with clients with anger management issues, his mom had been worried. Rowan understood it was potentially problematic to enter into a treatment niche that so closely resembled his troublesome early childhood, but that'd been *why* Rowan had chosen to work with these men.

He and his sisters rarely talked about their lives before moving to Tucson. Though he'd only witnessed his father's rage episodes until the age of five, Rowan also understood how lucky they'd been. His father had only taken his fists to the drywall or to the faces of the patrons at the bars he frequented. After his third imprisonment for aggravated assault, Rowan's father had done a surprising and merciful thing. He'd granted his mother the divorce she'd been wanting for years.

By working with these men, Rowan presented strategies to manage the poisonous emotion that had led to jail time. He could also commiserate because the same fury that flowed through his father's veins also pumped through his. It'd been an unexpected thing that popped up in puberty—a lot harder to manage than pimples.

Fortunately, Rowan had had Augie, who'd given him the skills to deal with the angry impulses that always jumped first. Working with Augie to find different techniques to manage his anger had inspired Rowan to choose this career. While pursuing his degree, Rowan had learned additional strategies—ones he implemented almost daily.

Even now, his anger simmered beneath the surface. Rowan took an extended breath sequence and channeled his energy into displaying compassion and understanding instead of responding to Chad's aggression with his own.

"You seem upset. Is everything okay?"

"Other than you being late?" Chad snapped.

Rowan simply tilted his head and waited, not bothering to point out that Chad had been early.

Chad fidgeted, changing his position on the couch three times before admitting, "Stella won't answer my calls . . ."

Chapter 15

It'd been *incredibly* childish, but Claire had run the shower for the entirety of Rowan's thirty-minute lunch. Sneaking out via the backyard, cutting through the desert, and taking a long walk down the road before being picked up by a rideshare after lunch had also been juvenile, but Claire had slipped into a cancellation slot for the DEXA scan this afternoon. There was no possible way she'd ask Rowan to cancel his appointments at the last minute for a fancy x-ray.

Not after he'd essentially told her she'd been in his way these last two weeks.

At least, this time, the onslaught of her mother's words only came in clips and phrases instead of the long-winded soliloquies Claire had experienced growing up. Regardless, the most harmful parts stabbed through.

"*. . . stuck with you . . .*" "*. . . such a burden . . .*" "*. . . biggest mistake of my life . . .*"

Claire pressed her eyes closed firmly before focusing on the *I'm with the Banned* book poster on the far wall of the library. Hiding out after her scan appointment was also immature, but Claire needed time to think. Time without Rowan's stern mouth frowning at her, without his fingers melting her skin, and without his gruff voice barking orders that she'd undoubtedly obey.

She *had* been restless all week, but not for the reasons Rowan thought.

It'd been challenging to stay still because whenever Rowan leaned over her to place a dirty dish in the sink, or when he mindlessly pulled out his crocheting while being engrossed in their shared TV show, or when he casually wished her *sweet dreams* before bed, something deep inside her stomach tugged.

Fighting her growing attraction had made her jumpy. Although Claire had viewed Rowan as her brother for years, she couldn't put him back in that mental box now—no matter how hard she tried. She'd already admired Rowan and wholly liked him as a person, but now *impulses* kept bombarding her.

Impulse control was never one of her strengths.

This change, combined with how this week had mimicked her teenage imaginings of a loving relationship, made everything harder. Claire felt stupid for being eviscerated over something as simple as sharing easy conversation, enjoyable meals, and snuggly TV shows with a man, but she never claimed to possess emotional maturity.

Case in point, her current behavior.

Since she'd already memorized Rowan's predictable work schedule, his last client of the day would be slipping out the door right now. Claire pulled out her phone and texted.

Claire: *Enjoy your evening with Zane. I'm already out with some old friends.*

It was ridiculous that her heart pounded in her ears as her fingers gripped her phone, waiting for his response.

Rowan: *I'll see you when you get home.*

She tried not to interpret the tone in that message. Was it the commanding one that infiltrated his words at the most unexpected times? His usual friendly, neutral one? Or was it the masked, apathetic one he'd used with her before she'd been hospitalized?

Rowan was meeting Zane at six-thirty, which meant she only needed to stall in the sublimely icy library for another half hour. Originally, she'd planned on staying out late, but what was the point? She had nowhere else to go. Claire opened OnlyApp and responded to comments on today's post of the Tanque Verde Ridge Trail.

Later, when Claire opened Rowan's front door with the spare key, turmeric and cumin accosted her nostrils a second before the sound of sizzling vegetables hit her ears.

Shoot.

Claire had expected him to be gone already. Her heel bounced a few times before she turned to slowly close the door as quietly as possible.

"What's the plan once you stealth-close the door? A ninja-level attack?"

Claire spun with a startled shout, fists already in front of her.

One glance at her raised hands and Rowan stepped back, making the narrow hallway feel less like a squeezing crevasse. The matted and framed photos of Rowan with his parents and sisters were also grounding. She wasn't stuck in a tight spot with someone dangerous. She was safe at home with Rowan.

"Would you have hit me?" It wasn't asked in a way that showed disbelief in her abilities, but odd curiosity.

"In the throat." Claire nodded while lowering her hands. "Do you think I've lived nine years on my own and can't defend myself? Once a year, I take a refresher self-defense class." Her chin tipped defiantly. "And I don't carry bear spray for the bears. I've never had a negative encounter with an animal. Men, however . . ."

Rowan's shoulders rose as he stepped forward, unguarded in his displeasure over hearing something that he should fully understand. He had *two* sisters. Surely he knew that the world was drastically different for women than men.

"If anyone touched you, I would—" The angry words halted when Rowan noticed his palm was inches from brushing over her cheek. His eyes squeezed shut as his fingers tucked into his pocket instead. "Never mind."

He would what?

It was mentally unstable how desperately Claire wanted to know the end of that threat. You're not supposed to be attracted to hotheads who blindly defend your honor. We live in a society where fist fights can end in jail time. But something about restrained Rowan losing his mind over the idea of her being harmed was more alluring than a pillow-top mattress after a week of sleeping on the ground.

The brutality in that broken sentence trampled what fragment of impulse control remained. One large step, and Claire's fingertips were gently but quickly freeing Rowan's auburn-brown waves from his hair tie. There were so many parts of this version of Rowan her fingers wanted to explore—his massive shoulders; his trim, muscled waist—but Claire started with his hair. There was a faint memory of what it felt like, and she needed confirmation.

Rowan's eyes widened, but he didn't pull away, just swallowed roughly as the ends of his hair fell to brush the edges of his unbuttoned collar.

"What made you grow your hair out?" She barely recognized the huskiness of her own voice.

"My ex asked me to." Rowan's gaze dropped to her bay leaf tattoo as his shoulders rose unevenly, touching the undersides of her forearms.

Even though that sentence was a punch to the belly, the sensation of Rowan's freed strands softened the blow. "But you kept it long after the breakup."

"Cutting it twice a year instead of every six weeks has its advantages."

When Claire ran her fingers through backward, cradling his skull, Rowan's lashes blissfully fluttered closed. That jaw. How had she never noticed it before? All she wanted now was to run her tongue along its sharp ridge.

A determined inhale filled her scattered lungs a second before a playful triple knock made them both jump.

Rowan startled a second time once his gaze landed on her, pulling himself from her grip. A few strands of his hair fell over the sides of his face before he turned, striding away and tossing his hoarse words behind him.

"Grab that. Won't you, roomie?"

Disorientation swept her limbs, making them heavy, but Claire managed to pull the door open to see . . . Zane?

Rowan's friend seemed just as shocked to see her. He blinked twice before adjusting his black-framed glasses and softening his lips into a smile. "Claire. Hey. Good to see you."

Her already flushed cheeks felt even hotter as she murmured her way through her own greeting. "Hi. It's been forever."

The bridge of his freckled nose seemed to redden as he walked past her, explaining he'd seen her at a wedding recently. Claire was half-listening to Zane recounting her leading the Electric Slide when she found Rowan behind the stove, hair up, as if nothing had happened. His strong back shifted as he effortlessly tossed the sauteed onions in the frying pan.

"Hey, Zane. Dinner's almost ready. Claire ended up getting home early. Okay if she joins us?"

Her forehead wrinkled so severely it tugged painfully against her ponytail. Rowan knew Zane had been coming over? Why had he allowed her to . . . to what? Get three seconds from placing her lips on the corner of his jaw, threatening to ruin everything, because her dumb brain had been too distracted by his growly promise to destroy whoever dared to touch her?

Claire had never been one for fairy tales. Her early years hadn't consisted of orderly bedtimes with her mother reading from a picture book. As a child, she usually passed out on the couch while her mother watched TV or in a quiet-ish corner if she'd been dragged to one of her mother's parties.

She'd bungled her way through high school-required reading, never managing to get into books the way Meg had—particularly romance. Those stories were even more unbelievable than the magic in faerie kingdoms. But Rowan's possessive demeanor and the way his auburn-brown hair had fallen over his scruffy jaw had made him a dead ringer for a Viking romance cover model. He just needed to replace his shirt with a fur shoulder pelt and oil his chest.

The sound of her name stopped her imagination from running wild with that idea, but not before Claire realized she'd been rubbing her lips.

She slammed her hand into the back pocket of her shorts. "What?"

"Where are you traveling to after this?" Zane repeated.

Her eyes automatically went to catch Rowan's, but he was focused on plating food.

"South Dakota. Right?" Rowan said, not looking up.

"Um. Yeah." She offered Zane what she hoped was a convincing smile. "I haven't explored the Badlands yet."

Zane chuckled. "It'd be perfect now. Much cooler than Tucson."

The plates had been situated so that Rowan sat on the counter's edge, kitty-corner to Zane, putting her on the other side of his friend. After dinners sitting right next to Rowan, listening to him talk about his day, Claire felt the intentional distance as a slap.

Mentally, she reorganized her thoughts. Rowan's action was completely reasonable after what had happened in the hallway.

Claire cleared her throat and forced her lips up. It was time for her to do what she did best—entertain. Fortunately, Zane was an easy conversationalist. An hour had flown by before she'd even noticed.

"You did not."

Zane held his hands up. "Swear. I was picking up Caroline from summer camp, and two teenagers were filming frying eggs on the hood of their truck."

"Probably trying to go viral and get OnlyApp famous." She chuckled before grabbing another delectable mouthful of flourless chocolate torte.

"They probably ruined the paint job," Rowan grumbled while pushing his dessert around. He'd hardly eaten any of his delicious creation.

"I thought Ethan was the car guy," Claire teased before noticing Zane's raised brows.

"You've met Ethan?"

Claire twisted her fork before setting it down. "Once or twice during your college days. Rowan mentioned he liked sports cars."

Fortunately, Zane launched into a story about Ethan's particularity with cars that kept her from admitting that since she'd been living with Rowan, Claire had tucked away every minute detail he'd shared as if it were a treasure.

That feeling of being caught had Claire shifting her hands into her lap. The instant her thumb found her wrist, her chin snapped to her chest. Around her left wrist was Rowan's hair tie. It was a simple brown band, almost identical to the one holding her hair back, but for some reason, possessing *this* circle felt more intimate than the wedding ring he'd slipped on her finger at the courthouse. Claire quickly pulled it off her wrist and pushed it into her pocket before smiling at something Zane said.

After dinner, she'd feigned exhaustion when Zane invited her to join them at the movies. Once the garage door rumbled closed, Claire's shoulders finally sagged. She did a quick sweep of the house, making sure everything was tidy, before heading to the bedroom.

Squatting over her frame pack, Claire slid open the smallest zipper compartment. The pink-and-silver friendship bracelet Meg had given her at thirteen sat next to her spoon. Razor-thin knicks marred the beautiful rosette handle, trailing down the slender neck and ending in a large gash on the left side of the spoon's bowl. That slash always dragged against her lip while eating instant oatmeal beside a campfire, leaving behind a slightly metallic taste.

After a few months of living with Gram, this spoon had accidentally slipped into the disposal. Claire had expected her grandmother to yell at her for her mistake when the sound of metal being thrown between blades accompanied the hum of the machine. Instead, Gram had simply fished the utensil from the depths of the sink, washed it, and put it in the bamboo drying rack.

"You're going to keep it? But I ruined it." Claire's brow wrinkled even as her stomach tensed to receive a lecture about how she'd just proved how much of a burden she was.

Gram leaned her hip on the counter before propping her other foot just below the knee on her standing leg. "You made a mistake. The spoon's not broken. It'll still hold soup or stir coffee. It's just a little scarred." Her grandmother's eyes softened even more. *"Everything gets a little roughened up with time. That doesn't mean it isn't worth keeping."*

The unexpected swell burning her chest made Claire bolt to standing. Backpacking meant traveling light. Each ounce you carried had to be worth the sting of the straps digging into your shoulders. This spoon was the only thing she'd kept after Gram's passing. The only thing she needed to remind her of Gram's love.

She was being silly again, but Claire dug into her pocket before wrapping Rowan's hair tie around the handle of the spoon.

It wasn't until after she'd finished that Claire caught a glimpse of the yellow sticky note on her compressible travel pillow.

Please stay as long as you want. I like you being here.

Her thumb smoothed over Rowan's neat, even handwriting until the words blurred slightly.

The bridge of her nose stung not only from the sentiment but because Rowan had given her an easy way out. He'd written this even before she'd surprised him by coming home early. There hadn't been a moment afterward when he'd been anywhere near his bedroom.

Clearly, he'd figured out that her running the shower and being gone when he finished work was her avoiding the conversation about staying here. Since she had a history of running away from difficult things, Claire supposed it wasn't such a hard conclusion to draw.

Still . . . he'd seen her for what she was and asked her to stay.

Something transitional stirred in her chest, rotating in clicking degrees.

Claire drew in a sharp breath, forcefully pushing the sensation away.

Zane knocking on the door earlier had been a gift. It'd be best if she didn't squander it.

Rowan had told her he'd loved her once. Even if that'd been a young man's romantic dreamings instead of real love, she didn't want to hurt Rowan now. Since Claire couldn't trust herself not to run if things got hard, it was best if she kept things platonic.

Claire set her shoulders, striding into the kitchen. The sticky note pad was in the junk drawer along with a random assortment of obsolete chargers, safety pins, pens, and twist ties.

The pen hovered over the paper for a halting beat. What if she wrote what she really felt?

I like being here too. So much it scares me.

Pressing hard into the pad, Claire wrote, *Thanks a bunch, Roomie.*

It was work not to add *Me too* to his *I like you being here*, but Claire kept it from scratching the paper. After setting the note on Rowan's stack of linens on the couch's end table, Claire folded her note from Rowan into a tidy square. Once she'd shut the door to the bedroom, she only hesitated a second before zipping it into her pack next to her spoon.

Chapter 16

If the previous week of being Claire's "roomie" had been tolerable, this week had been pure torture. The memory of Claire's nails scratching up his scalp still singed Rowan at odd intervals, making him shudder. It fought against the sensations of their courthouse kiss for his favorite memory of Claire.

Both thoughts were in a heated standstill—much like the two cowboys staring down on the dusty stage in front of Rowan.

Tonight's Fun Pact activity was a Pistoleros Wild West Show at Trail Dust Town. It was admittedly better than the spoken-word poetry reading Claire had taken him to on Wednesday. Literary art just wasn't for him. Last Saturday had been a triple-A baseball game because the main hydraulic pump at the water park had burst.

"I can't believe I let you talk me into this. This is so hokey," Rowan grumbled.

Keeping up a playful repartee became an unspoken agreement to avoid discussing their hallway encounter.

"Shhh." The sound was made directly over his ear. Rowan barely kept his eyes from rolling back. "I haven't seen this show since I was a kid. And it's not hokey. It's incredible."

The only thing separating them from the now fighting stuntmen was an old rope strung between wooden posts. Beyond the grunting men, an elaborate Old West backdrop, complete with lots of balconies to fire pistols and fall dramatically to the ground, stretched into the purpling night sky.

An unexpected explosion rocketed from stage left, flinging a third stuntman through the air. The acrobatic action was incredibly impressive. How these actors didn't break something every time they did a show was simply mind-boggling. Heat from the pyrotechnics flashed over his skin before the warmth of Claire clutching his arm replaced it.

"Sorry." The nervous look on her face was tearing him apart, piece by piece. "I didn't expect fire."

She pressed her palms together and slid them between her bare knees, just below the layer of fringe of her denim skirt. Before entering the recreated western-themed town, Claire had made them go to Goodwill to find cowboy outfits. He'd been lucky in that she seemed happy with him wearing his own jeans with a store-bought flannel and steer skull bolo tie. Claire topped her skirt with an oversized, rhinestone-studded, white button-up, which she'd rolled up to the elbows and tied at the waist. Every time she leaned forward, the edge of her shirt would slip up, exposing a distracting sliver of skin.

The rest of the thirty-minute show was a blur of trying not to acknowledge the settling in his spine when Claire laughed at a slapstick exchange between actors, or when Claire booed when the "bad guy" took one of the cowboy's daughters hostage, or when Claire gave an enthusiastic two-finger whistle when the actors took their final bow.

"What do you say, partner?" she asked once the crowd began to disperse. "Should we belly up to the bar?"

Rowan's head shook automatically as his heart became too big for his body. *This* was his Claire. It was as if she existed on some other astral plane, illuminated from within. She'd been so anxious this whole week that the light that had always flashed under her skin seemed dulled. Rowan had worried maybe that he'd done that, that being around him was hurting her.

They'd always balanced each other before. Her playful personality seemed to round out the rigidity in his. Rowan had always loved Claire's spontaneity, her ability to find joy in even the most mundane circumstances. She could pull him from the darkest recesses and make him want to join in the fun like no one else could.

Claire mistook his movement for resistance and huffed. "We can order Shirley Temples if you're not up for whiskey. Don't get your unmentionables in a bunch."

"I don't think a lady such as yourself should be speaking of unmentionables." His words slipped into a rusty drawl. The poorly attempted accent landed nonetheless, pulling a broad smile from Claire.

"Miss." He stood, offering his arm.

Claire's fully dimpled grin soothed that ache that'd been tightening his muscles all week.

"Thank you, kind sir." She took his arm, her accent slipping more Southern than Southwestern.

They slowly strolled past the gazebo into the main square. The building facades held signs and displays for a barber shop, bank, and apothecary while being filled with Western-themed boutiques. Children marveled over barrels of old-fashioned candies and tchotchkes within the general store.

Old piano music surrounded them once they pushed through the saloon doors. The middle-aged man wearing a vest and black arm bands around his white shirt, inclined his head as they found two open seats at the large wooden bar.

"Be right back, folks. I've got to switch out the tap."

Claire relaxed against the armrest of her wooden-backed barstool with a smile. "What'll it be?"

"Sarsaparilla. Only a real man can handle sarsaparilla." Rowan thumped his fist against his sternum. "Puts hair on your chest."

When Claire snorted into her hands, every cell in him sang. "I'll get one too."

"You sure about that?" His every facial movement was exaggerated, but it kept that effervescent smile on Claire's lips.

She leaned away from him with a raised eyebrow. "Don't think I can handle my sarsaparilla? I'm going to drink you under the table, you scallywag."

A chuff left his nose. "I'm pretty sure you slipped into pirate territory with that one."

Their chuckles halted when a man in jeans so tight you could see the chew tin in his back pocket leaned over Claire from the other side. "Hey, sugar. Can I get you a drink?"

The way the interruption had ruined their sweet moment sent an irritated flush roaring over his skin. Rowan resisted the urge to fist his hands, focusing on the toile wallpaper beyond the man's shoulder.

"No, thanks," she said, not glancing up.

"I like those boots." The man gestured to her hiking boots with the toe of his cowboy ones, further crowding her on the wooden stool.

Rowan was two seconds from physically removing the man from Claire's presence when she turned to Rowan and winked. Confusion swept through him before she spoke again.

"I think it's best you moved along," she said loudly, her Western accent nearly as bad as the man's scraggly mustache.

A few patrons seated around the nearby barrel-based high-top tables looked up, muttering to each other while watching.

The arrogant smirk the man sent Claire tightened Rowan's shoulders. One of his feet hit the floor as his hand gripped the rounded edge of his armrest.

"Naw," the man continued. "We're having a conversation here."

"We're not." Claire's drawl dropped as her tone iced. "I generally don't converse with men who can't swim."

That one hit. The man's smile faltered for a breath. Even a few onlookers tittered.

Seemingly noticing that he had an audience, the man doubled down.

"*Hooo.*" The sound echoed off the wooden cash register as he took off his gallon hat to scratch at his forehead. "Good thing I like 'em a little feisty. You're a piece of work."

Rowan's fingers crushed the armrest, but Claire simply tilted her face up with a poisonous smile. "Strong words from a man who cuts his own hair."

Rowan's eyebrows shot up as snickers sounded from the peanut gallery. He'd never heard Claire whisper a cruel word, but she was slicing this man to the quick.

Casually leaning her elbows on the bar, Claire asked, "Do women tell you they like that piece of scruff on your face? I know it's a trend, but you, sir, can't pull it off."

The languid look the man traipsed over Claire's body made Rowan's stomach roil. "Oh, sweetheart." He tsked, slowly shaking his head. "There are better ways to ask for a mustache ride."

Rowan shot to standing, nearly toppling his barstool. "That's *enough.*"

He didn't fault Claire for messing with this man when he'd clearly ignored a polite refusal, but this had gone too far.

The bar hushed, the rest of the patrons clearly thinking this scene was a continuation of the stunt show they'd watched on the outdoor stage.

"I'll say when we're done." The man tossed his words at Rowan before glancing down at Claire.

Rowan was stepping forward to put himself between this jerk and Claire when the man's gaze snagged on Claire's upturned forearms.

"That's a shame." The man trapped her left arm with one firm hand before knocking his other knuckle to the center of her tattoo. "Marking up your pretty skin like that."

Blinding white flashed over Rowan's vision before everything became oversaturated. It was as if someone had turned up the contrast on everything in sight. Voices blurred. The tinny sounds of "Maple Leaf Rag" were replaced by insistent ringing. Shocking electricity sprinted through his body, igniting every muscle into action. This odd sensation of being outside of himself murmured in the background as his barely banked anger wholly took over.

"Get your hands off my wife." His words were their own impact before Rowan ripped the man's hand away from Claire.

He folded the man's arm behind his back while pressing his slimy face into the bar. A discarded glass of water tumbled over, sending ice scattering to the ground. Several gasps rang out from the crowd, and Claire's stool toppled over as she jumped from it, but Rowan was beyond caring.

No one touched Claire.

No one.

The muscle in his jaw ached as Rowan decided what to do next. Should he knock a few teeth loose? Bloody the man's nose? Use the nearby martini shaker to break the knuckle that dared to grace Claire's perfect skin?

An inhuman sound accompanied Rowan wrenching the man's arm higher on his back, putting his full weight into the movement. Those dirty hands had touched his wife. The grime beneath the man's fingernails made an odd piece of trivia zip to the front of his mind. There were twenty-seven bones in the human hand. How many hits would it take to pulverize them all?

Rowan was reaching for a half-filled whiskey bottle to use instead of the shaker, drowning in the violence coursing through his veins, when Claire's fingertips rested on his back. The sensation was in exact opposition to everything burning his soul—slight, soothing, cool—but Rowan wasn't sure it was enough.

If anything could be enough to save him from himself.

Chapter 17

All Claire could see was Rowan's back. Rowan's massive, heaving back as he separated her from the cowboy.

"I'll leave her alone. I promise. Just let me go." His previously jerky tone was replaced with whimpering fear as the man attempted to bargain his way out of Rowan's unyielding grip.

"Rowan." Claire smoothed her palm flat, leaning her forehead onto him. "Let's go."

"Fine," he gritted, unhappy but relenting.

The second he released the man, Claire grabbed Rowan's forearm and pulled him toward the exit. Confused applause accompanied their swift retreat, but Claire didn't stop until they were through the swinging doors, down three storefronts, and around the far side of the building. A part of her wasn't sure she'd just witnessed her reserved, childhood friend physically restrain a man like he'd been trained in takedown tactics. Rowan certainly had the strength to do bodily damage, but she'd never seen him lose control like that.

The whole scene should have scared her, should have made her ask Rowan what the heck he'd been thinking, but the only thing circling in her mind was Rowan's growly command.

Get your hands off my wife.

Rowan collapsed against the building, cradling his head. "I'm sorry. I shouldn't have done that."

The shameful remorse in this tone ignited something in her. Bar fights ended up in lawsuits and real-life consequences. Rowan knew better. How dare he threaten his livelihood because a man touched her skin, even though the desire to wash her wrist was still making her nauseated.

"No, you shouldn't have." Her hands balled on her hips. "You're not supposed to get all macho-aggressive, *'I'll kill you if you touch my woman.'* You— You crochet for goodness' sake!"

A covered wagon blocked the light from the antique gas lamps, casting Rowan's face almost entirely in shadow, but Claire still caught his wince.

She began to pace in front of him, just to give this flustered sensation somewhere to go. "You can't be smart, sensitive, build like a Greek god, *and also* spine-meltingly possessive."

Even in the dark light, Claire could see that line between his brows.

"What am I going to do with you?" After three aggressive strides, she pressed the heels of her hands over her eyes.

It felt like her insides were melting. Claire couldn't catch a solid grasp of any of the emotions swirling in her stomach.

"I'm sorry."

An agitated groan left her lips as she stepped in front of him. "You don't even know what you're apologizing for."

His adorably confused brow only made him more irresistible. "Slamming that guy into the bar isn't the problem?"

She growled in response.

Rowan's gaze raked down her arms, stalling on her flexed, twitchy fingers before returning to her face. "Then tell me what is, and I'll fix it."

"No. Let's go home." Claire turned to walk toward the parking lot, but Rowan caught her wrist.

His calloused fingers settled right over her tattooed pulse point.

Right where they *belonged.*

Rowan's reassuring grip instantly washed away the lingering tarnished feeling. In its wake, a grounding sensation shimmied down her arms and legs until the soles of her feet stung. Her eyes drifted closed as understanding sent goosebumps pricking in defiance to the summer night's warmth.

She was done.

Done fighting how much she wanted this, wanted him.

How had Rowan felt like this for months when they were younger but never acted on it? She'd barely made it a few weeks.

"Claire. Let's talk about this."

The speed with which she spun to him and caught his jaw in her free hand took Rowan by surprise. Claire could see it in his gorgeous hazel eyes before she closed hers to kiss him. But the instant her impatient lips covered his, Rowan's hands spread wide over the small of her back, pressing her firmly into him.

A needy noise escaped her when those hot hands began to slide up slowly, like they were memorizing her. By the time his fingers smoothed over her neck and into her loose hair, Claire was shaking. Never in her life had she been this affected by a man. She'd never trusted anyone enough to fully let go.

Rowan hummed an appreciative sound that unfurled something shadowy and enigmatic in her soul. Her brow tensed until one of his arms banded around her waist, fully supporting her, and his other hand angled her jaw with geometric precision. Then she was truly lost—lost in the kiss, in him, in the sawdust scent surrounding them, in the deepening starlight above them.

The ability to release, to not have to be in control, was so achingly sweet.

Claire could have continued returning Rowan's deep kisses until the sun rose, except a man in spurs and a shiny six-point star cleared his throat.

"Let's keep things PG. Trail Dust Town is a family attraction."

"Yes, sir," Rowan answered respectfully despite his breathlessness.

Claire simply blinked, wholly distracted by the stinging sensation still resonating in the center of her chest.

The sheriff tipped his hat at them before sauntering away.

"I can't believe you got me in trouble." The wry way Rowan breathed that over her ear while one hand still gripped her waist made this uncontrolled laugh bubble at her throat like shaken champagne pushing on a cork.

It was too close to the words he used to angrily throw at her before stomping off to his room when they'd been kids. It felt like the eighty-seventh time that reality merged with a memory.

So many parts of herself were mixed with Rowan—like two paint colors swirling together, forever intertwined.

The eight-year-old boy whose bony knees she used to lean against while she joined him for another episode of *Curious George*. The reluctant teen who let her coerce him into joining another one of her and Meg's schemes. The young man who'd stood by her side at Gram's celebration of life ceremony, his steady fingers wrapping her wrist, his voice soothing as he asked what he could do when he'd already done the one thing she'd needed. The man who swore to love and cherish her before placing a wedding band on her finger.

They were all the same person.

That persistent throbbing behind her breastbone couldn't be good. She should probably make an appointment with a cardiologist in addition to following up with her gastroenterologist.

Sudden panic infused with the remnants of that breathtaking kiss as Claire's body completely malfunctioned. Was she going to vomit? Hyperventilate? Laugh? Perhaps all three? Her shaking shoulders had apparently decided that laughing was the best way to dispel these too-big emotions.

Fortunately, Rowan interpreted her existential crisis as that of being embarrassed by being caught by the fake sheriff.

"Go ahead." The corner of Rowan's mouth quirked. "Let it out."

It started with a snort that melted into a glee-filled giggle so heavy and full it felt like years in the making. Claire laughed so hard her eyes watered, and she had to catch little ungraceful dribbles of spit before they stained her shirt. Her, "Oh, no!"

while wiping her mouth finally made Rowan chuckle along with her. She heaved with another snort, pressing the crown of her head into the center of Rowan's chest while gripping his shirt sleeve to keep from dropping to the ground.

"I can't believe we—" The rest of that sentence died with her mirth when Rowan lovingly pushed her hair behind her ear.

Claire bit the corner of her lip, needles shooting over her shoulders. The *way* he was looking at her. She shouldn't be at the receiving end of that much wholesome affection.

"I'm sorry." Claire stepped back, the absence of Rowan touching some part of her was like a whip crack against raw skin. "I shouldn't have— We shouldn't be doing this." She flapped her hand between them in an awkward gesture.

His head tilted slightly as a devious smile tipped his lips. "You sure? You seemed to enjoy it."

Really?! Right at this moment, he's going to add cocky confidence to his repertoire of desirable traits?

"It's not that. It's just—" Claire took a shaky sip of air.

All the reasons she'd complied last week—*really good reasons*—got jammed in her throat.

"It's just that I don't . . . I'm not . . ."

A small voice whispered, *I'm not good enough for you.*

When Rowan's fingers framed her face, her scattered words finally found purchase. "I'm going to hurt you. I don't want to, but I will."

If she could barely handle kissing Rowan in public without having an emotional meltdown, there was no way she'd be able to manage the more serious parts of an honest relationship without messing something up.

That insidious thought spiraled until its icy claws lanced her spine. Rowan deserved better. He deserved someone smart and mature, not someone who barely made a living running from her problems and posting pictures of herself on the internet.

His deliberate, measured breath caused dread to seep through her stomach because Rowan would make the right decision—the practical decision—and that meant *not* choosing her.

Good.

It was good that one of them had a sane mind and wasn't completely driven mad by the idea of repeating that reality-shifting kiss.

"I think it might be worth it." The hoarse words were accompanied by Rowan's hazel eyes drifting to her lips.

Her head shook automatically, stifled by his gentle grip on her jaw.

Rowan let her face go, and she wobbled a bit without his hands grounding her. "What do you want?"

"I—" she stammered. "I can't just have—"

"Because I have wanted you for a long time. If you—" He blew out a slow breath. "If there's a chance that you want me back, even for a short while, I think I can live with whatever comes after that."

"No. That's not fair."

His hand collected her wrist, pressing his thumb into the center of her heart tattoo before bringing his lips to the same spot. "Life is rarely fair."

Her eyes helplessly blinked closed. Rowan made her feel simultaneously safe and completely undone, and her fragmented brain was quickly losing its battle because the rest of her wanted Rowan with a ferocity that frightened her.

When her eyes fluttered open and caught the tension in his jaw, her breath caught. Rowan was right there with her, barely resisting the urge to throw her over his shoulder like a caveman.

She tore her gaze away. "I still don't think—"

"Let's do this instead," he interrupted her. "Let's see how things go for one week. Seven days. That's it."

Leave it to Rowan to put nice tidy lines around things. Though, the idea of a deadline did help ease the incessant ringing in her ears. Could Claire get her fill in seven days and then extricate herself from his life before she did too much damage?

Maybe.

"I have one request." She worried her bottom lip. "That we don't—"

Claire had never had issues talking about intimacy before, but she was blushing *hard*.

Rowan's mouth curled into an entertained smile. "That we don't consummate our fake marriage."

"That." She pointed at the air.

His chin dipped once. "I give you my word."

"And . . . and we keep our Fun Pact."

Leverage. Somehow, she always needed leverage.

"I'd expect nothing less." The snarky way Rowan tossed that at her made her fingers flex again.

His gaze found her hands before his shoulders rose in a halting inhale. "You do that when you want to touch me, don't you?"

Rowan knew about her preference to explore the world tactilely. When they'd hiked together as teens, he'd always point out spiny thistle blossoms, plump pieces of moss, or tiny, grouped mesquite leaves for her to run a finger over.

"No." She tucked her twitchy fingers into the back pockets of her denim skirt.

Whatever restraint he'd been harboring, she'd apparently decimated it with her bold-faced lie.

"All these years." His hand roughly rubbed his jaw as he shook his head. "I can't believe that after all these years—" The sentence cut off when his lips covered hers, his groan vibrating down her throat.

"I thought I told you two to move it along." This time the sheriff was rough with his delivery.

"Right. Sorry!" Claire grabbed Rowan's hand and pulled him toward the parking lot.

Six steps in, Rowan sweetly wove his fingers between hers.

A deep breath filled Claire's chest as she pushed back against the impending panic. Instead of predicting how she'd eventually find a way to mess this whole thing up, Claire was going to give herself a break. She would let herself enjoy this for a week.

Seven days.

She could pretend to be normal for seven days.

Chapter 18

Rowan was mid pull-up the next morning when Claire padded barefoot onto his patio. The sight of her in her rumpled sleep shorts and tank only halted his movement for a second, but Claire's small smile as she closed the sliding door meant she'd caught his hesitation.

It's not like it was *his* fault. Couldn't she sleep in something looser? Something that didn't hug her curves so nicely? Even the early tendrils of light seemed to revel in curling around her body.

"How many of those can you do?" Her tumbleweed hair made his chest ache more than the strain in his shoulders.

"Good morning to you too," he said, seamlessly continuing his set.

Claire crossed under his climbing beam before pulling back a chair from the dining table and positioning it to watch him.

"Really?" Rowan dropped to the ground, wiping his forehead with the back of his arm.

He'd only been out here for twenty minutes, but his t-shirt was already drenched with sweat. Normally, once Claire had left for her morning hike, he'd do his workout shirtless. But since the door to his bedroom had still been closed when he'd woken this morning, he'd put on the extra layer and forwent listening to his professional podcast so he wouldn't miss her. He'd never expected Claire to track his every movement like a lioness on a hunt.

The flirty grin she sent him shot straight down his spine. "Really."

"Have you no shame?"

Claire bit the corner of her lip as she shook her head. "Not a drop."

Chugging half of his water bottle gave Rowan the pause he needed not to stalk across his paver patio and kiss that smirk off her face. He was still reeling from the possibility of it. That he *could*. He could kiss Claire Winesett whenever he liked. After wanting Claire for half his life, this knowledge short-circuited his organs.

Claire caught the exact second he gave in, because both dimples peaked before he'd even taken a step in her direction.

The self-satisfied way she simply tilted her face up at his approach made something unexplainable streak through his muscles. Instead of crashing his lips to hers, Rowan stood a step away from her crossed legs and gently gripped her chin with his thumb and forefinger.

"Good morning, Rowan."

Those whiskey irises flashed before she repeated his sentence. An appraising hum vibrated in his chest as he smoothed his thumb over her bottom lip before slowly bending at the waist. Her mouth parted slightly, her lashes fluttering.

"Good morning, Claire," he said, barely brushing her lips with his.

When he straightened, Claire almost knocked him over with the force she shot to standing. Then her lips were on his again. Claire reciprocating his feelings had always been such a far-fetched idea that Rowan hadn't anticipated the intensity of that reciprocity.

Apparently, when Claire wanted something, she went all in.

Eventually, Rowan pulled away, smiling as a little pouty noise left her throat.

"As much as I'd love to continue swapping saliva all morning, I've got to get showered for group." Normally, he'd be meeting with his college friends for coffee today, but once a month, he ran a group therapy rock-climbing session on Mount Lemmon.

Claire play-gagged. "Ugh. Why did you have to call it that?"

A smirk tugged at his cheek. "Because otherwise, you wouldn't stop. You can barely keep your hands off me."

Her twitchy fingers were still on his waist as her gaze traced the muscles showing through his soaking shirt. "Okay. Fair. I should have warned you last night. I have zero impulse control."

A breathy chuckle left his mouth as he dropped a kiss on her unruly cowlick. "Lucky for us, I have loads of it."

When Rowan looked up, he caught Herbert Nenninger padding toward the terra-cotta plant saucer he'd filled with water before starting his workout. "Look."

Claire followed his eyeline toward the edge of the backyard space, rotating in his arms. "He's real. I was beginning to think your bobcat friend was a figment of your imagination."

"Meg was the one with imaginary friends, not me."

Herbert froze between a sun-scorched sage bush and a barrel cactus, one paw up in the air. His spotted coat—blending tan, white, black, and brown—made him nearly indistinguishable from his desert surroundings, but his bright amber eyes never left the two of them.

"Morning, Herbert," Rowan said softly.

The early sunlight seemed to reflect off the bobcat's whiskers as it tilted its head before dipping its tongue into the water.

A satiated sigh resonated from Claire as she sunk against his chest. Rowan tightened his arms, memorizing the feel of her. "You should introduce yourself."

Claire's giggle bounced against him. "It wouldn't be the first time I spoke to a wild animal. On one lonely hike, a racoon and I went toe-to-toe about string theory versus loop quantum gravity for a solid thirty minutes."

"Herbert and I don't go that deep. Usually, we debate who would be the better best friend, Emma Stone or Jennifer Lawrence. I'm one hundred and fifty percent in the JLaw camp, but Herb is stubbornly Team Emma."

Claire was shaking with her effort not to bark out a laugh and scare the bobcat away, her breath unevenly leaving pursed lips.

That overwhelming sensation flooded his veins again. Rowan wanted to kiss the crook of her neck, the tip of her nose, and each one of her fingers all at once. One week would not be enough time with Claire. He'd only given Claire the deadline because she'd needed something concrete. Rowan wanted her here . . . always.

Taking a deep breath, Rowan closed his eyes and reminded himself to stay in this moment, to now allow himself to fall into the trap of foreboding.

You have this moment with Claire now. Savor it.

His chin dipped to take in the delicious scent of his body wash on Claire's skin, the softness of her sleep tank against his forearms, the sight of the desert waking for the day, the sound of her peaceful breathing, and the remnant taste of her minty tongue.

When Claire rotated in his arms, her fingers smoothing over his jaw, Rowan didn't fight her or remind her there were things to do. Instead, he took his time kissing the woman he loved.

◊◊◊

"You got this, Liam." Several other iterations of Rowan's words from the men around him followed Liam's sweat-covered back up the steep rock face.

Though this route was perfect for beginners, those who'd never rock climbed before usually ended up with Elvis leg if they hesitated too much with their progression. Rowan anticipated this of Liam and made him climb last, allowing him to observe the other clients' hand and footholds. Rowan leaned back on his harness, waiting and watching.

"Okay. Okay." Liam was speaking mostly to himself, but Rowan released the tension in the rope so Liam could ascend.

Taking a few select clients to climb the sandstone rock faces on Mount Lemmon had been something Rowan had wanted to do for years and enacted a few months ago. It was amazing to watch how being outside with literal rocks to ground them helped his clients break down walls that were sometimes immobile inside Rowan's therapy office.

Meg had loved the idea too, screen-printing him a custom orange t-shirt for the occasion. She'd printed "Mental Health *is* Health" in huge white letters across the back. So when Rowan climbed up first to anchor the top rope, his clients were reading those important words.

Sometimes when his sister meddled, she got it right.

After three more pushes, Liam slapped the top of the rock, hooting like a wild man. "I did it!"

The rest of his clients joined in cheering for Liam as he wiped his eyes. Having a breakthrough at the summit wasn't uncommon. The rush of achievement, adrenaline, and endorphins all culminated after reaching the peak.

Rowan gave Liam a moment before calling up to see if he was ready to be lowered.

Each man was working on something different today. Liam was continuing to focus on gaining confidence and stepping out of his comfort zone. Thomas was practicing controlling his temper on the climb. This was his third month attempting to complete the course. Today had been the first time he'd done so without slamming his palms into the cliff. Alejandro had only been able to go up six feet above the ground—where he could comfortably jump down—instead of to the forty-seven-foot apex. Since Alejandro struggled with trust and this was his first climb, Rowan was proud of his progress.

The second Liam's feet hit the ground, he accepted Rowan's high-five with a huge smile. "What do we do now?"

A chuckle left Rowan's lips. "I'm going to clean the top rope anchor while you all have a snack."

After organizing all the gear, Rowan settled on the smaller boulder beside the route and accepted a protein bar from Thomas. They'd have to hike a bit to return to the small turnout parking lot. He'd intentionally selected this crag because of its obscurity. The last thing Rowan needed was to contend with other climbers while also talking to his clients about their experience.

The boulder faced the Tucson valley, giving them a spectacular view of the city. The hazy desert expanded around the city center, other mountain ranges stretching out in the distance. The long, two-lane road up the mountain looped below them, a pack of cyclists whizzing downhill. Though it was well over a hundred degrees in Tucson by now, the upper-seventies breeze was tinged with the scent of sun-warmed pine needles. The fact that an hour drive could take you from the roasting heat of the desert into the company of towering Ponderosa pines and mixed conifers often meant the road to Summerhaven, Mount Lemmon's small mountaintop village, was often crowded on the weekends.

Rowan allowed a few more moments of relaxed silence to pass before beginning the therapy part of today's session.

Just before he was about to speak, his phone pinged with a text.

Claire: *I know I've already satisfied my allotted two activities this week, but I found something fun for when you get home. Are you up for an adventure?*

Rowan knew he was grinning like a lunatic, but he honestly didn't care.

Rowan: *Depends.*

Claire: *On what?*

Rowan: *Lots of things.*

Claire: *Don't be contrary just for the sake of being contrary.*

Rowan: *Why not? Your cheeks pink brighter than prickly pear fruit when you get annoyed.*

Claire sent a photo of herself, face flushed, with the caption, *You win.*

A laugh burst from him before he remembered his surroundings. Rowan needed to focus on finishing out this therapy session, not on his adorable wife.

That modifier was dangerous, but Rowan decided to ignore the warnings flashing in the corners of his mind.

Rowan: *I'll be home in two hours. I'm up for whatever you have planned.*

Pocketing his phone, Rowan turned his attention to the men around him. "Before we hike out, did anyone want to share something they learned about themselves today?"

Chapter 19

One foam ball clenched in each hand, Claire waited for the whistle. A semi-bored teenager in a striped referee shirt looked between the two lines of people. The black trampoline beneath Claire's sticky-soled jump socks trembled as the ten-year-old next to her bounced a bit in preparation. A lime-green pinnie covered her t-shirt while an orange one covered Rowan's. Both of them were wearing athletic shorts to compete in this epic trampoline dodgeball game.

Rowan shook his head slowly, mouthing, *'You're going down,'* from his position across the invisible scrimmage line. The average age of her fellow teammates hovered around twelve, but Claire didn't care. This was the perfect activity to celebrate her positive DEXA scan results. Having the bone density of an ox meant Claire didn't need to worry about fracturing a femur while jumping.

The indoor park consisted of four sections—the main bank of trampolines, trampolines with basketball hoops, a small

American-Ninja-Warrior-inspired obstacle course, and a giant foam pit—all of them fair game for the dozens of dodgeballers.

A whistle blast sounded, and Claire chucked her ball straight at Rowan's head. He caught her ball and a second one thrown by a tween in a sparkly pink shirt before ducking a third and slamming the ball in his left hand directly into Claire's stomach.

His hand-eye coordination and reflexes were insane . . . and *hot.*

Before she could fully unravel that thought, Claire bounced away. She'd need to figure out a better strategy in order to pummel Rowan. Unlike normal dodgeball, when you're out if you get hit, this was more of a constant barrage of balls flying with no outs. Fortunately for her, the green team didn't take kindly to an adult on the opposing team. It quickly became a game of pelt-the-grown-man as often as possible.

The sound of Rowan's hearty laughter slipped around every child hurriedly rushing from one side of the park to the other. At one point, Rowan picked up a boy, using him as a human shield before the referee blew a whistle at him.

Oversized chairs that normally would've been for lounging had become a penalty box, and Rowan bounding toward them was the perfect opportunity to whap him in the back of the head. As stealthily as she could, Claire rounded the basketball hoops and hurled her last ball at him.

When his large hand caught it in his peripheral vision before he even turned his head, Claire groaned. "Come on!"

"This was your idea." He tossed the ball between his palms, his smile wicked.

One of the refs snagged Rowan's ball and threw it back into the fair-play area. By the look on his face, you'd have thought the referee had just peed in Rowan's shoes. Claire laughed as two balls hit her back before a third smacked her upside the head.

"That's it!" She stooped to pick up as many balls as she could before springing toward the foam pit to enact her revenge on the gaggle of nine-year-olds.

Claire was mid-battle, siding with two teen girls against the three boys, when Rowan plucked her off the edge of the foam pit and tossed her in like she was as light as one of the balls sailing through the air.

"No fair." Struggling to gain purchase over the square blocks of fluff, Claire scowled at him.

Rowan simply smiled, bouncing once on the trampoline beside the foam pit, tucking into an effortless flip, and landing a few feet beside her. Then, his hands were hot on her waist, lifting her back out. Her shirt slid with the action, leaving his pinky searing the delicate skin below her ribs.

"I could have gotten out on my own." Claire crossed her arms from her seated position on the edge, feet dangling into the pit.

"I know." Rowan pulled himself out, booping her on the nose. "You don't need anyone."

"Hey!" Claire tried to keep the flustered sound out of her voice, but Rowan was gone, kids swarming him like blood-thirsty mosquitoes in a swamp.

At the end of the hour-long game, they were both sweaty and beaming like the surrounding kids.

"That was fun." Rowan handed her a sports drink from the vending machine and sat beside her on the narrow bench to change back into his shoes. "If you're up for it, I have something to add to the fun list for tonight."

"Oh?" The bottle top cracked as she twisted it open.

"Yeah." The shy smile on his face as he pulled off his jump socks twisted her chest. How had she never noticed how sweet he was? "But I'll keep it a surprise, like you did with this, if that's okay."

"Do I get to shower first? I'm more sweat-soaked than Erin after she tried to change her own oil."

History weaved seamlessly with the present as the two of them recounted the shared memory of his sister stubbornly refusing to pay for oil service in the middle of the summer. Rowan laughed, the sound of it slipping into the spaces between her ribs. So many times during their conversations over the last few weeks, they'd share a memory—picking it up, dusting it off, noting the different aspects of each of their versions before setting it back into space.

"We've got plenty of time to get cleaned up and eat dinner before it starts."

Claire took a gulp of her drink, wiping her lips with the back of her hand. "What are we having?"

"I thought we'd make something together." The casual words were aimed at his fingers as they tied his laces.

Just like something a real couple would do.

So far, Claire had mentally referred to their Fun Pact activities as things friends would do together—with the exception of kissing him, of course. But she'd altered something fundamental with her impulsivity last night. Claire could feel it with every breath she drew.

It'd always been easy to be around Rowan. They'd grown up together. She knew where to poke to elicit a scowl or a laugh from him. But the idea of truly opening up and letting him see all the jagged, ugly parts of her made her want to buy a bus ticket to the nearest national park.

Even Meg didn't get to see those parts. Early on, they'd both agreed to ignore their flaws and live in the moment. It was unorthodox as far as best friendships went, but it worked for them. Heavy topics were never discussed. Somehow, Claire knew Rowan wouldn't let her off the hook quite as easily.

That dipping sensation curdled her stomach, but Claire made sure her smile was even as she replied, "Sounds good."

◊◊◊

Hours later, when they stood in line for entrance into the club downtown, Claire bit her lip to keep from smiling too big. She should have known this surprise activity was going to be something good based on the fact that Rowan had asked her to wear her black dress while a white collared shirt topped his jeans.

One glance had Rowan rolling his eyes at her. "Stop it."

"I didn't say anything." She pointed at the salsa-dancing lesson sign beside the main door. "I'm not one for conformist gender roles. I actively rally against the notion that women can't be fully independent. What's wrong with a man wanting ballroom-dancing lessons?"

"Salsa lessons. It's different." Rowan gave her a slitted stare before turning to pay their admission.

Though they'd arrived early to take the lessons before a live band was to play, the popular club was already near capacity. Several couples were dancing to the low music playing through the speakers. Papel picados ran back and forth over the black ceiling, lines of dimly lit Edison bulbs separating each strand. A mirror ball centered the dance floor while low-backed red couches lined the space not occupied by the stage or the large bar.

"I'm pretty sure they salsa on *Dancing with the Stars*." If Claire wasn't careful, she'd draw blood on her lip.

Rowan stopped abruptly, causing her to slam into his back before he spun around. "Are you going to tease me the whole time we're here?"

"Probably." An affirmative head bob accompanied the squeaky word.

Claire didn't catch his mumbled response, just followed Rowan to the place where they were conducting lessons. The two leaders were dressed in a slightly toned-down version of a dance outfit you'd see on the aforementioned show, but Rowan simply shook his head when she pointedly flicked her eyes at them. Each of them wore a mic, displaying the step pattern before allowing everyone to follow along. They started learning in lines before partnering up, holding hands.

Rowan—curse his preternatural athleticism—mastered the dance steps quickly. She managed while dancing in lines but consistently went the wrong way when partnered with Rowan. Claire was grateful she'd worn her Tevas instead of her boots for the number of times she'd crunched on Rowan's toes.

"It's the same steps from when we were standing side by side." He counted for her.

"Tell that to them," Claire said, frowning at her uncooperative feet.

"Maybe you should allow me to lead. Do you think you can do that?" His raised eyebrows made her want to poke that ticklish spot on his side, but her hands were between his.

Rowan placed a hand around her upper back, tugging her into a more traditional dance stance while still keeping the distance between them. "Meg saying I'm rigid when her best friend can't relinquish control during a dance is a little narrow-minded, don't you think?"

Claire simply scowled.

The position change did allow Claire to mirror better, and eventually, the gentle guiding of Rowan's hands felt more natural. When she returned from a spin and didn't clobber his shoes, he purred an approving, *"Good,"* that vibrated over her skin.

"Okay, everyone," the female instructor called attention back to the front. "We're going to quickly cover bachata."

Claire was grateful to be separated back into lines. She still felt every syllable of Rowan's praise shimmying down her spine. They learned the second set of steps, but before they partnered back up, a trumpet blasted from beyond the stage.

The band didn't just play their way onto the stage, they danced as well. The energy of the room felt like it'd been doused in lighter fluid. Couples that had been waiting while lessons had been given flooded the floor. Rowan simply raised a brow with a proffered hand, and they stepped into the mix.

Before long, they were both as sweaty as they'd been when bouncing around the trampoline park. Once she'd gotten a hang of the basic partner steps—four songs in—Rowan started replicating the moves of other couples, twisting her this way and that.

The club was too noisy for conversation, but Claire was glad for it. Having to speak while also following along and not getting lost in the searing sensation of Rowan's hand over her shoulder blade would've been impossible. After a while, the music's pace slowed as the lead singer called out something in Spanish. The crowd erupted, falling easily into the bachata steps she hadn't yet figured out.

"It's okay. Just keep following along." Rowan pulled her closer, his hand sliding up to palm the back of her neck.

The effort of keeping her breathing even was gargantuan. Move over, tango. There was no hotter dance than bachata. As much as salsa had consisted of spins and quick steps, bachata had a sensuous movement that kept ratcheting the tension. Pressed so close to him, moving completely in sync, the hiss of the güira felt like it was sizzling down her forearms. Half a song was all Claire could handle.

"Rowan?"

"Yes, baby?" The scruff of his jaw rasped her ear.

When had she become *baby*? Claire's knees wobbled a little. He should stick *this baby* in the corner and kiss her senseless, because she had no strength to continue dancing.

"Can we go home?"

His considering hum rumbled *into* her body, burning its way to her toes. "No. We can't do that."

She leaned back enough to catch his gaze. "Why not?"

Rowan's chest rose as his eyes slowly savored her face. "Because I won't be able to keep my word to you. Not right now."

The honesty of that statement slammed into her like rain crashing onto metal—loud and startling. Her halting inhale left her lips parted. "Oh."

Those hazel eyes swept her again before he pulled back slightly. "Maybe we should get some water."

It'd take a glacier to cool her off at this point, but a glass of ice water would be a good start. "Okay."

The sensation of loss radiating through her when Rowan stepped away was so overwhelming her feet caught. He spun and steadied her in an instant.

"Why don't you sit down?" Rowan said, finding her a vacant seat on a couch. "I'll be back in a minute."

Claire watched his purposeful strides to the bar with a kind of helplessness. Claire pinched her thigh and focused on the rhythmic slap of the bongos to center herself. The thoughts she often told herself—that she was fine on her own, that she didn't need anyone—felt hollow after dancing in Rowan's arms. Even *that* knowledge made her feel foolish. Existence didn't alter after being held like something precious. Right? At this point, Claire had no clue. She'd never felt so discombobulated after something as simple as a dance.

Half a dance.

Gratitude thrummed in her chest that Rowan had again shown restraint, that he'd made the right decision when she'd been willing to dive headfirst into disaster.

When Rowan returned with two plastic cups filled with water, Claire made sure to keep the conversation light. When they ventured back onto the dance floor, they fell into the open salsa style, hands gripped between them. And when a bachata song played again, they agreed it was time for some late-night ice cream.

Chapter 20

Whose brilliant idea was it to spend the afternoon with Claire in a swimsuit? That was the thought that kept bothering Rowan the next day. Her navy, high-neck tankini was more modest than eighty-six percent of the bathing suits surrounding him, but it didn't matter. Every two seconds, Rowan had to remind himself not to stare, particularly at her toned legs.

He'd barely kept his hands to himself last night while salsa dancing, and his admission had altered the course of the evening, setting them back into a wobbly friend-zone. Even Claire hadn't demanded a kiss before they'd gone their separate ways for bed. This morning, they'd slept in late, which was unusual for both of their internal clocks, and had enjoyed an episode of their shared TV show before Claire announced it was "water park time."

"What's next? Lazy river or slides?" Claire asked as they paused beside their bags resting by an arrangement of fake palm trees. It'd been her idea to take a quick dip in the wave pool since they'd been sweaty from the short time in line buying tickets.

The mid-June sun beat upon them like some ruthless kid had held a magnifying glass to it. Rowan had slathered his chest with sunscreen, but it felt like a culinary torch was frying his skin. At least there was a slight breeze today, so evaporative cooling could do its thing.

"What about . . ." The rest of that sentence died in his mouth as Rowan caught sight of several familiar faces walking up the sun-bleached sidewalk.

"Hey, Rowan!" Tessa called, waving her free hand overhead while the other one held her daughter Caroline's. Tessa's boyfriend, Isaac, held Caroline's other hand.

Everybody—absolutely every single one of his friends and their significant others—was wearing blue wristbands and carrying various aqueous accoutrements.

"Surprise," Claire whispered.

His head snapped in her direction. "You did this?"

She rolled her lips together, twisting the towel in her hands. "I thought it would be fun to have everyone together since you missed hanging out with them yesterday."

"But how?"

"OnlyApp." She pinned him with a look. "You know, it's a little weird that one of your best friends developed the social media app to end all other apps and you don't even have a professional account for your therapy practice."

Rowan grumbled. "I don't need an account. I get more than enough referrals as it is."

Staying off OnlyApp these last few years meant he'd been less tempted to look through Claire's travel posts. It had been bad enough that Meg had brought Claire up at family gatherings, often bragging. Like how Claire had used her social media success to raise money to support nonprofits that provided support for single mothers in small towns, or trail maintenance in hard-to-reach communities, or wildlife rescue efforts.

"Besides," Rowan continued, "Ethan understands my position. *He* doesn't even have an account anymore."

"Okay, grandpa. It's good to know you and your grandpa buddy are on the same page." Claire rolled her eyes before turning to hug Zane. "Hey, Zane! Good to see you again."

Zane smiled, introducing her to his girlfriend, Ann, while Rowan was pulled to the outskirts of the group by Kevin and Kyle.

"Okay." Kevin rubbed his hands together. "This should be an easy divide-and-conquer. There's enough of us that we should split into groups. Obviously, you and Claire should be separated."

"Why didn't you tell me you were coming?"

"And lose the opportunity to walk in like a hero?" Kevin scoffed. "Not on your life."

None of his friends knew that things had shifted between him and Claire Friday night. They still believed that he was avoiding her whenever possible. Rowan opened his mouth, but Kyle spoke first.

"We'll keep Claire busy so you can enjoy the park in peace." Kyle craned his neck to see Claire shaking hands with his fiancée, Dani. "What do you think about boys vs. girls?"

"Are we in middle school?" Kevin quirked a brow.

"It works, doesn't it?"

Rowan watched Claire laugh at something Becca said before crouching to answer a question from Caroline. The idea of setting his friends straight teetered on his tongue, but since that would've undermined their good intentions and Rowan really didn't know where he and Claire stood, he simply agreed. At least it would nullify the staring problem.

"Sure. Let's split up."

◊◊◊

"Are you sure Claire's never done any acting?" Kevin asked a few hours later. His friends were sprawled over a few uncomfortable tables under a ramada next to the taco stand for dinner. Misters hissed overhead, sprinkling them with a cooling reprieve.

Though the groups had shuffled several times, he and Claire had always been separated. Even now, she was two tables away, chatting with Tessa and Becca.

Rowan pulled his gaze back to Kevin, his forehead wrinkling. "No. I don't think so. Why?"

"That woman's chameleon skills are impressive. She effortlessly morphs into someone warm with Ann, jokey and teasing with Zane. With me, she's a downright riot. She's gossipy with Tessa and Becca but reserved with Dani and Kyle. It's like she picks up on each individual's personality and mirrors it back at them."

Claire took a bite of her corn-tortilla taco, smiling before turning her attention to Tessa. Tacos were one of the few foods that hadn't altered in some way with her celiac diagnosis, since Claire had always preferred the corn tortillas that many restaurants in Tucson made fresh-to-order.

"I've never noticed that." A deep frown tugged on his lips. "When she's with me or my family, she's always been the same person."

Kevin barreled on. "It's no wonder she's got such a large following. That woman is pure charisma. And Sparkplug?" His friend laughed. "What a perfect trail name for her."

Rowan hadn't even thought to ask what name other hikers had bestowed upon Claire. His throat tightened, realizing she had an entire life he wasn't a part of.

"I mean, did you see her with Caroline? I've never seen that girl smile so much. Her little face is going to hurt tomorrow."

"Yeah." Rowan ran his fingers over the diamond-holed pattern of the tabletop. "She's, uh . . . really good with kids."

The thrumming sounds of hydraulic pumps, rushing water, and infinite voices were nothing compared to the anxious sloshing in his ears.

Kevin slapped the table. "I can't have her stealing my role. Everyone knows *I'm* the fun uncle."

"Pretty soon you're going to be the fun dad." Becca's smiling voice beside them drew Rowan's gaze.

Kevin and Becca waited three long years to become adoptive parents and just learned that their daughter will be born in August.

She smoothed her hands over Kevin's shoulders with a peck to the cheek.

"I can't wait." When his friend caught his wife's lips in a less-than-PG kiss, Rowan took the moment to throw out his trash and give them some semblance of privacy. They'd always been a little handsy, even in public.

"Hey, rock climber, go on the Free Fall with me. No one else will do it." Claire tossed her soda can in the recycling bin.

Rowan took a step with the intention of notifying the group, but Claire grabbed his hand and smiled with that mischievous smirk of hers. "Just us. I haven't seen you all afternoon." She tugged on his arm. "This way."

Claire wove him around the back of the taco stand, shouting hello to the workers as they ran past. They were both breathless from laughing and sprinting through the park when they finally reached the painfully long line for Free Fall. It was so reminiscent of times she'd dragged him on various zany activities when they'd been younger that when Claire turned her face up to smile at him, he'd been surprised to see the subtle age lines creasing her joyful eyes.

"Let's play Never Have I Ever to pass the time." Claire lifted her hand, spreading out five fingers.

"Not sure how well this will work since we already know—" Claire's shove to his shoulder put her palm too close to his heart to finish that sentence.

"Play along," she admonished.

"Yes, ma'am."

Her eyes flew wide. "Did you just *ma'am* me?"

"You are four whole years older than me." He bit the inside of his cheek to keep his smirk from deepening.

They climbed up a few steps while Claire huffed. "Never have I ever rock climbed."

Rowan bent his first finger while his lips firmed into a playful line. "Never have I ever gotten a tattoo."

A few more steps brought them into a slight breeze, and they tilted their sweat-dotted faces into it. Since they were on the outskirts of the water park, they had a bird's-eye view of the surrounding desert. Big fluffy clouds dotted the usually vacant sky. Their stark white hyper-accented the deep blue beyond. Hopefully sooner than later, those clouds would darken and release monsoon rains on the parched brittle bush and desert grasses stretched out in every direction.

"Um." Claire chewed her lip as she thought, forcing Rowan to shift his gaze over the railing so he wouldn't catch those lips in his. It'd been over twenty-four hours since he'd felt their softness. "Never have I ever bought a bouquet of flowers for someone."

He put a finger down while asking, "I thought you get flowers for Meg every Valentine's Day?"

Claire's head shake dislodged a few droplets from her hair, one of them hitting him in the abs. "No. Chocolates."

His head tilted in a slow nod. "Never have I ever been to Minnesota."

With another finger down, Claire frowned comically. "You're right. This is boring." She flopped her hand to her side, signifying the end of the game, before leaning over the railing. "I wish it'd rain."

The corner of his mouth tipped up. "I was just thinking that."

The anticipation of monsoon season for Tucsonans was akin to leaf-peepers breathlessly awaiting that first turn of yellow.

Claire smiled to herself while still gazing at Dove Mountain in the distance. "Sometimes when I'm in other places, I swear I can still smell it. The way the desert comes alive with that bright-green scent layered over an extinguished campfire undertone."

"From the creosote bushes." His gaze darted between the short, scrubby plants dotting the sandy expanse.

"Meg sends me a little bag of dried creosote leaves every year for my birthday. It's nice, but it's not the same as being here, feeling that pressure in the air as the humidity rises. The sound of the cicadas buzzing in anticipation."

Since the weather in Tucson typically contained clear skies and hot, hotter, to hottest temperatures, the drastic changes during monsoon season always felt special.

Her smile shifted, becoming contemplative. "Then there's that sensation that something bigger than yourself is coming as the high winds pick up before that first thundercrack. And the overwhelming peace when the rain finally pounds the packed earth, blurring the view of the mountains."

Claire was still staring out at the landscape, but Rowan couldn't pull his gaze from her.

A kid yanked him from his reverie by pointing out the growing gap in the line. They bounded up half a flight before stopping beside a slow drip of water plummeting from the upper decks. Rowan shifted himself out of the way, but Claire purposefully positioned herself so the water would plop on her shoulder.

"What's the deal with this slide anyway?" he asked, gazing up the staircase.

"You stand on a hinged platform that drops you into a straight, seventy-five-foot freefall."

The clenching sensation wrenching his stomach was instinctual.

"What? What's that face?" Claire playfully poked him in the cheek, snatching her hand back before he could capture it and kiss her palm. "The rock climber can't be afraid of heights. That's why I asked you to go with me."

"I'm not afraid of heights," he said before clearing his throat. "I'm afraid of falling. Every climber is afraid of taking a whipper."

"A whipper?"

"It's when you're lead climbing and fall from above your last clip. It whips you in an arcing motion."

"Oh." Her chin dipped once before the corner of her mouth twisted up. "But this time you're intentionally falling into a tube that will deposit you safely into a pool."

Rowan gave her a wry glance before climbing a few more stairs.

They didn't speak again until it was time for them to step onto the topmost platform. The trap door was encased in a clear, rounded tube. It looked like one of those gameshow tubes where you'd have to grab all the money swirling around you. Except, the only thing surrounding you was various thoughts of your own demise. Then, you'd wait with your arms and legs crossed for the trap door beneath your feet to release.

Claire tapped his white knuckles gripping the handrail as they watched the couple in front of them go down the slide. "It'll be fine. It's just a ride."

"But I've been counting." Rowan swallowed roughly. "The door never drops at the same time. If it was after four seconds every time, I'd know when to expect the fall, but it's randomized. Sometimes it's four, then seven. Nine. Six. Six again. There's no pattern. We've been standing within earshot of the door opening for five minutes, but there's no rhyme or—"

His words dried up when Claire smoothed her fingers over his gripped ones. "Rowan." Her eyes bounced between his as her other hand rested on his upper arm. "Deep breath."

Claire demonstrated the breath he was supposed to be taking, allowing his brain to disregard the exquisite sensation of her fingertips on his warm skin long enough for him to join her in a second breath.

Her gaze darted briefly to his chest. "Do you want me to go first?"

"No." Why was his voice coarser than the side of a jagged crag? "That would be worse."

Her light-brown eyebrows scrunched together. "Why would that be worse?"

"I can't watch— Never mind," he mumbled.

There was no good way to explain that seeing Claire go first would only worsen the seizing sensation spreading over his ribs. Watching her fall first would too closely mimic the memory of her collapsing in his kitchen, of not knowing if he'd lost her for good.

He'd only really had Claire as his for less than two days. Two beautiful, blissful days. But would there be more after they reached seven, or would she run away again?

"Rowan?"

When Claire's hand slid up to frame his face, Rowan almost took her lips in his. The concern etching her irises made his heart squeeze. The only thing stopping him was the teenager beckoning him toward the ride and the group of excited ten-year-olds waiting behind them.

"It's fine. I'm fine." He stepped onto the loading platform just outside the slide.

Her worried brow followed him until it broke with such an exuberant expression his chest squeezed. "Hey, everyone! Let's cheer on my friend Rowan."

Claire started a lunchroom chant of his name that immediately caught on with everyone on the platform and stairs. The teenager overseeing the ride laughed at Claire's antics before reiterating instructions and sealing Rowan in his cylindrical coffin.

"Just focus on me," Claire said, stepping on the loading platform and meeting his gaze through the scratched plastic.

Rowan forgot to count as her whiskey eyes never left his, her full-dimpled smile on her lips as she continued cheering his name.

When the trap door dropped, Rowan recognized the sensation instantly. It was an exact duplicate of what it felt like to fall in love with Claire Winesett.

Chapter 21

"Oh, hey." Claire looked up from the blank notepad when Rowan closed his office door the following Tuesday afternoon. "I was just going to let you know that I'm heading to the store for a bit."

"The store?" His beautiful brows crinkled. Today's hunter-green shirt over his dark-gray slacks made the slight red in his hair more prominent.

"Yeah. Erin texted me about a business idea. She wanted to talk about me leading group hikes sponsored by the store since I'll be in town for a while."

Rowan's pace slowed slightly. "You'd be interested in that?"

They hadn't discussed her leaving again. They hadn't discussed *anything*, actually.

Claire was certain Rowan was letting the two of them live in this limbo on purpose. She knew he'd rather hammer things out. He preferred clean lines and knowing where he stood. It was obvious Rowan was letting her lead these last few days. He never kissed her unless she initiated. Though, once she did, the relief wafting off him was strong enough to loosen the tight chains around her heart.

Pressing the pen tip to the pad, Claire swallowed against her mounting anxiety.

Talk. Communicate. Like a human. He deserves that much.

"I like hiking."

Shame flooded her bloodstream at her failed attempt to say what she really meant. This trial period—these seven days—would end Friday night, the day after her scheduled endoscopy. If staying was something she was capable of, Claire needed to find a way to live here.

Rowan's face only softened, as if he could sense her effort and was patiently waiting.

"And I like the store."

The tug at the corner of his mouth was nearly imperceptible.

"And your family."

And his friends. Spending the afternoon at the water park with them on Sunday had been unexpectedly enjoyable. Though she'd met Kevin, Kyle, and Zane when Rowan had been in college, she'd never really spent any time with them. Seeing how each of their various personalities complemented each other had reminded her of the solid familial bond the Bellamys shared.

Her mouth opened to say the hard part.

And you. I really like you.

Claire dropped her gaze to the countertop with a hard exhale when the rest of the vowels and consonants got jammed in her tight throat.

"I was coming to tell you that my last client just canceled. Do you want me to go with you?"

She blinked up, heaviness slackening her arms. "You don't mind?"

Three slow steps and Rowan's hands framed her face, his thumb brushing her cheek. The tenderness in his gaze was nearly incapacitating. "No, Claire. I don't mind."

When he brought his lips to hers, Claire couldn't help the sigh leaving her rigid lungs. This time, the feeling of being cherished, of being loved, didn't feel as terrifying as it had yesterday. It was almost as if Rowan was micro-dosing her with it each day until her body grew accustomed to the feeling, the idea that maybe this—being with him—would be okay.

◊◊◊

Rowan kept her fingers intertwined with his over the gear shift the entire drive to Canyon Outdoor Supply Company. Two quick squeezes and he let go once they'd parked in the back lot against the row of Palo Verde trees bisecting the shopping complex from the midtown neighborhood beyond.

Claire hesitated, her hands on the door handle, glancing down the lot toward the back door of Blissful Desert Yoga.

"Heather would be happy to have you as part of the studio again if you decided you wanted that," Rowan said.

Her focus fixed on the purple Om symbol. "Maybe."

"There's no maybe. We all want you to be here."

Before she could respond, Rowan pushed out of the Jeep. The door shutting behind him felt like a punch to the temple.

As they quietly entered the store, her thoughts were tumbling over each other, tripping and falling like a stumble downhill. That helplessness swarmed her skin, realizing how incredibly hard it was to stop once momentum and gravity had you in its grip.

Erin had just ended a phone call when Rowan rapped his knuckles on her open office door.

"*Rowan.*" Her shock hovered for only a moment before Erin tightened her ponytail and gestured for them to enter. "I guess it's better this way."

When Erin crossed behind them and closed her door, adrenaline slammed the underside of Claire's chin.

Picking up a piece of paper, she held it out to her brother. "Who wants to start?"

Rowan barely glanced at it before tossing it on the desk and crossing his arms. Claire had never seen him go so rigid with his eldest sister. He'd often bristle with Meg, but Erin and Rowan had this tender connection that Claire had always envied.

Their stare-down lasted ten seconds before Erin shook her head. "This doesn't make any sense."

"The hospitalization had nearly bankrupted her." His hands flung upward. "You were there. You knew she needed more labs and scans. And now she needs another endoscopy. Our insurance is insanely good. This way, whatever she needs is covered."

"*Row.*" Erin rubbed her forehead with a heavy exhale.

"Do you want me to step outside?" It was selfish, but Claire didn't want to be there while they fought, even though she'd caused the argument.

"You know what? Yeah. This is a family matter." Erin strode to the door, swinging it open.

Even though the words stung more than a pricker bush scratching bloody lines over her legs, Claire ducked into the hallway. She only made it a few steps before Erin's harsh voice through the closed door halted her movement.

"Marrying her? Really?"

"I already told you—"

"You could have just given her the money. It's not like we each don't have abundant savings. You didn't have to marry her. You didn't have to commit fraud."

Rowan's silence allowed the pieces to click into place. Invisible strings pulled dozens of memories together until Claire stumbled back against the wall. Even before Meg's photography business had taken off, Meg had flown all over the country to join her on adventures, sometimes at a moment's notice.

Her best friend always had a viable excuse. The plane tickets had been her birthday present from her parents. She could afford to rent them a little beach house for a week because she'd received a big bonus from a wealthy couple after their wedding. Since the Bellamys had always lived modest lives, Claire hadn't put together how much each of them must profit from Canyon Outdoor Supply Company's success.

The fact that Rowan could have handed her thousands of dollars without blinking made bile surge up her esophagus. For someone who had subsisted on gas station taquitos and had to count change to ensure she could fill her tank, Claire should have noticed the stark difference in their lifestyles. Even Rowan's property, though the house itself was humble, must have been expensive.

"I knew her staying with you was a bad idea," Erin continued. "I should have insisted she live with me. I could see it at the hospital . . . you slipping."

Another haunting pause hovered, only the upbeat music from the front of the store and salespeople chatting seeping into the narrow hall.

"What are you talking about?" The wary tone of Rowan's words tightened Claire's shoulders.

"Come on," Erin scoffed. "You don't think I see the way you look at her? The way you've always looked at her? I'm the same as you, Row. Always surveying, always vigilant, making sure everything is okay. Because I had *five additional* years of measuring every tick of Dad's jaw, of making sure I took you and Meg out of the room before he snapped and threw a lamp at us. Why do you think we played 'fort' in my closet so much?"

None of the Bellamy siblings spoke much of their birth father. Meg didn't acknowledge anything prior to moving to Tucson, like she'd simply materialized into life at the age of nine. Claire knew from clips and pieces that their dad had been a lousy human, but not that they'd been in danger.

Claire took a step back toward the office, the urge to wrap her arms around Rowan's neck and hold him stifling. The stagnant backroom scent of cardboard and plastic swarmed her nostrils.

"I know." His voice was barely audible through the closed door. "You took such good care of us."

"So you understand why I can't let you shred yourself over her again."

A sigh preceded, "I'm already—"

"Hey, there. Can I help you with something?"

The kind words of the twenty-something employee made Claire jump, spinning away from the office.

"Oh. Um. I—" She rolled her lips together, resisting the impulse to turn back around. "I'm waiting for Rowan and Erin to finish up, but I can do that in the store."

It's not running, she told herself as Claire beelined to the hammocks and tucked herself into the cool parachute fabric. She shouldn't have eavesdropped for so long. It'd been a private conversation.

Staring at warm, wooden beams hung below the open ceiling, impotence saturated her stomach. The memory of gentle, quiet, eight-year-old Rowan watching *Curious George* while hugging a well-worn stuffie blurred her vision. He would have been five when Kelly had moved them to Tucson. Meg nine. Erin ten. Twelve years of not being wanted, of constantly being in her mother's way, paled in comparison to worrying about your safety on a daily basis.

Long minutes passed before her phone vibrated with Rowan's text. *Meet me at the back exit.*

Claire stared at the screen for a breath before climbing out of the hammock. Erin's office door was closed as Rowan leaned against the wall beside the back door.

"Let's go." His inflexible tone meant that he and Erin had not come to an agreement.

Agony over being the cause of so much trouble hummed louder in her ears than the engine during the drive home. Fighting the compulsion to pack all her things and leave the second the Jeep tires crunched over his gravel driveway had been immensely draining. When Rowan stomped into the house, leaving her in the open doorway, all her muscles tensed.

He spun around, noticing her trepidation. The devastated turn of his lips, the way that sorrow hollowed into his cheekbones and stained his beautiful multi-color irises, broke her.

"What do you want to do?"

It'd be so easy to leave. To turn away from all of this.

"I don't know."

Rowan flinched at her words but didn't look away. Something whispered inside of her, stirring softly. It tumbled and swirled until it felt like a steady pressure beneath her breastbone, and words materialized as easily as taking one step after another.

"Actually." The breath filling her lungs was steadfast and even. "What I want is to press my forehead against the pulse point in your neck, and I want to hear your heartbeat in my ears and feel your chest rise with soft, even breaths as I wrap my arms around you."

Rowan blinked, frozen for a few seconds, before a shaky hand ran down his chest. "Um . . . We can do that."

She swallowed, tension racketing her spine. "Okay."

Rowan's head twitched subtly as he watched her close the door and step toward him.

"Sit down, please." Claire gestured to the couch, the emotional exhaustion of the afternoon catching up with her.

He hesitated for only a second. Claire nestled close, banding her arms around his waist and lightly sighing when Rowan hugged her back. His erratic pulse had Claire loosening her front arm to gently stroke the long column of his neck. Minutes passed as his muscles sequentially slackened, until he was as loose and relaxed as he'd been when he'd kissed her in the kitchen earlier.

"I don't want to do a Fun Pact activity tonight," she said after a long while.

"No?"

Claire shook her head against him before lifting it to catch his gaze. "I want to make dinner with you, and then I want you to teach me to crochet."

The unrestrained joy brightening his entire face made her heart contort. "We can do that."

Tucking her forehead back into the crook of his neck, Claire made a promise. It felt like a concentric pulse, radiating out from where they held each other. She wasn't going to let anyone hurt Rowan any more—not even herself.

Chapter 22

*Y*ou're sure you don't want to do something tonight?

Rowan stared at Kyle's text before answering. *Claire has her endoscopy this afternoon, so I don't want to go anywhere if she needs me.*

It was a half-truth. Being separated during the procedure would be difficult enough. Over the last two days, Rowan had begun darting out between appointments just to brush his lips to Claire's. Every time he did, she obscured her notes in her small Moleskine notebook.

Last night, Claire had asked if he wanted to stay in and skip their Fun Pact activity, but he'd surprised them both by asking what she'd had planned. Claire had found a carnival on the outskirts of town, and they'd spent too much money on shaved ice and attempting to win a hideous stuffed monkey. Rowan *might have* thrown every attempt because each time he missed, Claire goaded him.

Kyle: *That's fair. Let's get together this weekend, though.*

Rowan: *Sure thing.*

Though tomorrow night was the end of their seven-day trial period, Rowan was confident that Claire wasn't ready to leave.

Mostly.

The notes she took could be about her next destination.

What Rowan knew for certain was how much he wanted Claire with him. He wanted her beside him on the couch each night, her feet in his lap as she made a mess of his yarn. He wanted to come up behind her while she washed dishes and kiss that sweet spot at the base of her neck. He wanted to read her sticky notes, telling him where she'd be, when he woke every morning. At first, they'd been on the kitchen counter, then the coffee table, then his chest, then his forehead.

Rowan took his time finishing out the therapy notes on his last client and reminding himself what he *needed* to do was focus on what Claire needed today. Not what he wanted.

The second he stepped out of his office, Claire's dramatic pout pulled a laugh from his stomach.

"I'm so hungry and thirsty." She draped herself across the kitchen counter, tilting sideways. "I used to go hours without eating without any issues, but you've ruined me with all your delicious food. Missing breakfast *and* lunch feels like going against the Geneva Convention."

Rowan chuckled. "I promise to feed you the second they let you loose." He ran his palm down her back a few times before asking, "You ready?"

She sat up on the stool, tucking her hands between her knees. "As I'll ever be."

"I'll be there the entire time. Even when they take you back, I'm still there."

Claire sucked in a deep breath while nodding.

"Here." He pulled their silicone wedding rings from his pocket. "We should wear these." When Claire only stared at his open palm, he added, "Since you're on my insurance as my spouse."

He wanted to say *as my wife*, but he'd been saying it far too much in his head already. *I love the way my wife laughs. My wife makes the cutest scowl when she pretends to be mad.* And when their kisses knocked the words out of his head, only a growly *mine* resonated down his spine.

The band rolled between her fingertips before Claire compressed it into an elongated oval. "That makes sense."

Rowan forced himself to look away when Claire slipped the ring on. "Let's get this over with."

◊◊◊

The tension in Claire's shoulders increased with every moment within Tucson General's walls, but Rowan kept some part of him touching her at all times, grounding her. Mostly they held hands, him stretching his thumb to trace her heart tattoo. This had confused her doctor, who muttered something about how she'd thought he was her brother. Claire had snort-laughed at that the second everyone had left her pre-op room.

Before long, the staff escorted Claire to the procedure area while Rowan was sent to the waiting room. He'd planned on reading a book on effective therapy techniques for the Highly Sensitive Person, but it hung limply in his hands. His mind was on a five second repeat of the tense expression Claire had cast over her shoulder before she'd turned the corner with the two nurses.

Rowan didn't see his ex-girlfriend Bethany walking up to him in her green scrubs until she called his name.

"Is it Augie?" She looked around for the rest of his family. "Did he have another MI?"

"No." The book slid to the seat beside him as he stood. "Dad's fine. Don't worry."

With his palms splayed in front of him in an *It's okay* gesture, Bethany's gaze caught on his gray wedding band.

"Oh." She took a step back, tugging her long blonde ponytail over her shoulder. "Oh, good. I'm glad to hear he's okay."

Awkwardness hovered for a few beats before she asked, "So you're doing well?"

Resisting the urge to slide his hands into his pockets, Rowan gave a small smile. "Yeah. I am. Are you?"

Bethany nodded. "Busy, but overall." A shrug lifted her shoulder as her pager beeped from the waistband of her scrubs. Relief smoothed her cheeks as she checked it. "I've got to go, but it was good seeing you."

Rowan responded in kind before returning to his seat.

"That was painful to watch." The older gentleman a few seats down gestured at him with his paper coffee cup. "I'm guessing that's the ex. Poor thing. The second she clocked your ring, it was like watching a coyote getting hit by a semi-truck." He ran age-spotted fingers through his thick white curls. "Brutal."

"I wasn't trying to upset her."

"No." His head reared back at the absurdity of it. "Of course not. Sometimes we get stuck on a person and can't let 'em go. That lady doctor was stuck on you."

Rowan cringed at the phrase *lady doctor* as his gaze flowed to the hallway where Bethany had disappeared. "That's why I broke it off. It wasn't fair to have my heart half into it when all I wanted was another person."

The man hummed his agreement. "You did the right thing. It'll work out for her. It'll just take some time."

Thankfully, that ended the conversation. It wasn't long before Rowan was pulled back to the PACU.

"You can't make me eat asparagus," was the response Claire gave when the PACU nurse tried to get her to have a sip of apple juice.

Rowan helped the nurse sit her up on the gurney. "The sooner you drink, the sooner we get to go home."

"Listen to your hubby," the nurse said, holding out the straw.

When Claire's hazy eyes drifted open and she dimple-smiled at the sight of him, the cacophony of the busy recovery room hushed.

"You're here." Her clumsy hands found his face before slipping to his chest as she slumped onto him. "I'm so glad you're here."

"Me too," he whispered against her ear.

Rowan dismissed her shudder as stemming from the lingering medicine still in her system, hugging her back.

Forty minutes later and you'd never have known that Claire had undergone twilight sedation besides some lingering nausea.

Dr. Reyes stopped by to state that everything looked as expected and that she'd put a rush order on the pathology. Claire's fingers crushed his hearing this, but she managed an agreeable smile.

Once back in his Jeep, Claire traced an incoherent design on the passenger window. "I'm too nauseated to eat, and I don't want to go home yet. Can we go to Target instead?"

His forehead wrinkled. "Target?"

"Remember that time we did that photo scavenger hunt at the one off Grant Rd.?" Her gorgeous lips lifted as the memory swung through his mind. "Let's walk around and look at stuff we don't need."

A few minutes later, Claire was halfway through trying on every hat in the women's section when she caught his gaze in the mirror. "Two Truths and a Lie."

The *Beach Please* hat was replaced by a black brimmed fedora. "I hate asparagus. I love sudsy bubble baths. And sometimes I feel like one of those sharks that'll die if they stop moving."

Rowan stepped behind her, close but not touching. "The bath one. You hated being in stagnant water even when you were on the swim team."

"You got me." Her voice wobbled as a pink sequined ball cap switched out the fedora. "Your turn."

"I'm afraid of snakes. Black licorice is my favorite." He hovered an inch closer. "And I knew I wasn't going to be able to stop after seven days, but I said that to get you to agree with me."

Claire's fingertips shook as she took off the cap. "Licorice. You can't stand the anise flavor."

When she turned and pulled a wisp of hair from her eyes, Rowan realized they were both still wearing their rings.

Rowan wanted to tell her the rest. That he'd said seven days that night because he'd needed her to kiss him again. That Claire wanting him was so much better than anything he'd ever imagined. That he never wanted to stop living with her, being around her. He already couldn't stop loving her. He wanted the marriage between them to be as real as it already felt in the marrow of his bones.

"Rowan, I—" Her gaze darted over his shoulder a second before a thunderous crack shook the foundation of the building. "It's raining!"

Her joyful face and firm grip on his hand as she pulled him to the exit almost made up for missing whatever she was going to say. Claire nearly slammed into the automatic door when it didn't open fast enough.

The cumulonimbus clouds that had been hovering since Monday were finally making good on their promise. Sheets of water pummeled the parking lot, sending patrons running for shelter. Rowan hesitated under the building overhang, but Claire ran straight into the rain with outstretched arms. The blissful look on her face as she closed her eyes and tilted her chin skyward arrowed straight through him. Rowan quickly memorized the sight before spinning her in a blurry circle. The laughter engulfing him was as warm and soul-clenching as the summer rainstorm.

But then his slightly untied shoelace decided to end their swirling fun as one foot came from under him, and Claire slipped on top of him. Fortunately, he was able to brace her fall and keep himself from flattening all the way on the slippery sidewalk. Claire laughed as she sat on his outstretched legs before holding her hands flat and creating a little shelter between their faces.

"What am I going to do with you?"

Love me, his heart begged.

Something must have shown on his face, because Claire's smile fell as her fingertips traced his temples, his cheeks, his jaw. Her gaze followed every touch until her wet lashes beat closed, and she brought her mouth to his.

People raced in and out of the store. Mothers huddled their children under umbrellas. The sky cracked open as lightning flashed beyond his closed eyelids. But Rowan ignored it all and kissed his wife in the rain.

Chapter 23

"Is the blindfold really necessary?" Rowan grumbled the next night as her yellow bandana covered his eyes.

"It wouldn't be on you if it wasn't." A playful huff left her mouth, the clean scent of Armor All slipping in with her next breath.

After realizing that there'd been nothing left to deep clean in the house, Claire had set her sights on washing and detailing Rowan's Jeep after she'd returned from Robles Pass this morning. First, she'd allowed herself a few moments to eat breakfast—a scrumptious egg souffle, cool herself in the life-giving air conditioning, and post the pictures she'd taken with her new sponsored frame pack. She'd set up her tripod to capture herself walking far down the trail as the sun rose this morning.

While she'd shuffled through comments, story shares, and new followers, Claire wondered what would become of her haphazard career if she stayed in one place. Even though the

Sonoran Desert was breathtaking—often a destination for professional photographers—her content had always been centered on novelty.

The next trail. A new location.

A part of her had known that she couldn't do this forever. Her body was already marred from her labor, her right knee sounding like a pepper grinder with each inclined step. But what would Claire do in place of capturing a misty meadow at sunrise, baby sea turtles tumbling toward the foamy sea, or the mesmerizing murmuration of thousands of starlings?

She'd spent the week scribbling ideas in her trail-notes notebook. Though Claire wrote out multiple possibilities, there was one option that kept popping up like an earworm. In order to make that idea work, she'd need to set up several things.

"You're being an absolute hamster right now." Rowan crossed his muscled forearms over his chest.

The barking laugh leaving her mouth efficiently pulled her from her tailspin.

When she'd been thirteen, Augie had heard her and Meg using a few choice words they'd heard on the middle school bus and staunchly informed them that those kinds of words were unimaginative. Adding "absolute" before any noun had instantaneously turned it into a cutting retort.

Absolute hamster. Absolute cactus spine. Absolute dinkhead.

That last one hadn't received parental approval.

Claire made a left turn onto Speedway. "This feels like a kettle/black moment. Weren't you telling me to relinquish control just last weekend?"

When Rowan simply slumped further in his seat, Claire's smile grew. His gruff was purely for show. She'd gotten into the habit of watching his facial expressions as he came out of his office and gauging if he'd seemed too mentally wiped to go out. Tonight, he'd crossed to her in four hungry strides before sweeping her into a breathless kiss. And when she'd asked—just in case—if he was game for a different kind of Fun Pact activity, his hazel eyes had only shone with intrigue.

"We're almost there," Claire said.

A few moments later, she opened his door, holding Rowan's hand to help him out of the car. Claire took one step to lead him toward the green-awning-covered building before Rowan tugged her to a stop.

"Do I get a kiss before we start whatever barrel of laughs you have planned for me tonight?"

The self-assured smirk on his gorgeous mouth short-circuited her nervous system. Claire *almost* leaned in out of habit before remembering her surroundings. "I don't know if you'd want me to do that."

His smile widened, thinking it a game. "Why wouldn't I—"

"You made it!" When Kevin's voice bounced off the rest of the cars in the All World Theater parking lot, Rowan's fingers stiffened.

"Surprise." Her whispered word held a hint of hesitancy.

Rowan pulled off the cloth, taking in his surroundings. "*Midsummer* doesn't open until next weekend."

"I can't believe you got him to come to Improv Night." Kevin was beside them now, vibrating with energy. "I've been trying for *years*. Even Ethan brought Haley before they left for Maryland."

"Clearly, it was against his will." Claire gestured to the blindfold dangling from Rowan's fingertips.

A resounding clap accompanied Kevin's laugh. "I knew I liked you," he said, tucking her under his arm and leading her toward the propped-open front door.

Claire and Rowan joined twenty other people in the intimate community theater as Kevin hopped on the low-lying stage to explain the various games and how they'd randomly call names to pick participants.

"The main rule is to never say no. If someone says, 'I'm a turtle,' your response should be along the lines of, 'Yes, and . . .'" His smile was luminescent. "For example, 'And your shell is so bright and shiny,' or, 'It's a good thing this bar caters to reptiles,' or simply, 'Me too. Let's be friends.' Does that make sense?"

Most of the audience nodded.

"Excellent. Let's play." Kevin plunged his hand into the oversized fish bowl containing the green squares of paper with their names on them.

They weren't drawn for the first few games. While four people held props and used them as anything but what they actually were, Rowan's breath warmed her ear.

"Why did you want to come here tonight?"

Claire barely subdued the desire to close her eyes and savor the sensation. "Kevin couldn't stop talking about it at the water park, and I thought it'd be fun."

That, and it was a welcome distraction. Today, while Rowan had made up his client appointments from Thursday, Claire had spent all day trying to figure out the best way to tell Rowan what had struck her like lightning while sitting on the rain-soaked sidewalk outside a Target.

You'd think a blast of clarity would happen somewhere transcendent, like the mountain peaks or seasides she'd visited. It ought to be accompanied by swelling music, raucous applause, or something otherworldly. But no. It happened in a Target parking lot as much-needed rain washed away oil slicks, months of built-up dust, and discarded debris.

Plump raindrops had run down Rowan's cheeks, the ridge of his nose, his full lips. Then his expressive eyes had asked a question that her heart had instantly answered.

She loved Rowan.

Truthfully, it'd been something she'd been thinking about for days. Every morning, Claire had woken after a fitful sleep, even earlier than normal. Rowan's whisper-soft snoring would fill the air as she padded into the living room, bringing a smile to her lips. His hand had rested behind his head, hair unbound. Claire couldn't remember a single time he'd slept in a different position. As memories layered upon each other again, one thought seared through—the same one that she'd tried to unravel as her boots crunched over the rocky desert ground during her morning hikes.

It didn't feel new.

It felt like something that had been hidden in an attic, covered in layers of dust. Waiting.

Kevin's voice pulled her back to the theater. "Next up is Claire. Jeremy. Natasha. *And Rowan*." He laughed, gesturing to the stage. "Come on up."

The bright lights made Claire squint as she listened to Kevin's instructions. "I'll give Rowan a slip of paper with a starting line. Then, Natasha will come up with the next line, followed by Jeremy, and Claire. You keep going down and back until it feels like a natural end. If you get lost, I'll jump in and end the scene for you."

The disapproving grimace Rowan sent Kevin as he received a slip of computer paper made giddy anticipation rise in her ribs.

"I am a pretty, pretty princess." The audience snickered at Rowan's deadpan delivery.

Rowan's slitted gaze shot to Claire's as a snort left her nose.

"And the kindest this kingdom has ever seen," added Natasha after a beat.

"No fairer a lady has ever been beheld." Jeremy even gave a small bow with his line.

Claire was biting her lip to keep from dissolving into a fit of giggles. "Your long locks are the envy of the land."

The audience chuckled again.

"Fantastic." Kevin beamed from beside her before gesturing for Jeremy to continue.

"If only I were worthy of such a maiden."

"Um." Natasha paused, glancing at Rowan. "We should be friends?" Her shoulders and palms rose with her inclining pitch.

"That's fine. Keep going," Kevin urged.

"If only I hadn't been dragged from my castle by a terrible wench." Rowan's playful gaze speared Claire from the end of the line.

"Hey! That wench is trying to introduce you to fun, new things," Claire countered.

Natasha timidly raised a hand in front of her chest. "Wasn't I supposed to go next?"

"Yes, technically," Kevin said.

Claire clamped her lips together while darting an apologetic glance at Kevin.

"Don't worry." Two gentle pats landed on her shoulder before Kevin drew another slip of paper and handed it to Natasha. "Let's start another round."

After having to come up with lines following, "Oh no, I left my wallet at home," and, "Officer, please don't give me a speeding ticket," they were dismissed, and a new group started a different game.

Rowan and Claire each played a second time, though separately. When the night came to an end, they lingered behind to say goodbye to Kevin before leaving.

"You're coming to opening night next Friday?" Kevin's warm gaze centered on her.

"Uh. Sure." Though Kevin beamed at her response, Claire caught the way Rowan stiffened.

She'd hesitated only because she and Rowan hadn't discussed what would happen after tonight. Seven days were up. Right *now*. From what he'd said yesterday during Two Truths and a Lie, Claire assumed Rowan would be okay with her staying, but they still needed to talk.

Her heart kept climbing into her throat and punching the underside of her chin the entire drive home. Twelve different ways to start this conversation sprinted through her mind, but they slipped away like sneaky salamanders before she could grip a single one. Claire would part her lips only to feel like a noose was crushing her windpipe, making speaking impossible.

When Rowan cut the engine but didn't exit the Jeep, relief pulsed through her. Rowan would start this conversation. He'd make things easy on her, just like he'd always done. But then an angry breath blew over the steering wheel before he stormed inside, slamming the garage door.

Something about being left behind seared her. All of the nervous anticipation shifted into a blaze that started at the tips of her fingers and raced to her ears. Claire punched into the house, finding Rowan in the kitchen, facing the sink with his hands on the top of his head.

"Why are you mad?" Her harsh words sliced through the air.

He had every right.

He had every right to scream at her. As messed up as it was, that idea softened her spine . . . because yelling would be easier. They'd never argued. Not really. But she'd fought with others. Could stand her own that way. Everything else, admitting softness and tenderness, seemed impossible.

This she could do.

His hands fisted before Rowan slowly brought them to his sides while turning to face her. "I'm not mad."

Lies. He was lying to her.

"Yes, you are."

The measured breath Rowan pulled into his body only fueled her indignation. "I'm not."

Her jaw clenched as heat burned over her cheeks.

"Fine." Claire turned a flustered half-spin before flipping back to glare at him. "If you won't fight with me, I'll just get out of your hair."

In her agitated state, Claire went for the front door instead of the garage. She stalked down the narrow hallway, ignoring the smiling faces of the Bellamy family. A family she'd always be tangential to—hovering nearby but never belonging. The sound of the lock sliding open was like a bomb blast in her head. Another cleaving. Another demarcation of before and after. Claire ignored the pointless tears pricking at the bridge of her nose, reminding herself she'd been alone before. She could do it again.

The door wrenched open only to have Rowan's hand force it closed over her head. She spun, flattening herself against the solid wood.

"Fight *for* you." Rowan crowded her, palms flat on the door beside her ears. His eyes darted between hers. "That's what you mean, isn't it? What you really want."

The simple answer sat trapped in her dry, open mouth.

Rowan's eyes closed as an agonized expression sullied his features. When his thick lashes flickered open, determination laced his hazel irises.

"I want you to stay." The gruffness in his tone melted. "I want you to be here with me always, but I will not force you. You have to choose. It's always been your choice."

How could she explain that the terror raging in her chest wouldn't allow her to? How this very second her heart was beating with a ferocity that would likely kill her? How, as much as her soul wanted all of this, Claire didn't think she deserved it?

Rowan's gaze traced from her heaving collarbones to her twitchy, flexed fingers. Understanding overtook his features as he nodded, his eyes rising to meet hers. "Okay, then let me start." The calm smoothing out his brow made her tense muscles soften a fraction. "I love you."

His words should have been a balm, but they felt like a blast of sand and shrapnel scarring her skin because something in Claire couldn't fully believe them. Even now, after weeks together, with the reciprocating equivalent sprinting through her veins. A sharp, shaky exhale left her lips as pain resonated behind her breastbone.

Rowan's hand traced her face with searing gentleness. "I have loved you since I was fourteen. I'm not going anywhere. I'm not going to stop loving you. I can't. I've tried. I worked so hard to forget you when you left. But I couldn't. It never worked." His thumb brushed away an escaped tear. "I don't know how to not love you."

The sensation of warm liquid on her cheeks was as foreign as it was alarming. So many years those tears seemed jammed in odd places within her body, their pent-up energy stuck and poisoning her.

"I'm going to fight for you, my love. Fight for us."

My love.

Her ability to breathe just ceased. Because that was who Rowan was—*her* love. Claire's lips parted to tell him as much, but only a wispy sound slipped out.

Frustration roared as everything in her body became itchy and hot, malfunctioning.

Why did she have to be like this?

"You don't have to tell me. I know." The way Rowan seemed to see right through her, understanding how hard this was for her, felt incomprehensible.

Claire shook her head helplessly. She didn't want to be let out of this. She wanted to say it back. She wanted to make her useless mouth form the words because her love for Rowan beat like a pulse of light whenever he grinned at her, or held her, or kissed her.

Rowan's lips only softened into a small, knowing smile.

A second set of tears streamed down her face. Rowan's gentle focus went to catching them in the tenderest way, murmuring how everything was going to be okay, that she'd get there in her own time. Her bodyweight had already been pressed to the door, but now her knees buckled as everything in her short-circuited. This was more than Claire could handle, more than she'd ever allowed herself to feel without spending months exhausting her body in an attempt to shake free her emotions.

"It's okay. I got you." It wasn't until Rowan stooped to pick her up that Claire noticed her hands had been fisting the fabric of his shirt.

Claire's head lulled onto his chest as he carried her into his bedroom, utterly exhausted.

The gentle way he tucked her under the covers sent forth another wash of tears. Rowan sat on the edge of the bed, his hand circling her back with even strokes. Once she'd settled enough and her eyes began to droop from mental depletion, Rowan moved to stand. The soft chuckle at her unyielding grip on his arm sent vibration darting to her toes.

"I'll stay." Rowan moved around to the other side of the bed, lying atop the covers and kissing her fingers as he collected them in his. "Rest."

She'd been determined to stay awake, to quickly recuperate and make herself say the simple three words people utter thousands of times per day, but fatigue drew her under. For the first time in years, Claire slept a restful, dreamless sleep without it following a twelve-mile hike. And for the first time in their marriage, Claire shared a bed with her husband.

Chapter 24

Hiking Linda Vista Loop today. Will you do Phone Line with me tomorrow?

That's what the sticky note left on Claire's pillow read when Rowan woke up halfway to ten the next day. He usually didn't sleep in, but Rowan hadn't fallen asleep until early this morning, thinking about their situation. Even with last night's tipping point, Claire might still choose to leave.

That uncertainty made his muscles twitch to be used, but being late morning, the summer heat would be unbearable. Opting to skip his workout, Rowan showered instead. Only when he entered the main room to make breakfast did Rowan notice the others.

Yellow sticky notes covered the entire kitchen counter like a blanket of fallen cottonwood leaves.

Unsure if the notes were independent thoughts or in a pattern, Rowan began at the top left corner. *I know Meg always complains about your snoring, but it's like the world's best sound machine.*

The right side of his mouth lifted before his eyes saw the note beneath it. *I'm sorry about last night.*

Rowan's head shook automatically, reading the note below that. *I want to be like you, be able to say what I'm thinking.*

His intestines twisted into a trace-eight knot. Communication wasn't one of Claire's strong suits, but that was something they could work on together.

Slowly. At her pace.

I want to get better, but for now, I'll tell you what I remember.

Now the thoughts flowed over different sticky notes, sometimes severing mid-sentence to be continued on another. Rowan's gaze followed to the bottom before darting back to continue down the next column.

I remember relying on all of you in the months following Gram's death. It felt like I was always leaning left. Like my body was permanently misaligned from the shock of it all. She was gone. The one person who chose me, who loved me even though I am so completely flawed. She was gone.

Rowan had to pause after that, closing his eyes and collecting his breath before continuing. It hurt that Claire had never understood how much he and his family had loved her too.

How was I supposed to be okay without her humming while making that horrible zucchini bread she loved? How was I supposed to know what to do with myself when my foundation was gone?

I couldn't handle it.

His own memories played before his eyes. Claire had allowed them to help initially, but after Anne Marie's funeral, she'd drawn inward. He'd scoured his psychology class notes and textbooks, looking for how to help someone through the loss of a loved one. But Claire had never wanted to talk. She'd actively remove herself from dinner, ice cream, wherever, the minute Rowan or anyone else started talking about grief.

That was when Meg began hosting movie marathons like they'd watched as kids, inviting him and Erin to join them. Erin rarely came, so Claire had sat silently between him and Meg. She'd sag onto Meg's hand-me-down couch, hugging a pillow, but by the end of the film, Claire's shoulder would be leaning against his.

Every time.

I began to slowly self-destruct, going out and not telling anyone. I'd be in some random club, letting the rhythmic pounding of the too-loud music vibrate through me. I thought I had to live twice as much to make up for Gram's stolen years. I'd dance until I collapsed, but it didn't help.

Rowan recalled Meg being worried when Claire wouldn't come home until the sun whispered over the horizon.

When that didn't work, I sought distraction in a string of terrible men.

Claire had seemed to have a finesse for finding the worst possible person to date, beginning even before Rowan had developed feelings for her. She'd kissed boys in middle school who had turned around and bragged about it, embarrassing her. She'd dated guys in high school who constantly berated her, almost as if it'd been a game. It wasn't until she started bartending that Claire began pushing back. Then she'd adopted a mindset of treating men as disposable as they'd always treated her.

Then, one night, you were at Meg's when I'd walked home in broken flip-flops after being abandoned mid-date. You and Meg were furious that I hadn't called or asked for help. But your family had already done too much. I'd been too much of a burden already.

Meg went searching the kitchen for wine while you set down a lasagna pan full of warm water to soothe my cut feet. Your fingers held my ankle in the tenderest way as you murmured to my toes that I deserved better. Our eyes met, and this burning sensation ran from where you touched me straight to the center of my chest.

I wanted to cry then. I wanted to release the tension that had been building for weeks. I wanted to scream at the unfairness of it all. But instead, I yanked my feet out of the water and declared I needed a shower. I didn't let myself think while standing under the scalding water.

I didn't sleep that night. The next morning, when the sunlight peeked through Meg's living room windows, I pulled on my old hiking boots and walked for miles. My feet stung, but the soft sound of each footfall on the silent trail quieted the incessant noise in my head.

That afternoon, when I got back to Meg's, I slept like I had before Gram had died. I knew what I needed to do.

Rowan swallowed, allowing himself a moment before continuing.

The plan had been to hike the PCT and return home. I'd figure out what to do after I'd proven I could survive.

But then you hugged me goodbye.

Whooshing blood clamored in Rowan's ears as his own recollection of that night flashed through his mind. He'd put his heart in his hands, and Claire had misinterpreted the gesture.

I knew what you meant when you said you loved me.

His heartbeat was a dizzying pulse trying to break his ribs. Even Claire's handwriting seemed to shift with this sticky note. It became more organized, switching into print rather than the scrawling half-cursive from before.

I understood, but I couldn't process it. You couldn't love me. I wasn't worthy of your love. I was broken.

An ink stain followed that sentence almost like she'd paused for too long.

I still feel unworthy of it.

Rowan's entire body seized. He'd spend the rest of his days showing Claire how worthy she already was.

I'm still broken too, but I want to do things differently now.

I know you've already been the most patient man on the planet, but please continue giving me grace. I'm trying.

I'm going to mess up. Often.

But I want to stay this time.

Rowan's thumb brushed over the last note as his sternum felt like it was splitting open. The dual impulses to press the note to his chest or laminate it like a giddy schoolgirl stretched him in different directions.

Claire wanted to stay.

With him.

Freaking *finally.*

Rowan ripped his phone off the charger in the kitchen, yanking it from the outlet.

"Breathe." Two rounds of focused breathing was all he could handle before Rowan pulled up Claire's text conversation.

On the off chance she was on a trail without service, he sent a message. Then, Rowan rushed to the garage, not caring if he was being silly. He was going to use packing-tape to laminate the whole blanket of sticky notes together. They were, after all, the first love letter from his wife.

Chapter 25

Come home.

Claire could feel the growly rumble in that simple two-word text scratching down her back. Though she fully understood the command, there were things that needed to be done first.

Claire: *Soon.*

If she went into further detail, Rowan would race to her side, always wanting to support her. Claire had to do this by herself. That was why she was biding her time in this gluten-free bakery and cafe, enjoying an egg, black forest ham, and avocado on sourdough breakfast sandwich. Poppy, acoustic versions of the latest rap hits swirled around her as she checked the time. In ten minutes, Canyon Outdoor Supply Company would open, and the first of Claire's three errands could begin.

In front of the store, Claire spent too much time staring at the ridges of Rowan's tanned back, working up the courage to stride through the large glass doors. If what she'd decided this morning was going to work, this was the necessary starting place.

Erin was the one Bellamy she'd have to win over.

Smiling at the puzzled young cashier, unironically wearing suspenders over his Canyon Outdoor Supply Company button-up, Claire explained that she was a friend of the family while crossing toward the back. Tension built between her shoulder blades and through her stomach with each step as she drew closer to the open office, but Claire only allowed herself one breath of hesitation before she stepped through.

"This is a surprise." Erin folded her arms over her tucked-in company polo, leaning back in her office chair. "I honestly thought you'd duck and run like last time."

Erin's arctic tone stabbed against Claire's collarbones, but she forced herself not to flinch.

"We need to talk about Rowan. About this whole situation."

Erin simply raised her eyebrows, waiting.

"I love your brother."

It was *so incredibly* frustrating how easily those words launched from her tongue when she'd been incapable of saying them to Rowan last night. Even in her notes, she'd danced around it, not writing the words outright. Telling Erin made the pent-up resistance that weighed her down shift and loosen like ice thawing in the spring.

"That didn't stop you from leaving last time," Erin said, unimpressed.

Her brows slammed together. How could Erin have known she'd loved Rowan nine years ago when she'd *just* figured it out? At the cafe, Claire searched the internet for why she suddenly felt like a vault had been unlocked within her. No matter what sequence of words Claire typed in the search bar, articles on denial kept popping up. Her brain felt like a tangle of impenetrable jungle vines, yet Erin regarded Claire as if she was as transparent as glass.

"This whole trust-issues, worthlessness, inability-to-accept-love thing wasn't cute in our twenties, and it definitely isn't a decade later." She circled her hand to encompass all of Claire. "If you want to have a relationship with Rowan, you'll need to do better."

Erin had just wrenched a serrated hunting knife through her sternum.

"I know." She swallowed, fighting against that insatiable impulse to spin on her heel. "I want to work on those things."

"You'll forgive me if I don't believe you until I see it in action. Words are essentially meaningless. It's what you do that matters."

Claire understood the rigidity in Erin's slim shoulders for the protectiveness it was.

"I am going to be good to him—*for him*. I don't want to hurt him."

Erin stared her down for a few more heartbeats. "You'll need therapy. Lots of it." She picked up her phone, tabbing away until Claire's phone vibrated in her back pocket.

A contact card for Painted Owl Psychology was attached to Erin's blank text.

"She works out of Phoenix but has virtual appointments. Considering how hard you're sweating talking to me, virtual might be the best for you anyway."

Beads of moisture accumulated on her brow and upper lip almost as quickly as they had once the unrelenting sun had crested the Rincon Mountains earlier.

Claire's chin dipped in a determined nod.

Therapy had been something she'd already considered.

Another tense beat passed, but Erin's frame softened subtly. "Are you going to tell Mom and Dad?"

"I'm headed to their hotel next. I wanted to speak with you first."

Erin unfolded her arms. "And Meg?"

"After your parents."

The AC clicked on in the ten-second pause Erin used to scrutinize every inch of her. "I like you, Claire. I always did, even though you and Meg used to drive me crazy. I just—" A broken sigh left her mouth. "Nothing matters more to me than my family."

"I understand."

Erin shook her head like she couldn't believe she was allowing this nonsense. The expression reminded her so much of the younger version of Erin that Claire smiled beside herself.

"It'll be different this time," Claire reassured her.

It had to be.

Erin simply took a deep inhale and waved Claire out of her office like she used to wave her and Meg out of her teenage room.

Kelly and Augie, it turned out, were *not* mind-reading wizards like Erin. Oblivious to the history between her and Rowan, they were overjoyed at the idea of them starting a real relationship but shocked that Claire was asking for permission to marry Rowan.

Itchiness had scratched at her forearms when she revealed that they were technically already married. She detailed the reasons for their secret marriage, feeling a bit like she was betraying Rowan's trust but needing honesty from here forward—not only between her and Rowan but between her and his family.

Claire had made several decisions while hiking in the early whispers of daybreak this morning. Crickets and toads had sung the praises of yesterday's rainfall. Even the prickly pears and saguaros seemed to preen with the renewal of water. The dewdrops still clinging to their spines acted as thousands of crystals refracting the growing sunlight.

Step after step in the fragrant landscape brought a simplistic kind of clarity. It wasn't like when she'd battled through the miles of the Pacific Crest Trail. It was almost like a satiated sigh.

She wanted to marry Rowan.

Honestly this time.

Claire wanted to repeat vows while her heart nearly burst with the truth held in every syllable.

Though she'd never thought this type of permanence—this kind of life—was something she'd ever have, it was already here.

I don't know how to not love you.

The memory of Rowan's words were like a blanket Claire could wrap around herself if she hadn't been sweating from the one-hundred-and-six-degree heat.

After telling Rowan's parents about her plans for a vow renewal, Kelly had nearly shattered her hand from how hard she'd squeezed Claire's fingers. And once she'd asked them to be a part of planning the event, she'd ended up in another parental sandwich.

Now, Claire needed to notify her best friend that her venue visions for Rowan's backyard could be actualized. Meg was going to skewer Claire for not telling her sooner, but hopefully, decades of friendship might soften that blow.

The Jeep's AC blew back wayward wisps of hair as Claire removed her cap and untied her ponytail to cool her sweaty scalp. Her best friend didn't pick up her video call after the two attempts, leaving only one errand left.

Some might consider Claire's next move impulsive, but she hoped it would demonstrate her sincerity for Rowan.

Erin was right. Claire had *so much* ground to cover, but working through her issues now felt like standing at a trailhead. Every journey started with a single step, and Claire was excellent at moving forward. Doing so with Rowan was more exciting than any adventure she'd undertaken in years.

There would be pitfalls. There always were. But she wouldn't get lost. Not if she stayed on the path.

And this time, Rowan would be right beside her.

Claire set her phone in the center console and shifted the Jeep into drive, a growing smile lifting her lips.

Chapter 26

"Hey, Row. Is Claire around?" Meg asked when he answered her video call.

"No." Rowan barely kept the gruff out of that word.

Claire had texted him *Soon* two hours ago. Since then, he'd been trying every distraction technique to prevent himself from texting back *Now*. Because as much as Rowan needed his wife at home with him—preferably kissing him—he didn't want to be a maniacal, controlling dirtbag of a husband.

"Why?" he asked, propping the phone on the kitchen counter and grabbing a spoon out of the silverware drawer for his Greek yogurt.

"She called me, but now isn't answer— What the heck is that?"

Rowan was already staring at the scratched, unfamiliar spoon in his fingers. "I don't know. It was in the drawer."

"Why is Claire's spoon in your drawer?" The frantic pitch of Meg's voice on top of Claire not answering her phone or being home yet ratcheted his blood pressure.

When Meg squealed, Rowan nearly dropped the open yogurt container on the floor.

"It worked! I can't believe it worked!" Meg's side of the call was shaking, her long hair flailing around the frame like she was jumping. "I'm finally getting a sister!"

"You *have* a sister," he countered.

"A sister who likes me, dummy!" Meg made another high-pitched squealy sound before talking to herself. "Okay. Calm down. She spooks easily. You need to pretend like you don't know what this means. Casual, Meg. You can do casual."

"Start talking sense." Rowan abandoned his snack, snatching up his phone with a strength that could crack the protective case.

His sister sucked in a deep breath and tried to straighten her lips, but they wobbled back up into a smile. "That's Claire's favorite spoon. The only thing she kept after selling Ann Marie's things. She never puts that spoon anywhere but in her pack. I've seen her use it, wash it, and put it right back in the pack next to the friendship bracelet I gave her when we were kids." Meg made little jagged gestures with her hands as she spoke. "If she left it at your house, that means . . . ." The sentence trailed off as Meg did another jumpy dance.

"What, Meg? What does it mean?" His voice had gone all growly and irritated, but it didn't touch Meg's incandescence.

"She finally trusts you."

With how she cried last night and her notes this morning, Rowan had surmised that Claire probably loved him, even though she still hadn't said the words. But for Claire, trust was even bigger than love. Meg continued to mumble something along the lines of how it'd taken him less than a month, when she'd tenaciously chipped away at Claire's defenses for years, but Rowan only cued back in when Meg's, "She loves you back," sailed over the line.

"You knew I loved her?"

"*Row.*" She gave him a sardonic glare. "Did you think I couldn't see how you've pined for her all these years? You're not that good at hiding your emotions." Meg snorted, cutting her eyes to the side. "It really was perfect that she ended up coming back to Tucson with nowhere else to stay. I couldn't have planned it better myself."

Too many sensations were running through his body. Rowan needed Claire here *now*. He needed her antsy fingers running over his skin to quell the whisper of doubt burning in his chest.

A threatening summer storm rumbled against the windowpanes. Claire wasn't still hiking, was she? The canyons were dangerous places during the flash floods that accompanied monsoon rains.

Meg went on and on about turning his backyard into a wedding venue, draping organza over the pergolas, stringing twinkle lights everywhere. He'd explain later that they were already married. Right now, Rowan needed to make sure Claire was safe.

"I'll call you back."

Rowan had no sooner hung up and dialed when he heard an echoing tone matching the ringing in his ear. He spun from the sliding glass windows, where he'd been nervously watching the growing storm, to see Claire sling her day pack onto the tile.

"Hey." A nervous flush pinked her cheeks.

"*There* you are."

A few steps and Claire was in his arms, kissing him back with equal fierceness.

"Thank you for the sticky notes." Rowan set one gentle kiss on her brow when he pulled back to look at her.

She wrinkled her lips, almost in a wince. "It was easier to write."

Rowan understood the implied end of that sentence—*than say aloud.*

"It's okay." He smoothed his palms up and down her back.

"I want to get better at . . ." Claire's frame heaved with a sigh. "Everything."

He opened his mouth to speak, but Claire continued, "What I figured out is that I work better with action. Movement helps. Touch helps." She ran her fingers up his arms and palmed the back of his neck. "So I did some errands after my hike this morning."

Those mesmerizing eyes centered on his with steady assuredness as thunder rumbled in the distance. "I talked to Erin about us staying together. And then I told your parents . . . everything." She paused, rolling her lips together. "I also tried to call Meg, but she didn't answer. I wanted—" A shaky exhale shook her shoulders. "I wanted everyone to understand that though this started as something fake for health insurance, it isn't anymore."

An expanding feeling was trying to burst from his chest.

Her gaze skipped all over his face before Claire leaned back against his arms, sliding her hands down his chest.

"Did you hurt yourself?" Rowan asked, seeing the gauze bandage on her hand.

"No." Thunder shook the house, as if the storm was on top of them. "This was something else I did this morning."

Claire's fingers were steady as she picked at the tape securing the gauze in place. The second he caught sight of angry red skin and inked lines, Rowan gripped her fingertips. In the center of a finely lined band was a tattooed stone. A letter was printed along each line of the pentagon shape, their tops stretching inward—R O W A N. The band surrounding the inked stone had a diagonal striped design that continued all the way around.

A wedding band.

A *very permanent* wedding band.

Rowan flipped her hand a second time, not quite believing what he was seeing.

When he looked up, Claire was watching him, her gaze achingly tender. "I don't like jewelry, but I love you."

His hands shook as they slowly burrowed into her hair, his thumbs firm on the corners of her jaw. "Say it again."

Claire's blissful tremble at the command in his tone lit unexpected places in his body.

"I love you, Rowan Bellamy." Her smile grew. "Will you marry me?"

He should have answered her, but he was completely incapable of not kissing her that second. Claire didn't seem to mind, meeting each demanding press equally. Her needy fingers snuck under the sides of his shirt, nearly tickling his ribs.

"Take. This. Off." Each word was a breathy plea between lips and tongues tangling.

Rowan obliged before kissing his way down her neck. An approving hum accompanied the taste of salt still on her skin. That sound seemed to throw his antsy wife into overdrive, because she pulled back long enough to jump and wrap her legs around his torso. Rowan chuckled at her forearms digging into his shoulders as her fingers tugged out his hair band. One hand tangled in his hair, but as the other snuck between them, sliding down his abs, Rowan leaned back.

Claire's mouth dropped open. "What?"

"Oh, my love." Rowan shook his head slowly, unable to hide his smirk.

Her puzzled expression sent dark effervescence tumbling through him.

"If you think for a second that I'm going to rush through something I've been wanting most of my life, you are sorely mistaken."

Claire's eyes fluttered half-closed as his words seeped into her skin.

His lips found the crook of her neck, kissing before giving a soft nip. "You are going to let me take my time and savor every inch of you. Do you understand?"

She shuddered, a languid nod dipping her head.

"Good." That single word over her ear was all it took for his wiggly wife to sag in that sublimely boneless way. This new dynamic between them was as foreign to him as he expected it was for Claire, but it somehow seemed to be the perfect layer atop years of friendship, trust, and love.

When he leaned back to catch her gaze, Claire's irises flashed in anticipation. The corner of his mouth lifted as the sky opened up, and rain pelted the roof, the raucous sound drowning out their labored breaths.

Claire's teeth tugged at her bottom lip, her smile growing. "It's raining."

"Finally." Rowan kissed her again, each step steady as he carried Claire to their bedroom.

Chapter 27

"I can't believe you've been married for three weeks and didn't tell me!" Meg's face attempted to glare at Claire over their video call, but her twitching lips betrayed her.

"I don't know what you're so mad about. Apparently, you were the evil mastermind of this whole thing." Claire's gaze drifted toward Rowan, who was sitting in a gray tattoo chair, his left hand extended over the artist's work table. "I thought we were supposed to scheme together?"

The buzz of Rowan's tattoo machine and two others harmonized like a chorus of cicadas.

When Claire had come out of the shower earlier, Rowan presented her with two yellow objects. The first had been a sticky note with the design for his wedding ring. The band had finely drawn diagonal slants between the edges—the style matching hers—but in the center of his ring held her name written in cursive. The second object had been her yellow wedding dress.

"When we get home, you can go as fast as you want the second I untie these." Rowan stood behind her and kissed the top of each shoulder where the dress straps were tied in bows. "I've been dreaming of doing that since you walked out of that dressing room."

Rowan's hazel eyes found hers, the memory of his promise heating his gaze. Bella, the tattoo artist who'd inked Claire's ring, paused to glance between them. A knowing smile tugged at her lips before her head bent to finish Rowan's ring.

"Um. Hello? Play googly eyes with my nerd brother later."

"Sexiest nerd I've ever seen," Claire murmured, still unable to pull her gaze away.

Meg made a gagging noise. "Don't make me regret pushing you two together."

The effort to pull her focus back to her best friend was gargantuan. Claire leaned against the exposed brick wall opposite the line of five workstations, careful to make sure her shoulder didn't make contact with the various framed designs.

"Why *did* you do that?" Claire wasn't upset that Meg had helped her get to this point, but she wondered if, like Erin, Meg had known her true feelings before Claire had clawed herself out of denial long enough to discover them on her own.

"Other than, now that you're married to Rowan, you're both my best friend *and* sister-in-law?"

Claire snorted. "Yes. Other than that."

"You're perfect for each other." Meg made it sound so simple.

That seed of doubt brewed in her belly. The one she'd been assiduously ignoring. "We're exact opposites."

"That's exactly why it works. Rowan likes routine and predictability, while you like to chase the next adventure. He'll ground you. You'll challenge him. Besides that, you're more similar than you think."

"We both enjoy the outdoors more than you, but—" Her eyes cut to her husband. *Her husband.* Claire was getting used to that word, how it grounded her in an unexpectedly comforting way. Even with the remnant warmth of that thought, insidious, tenacious doubt nipped at her temples. "Rowan's so smart."

Her best friend growled—actually *growled*. "I hate when you do that. Just because your intelligence doesn't come from doctorate study at an accredited university doesn't mean it doesn't matter. If there was a zombie apocalypse, I'd bet good money that you could survive in the wild for decades. Most people? Two days, tops."

When Claire simply stared, open-mouthed, Meg spoke again. "I never went to college. Am I stupid?"

"No. Of course not."

"So why doesn't that logic apply to you?"

Claire fidgeted. Meg never called her out like this. Usually, they kept things light. This week's soul searching had already left Claire craving a two-year sleep.

Rowan's eyes caught hers again, that line forming between his brows as he mouthed, "You okay?"

Her head dipped in a few quick nods before she answered Meg. "I'll work on that—along with the laundry list of things Erin gave me this morning."

"Oh no," Meg groaned. "We're listening to Erin now?"

"Something about emotional maturity and growing up." The careless shrug lifting Claire's shoulders felt anything but.

The corner of Meg's mouth tilted. "I guess that's worth pursuing. I'll even give it a try."

"Yeah." She scrunched her lips. "We can't wreak havoc our whole lives."

"Like heck we can't. I expect to be spiking Erin's protein shake with cayenne even when she's eighty. I'll just leave a bottle of antacids in her bathroom so her stomach lining doesn't combust." That mischievous smile peaked before Meg waved a hand. "Besides, you being with Rowan is one small—okay, *big*—change, but nothing else between us has to. I'm still your ride-or-die."

Claire smiled, warmth sweeping her exposed skin. "You're the best."

"That's right." Meg's expression tipped into smugness. "Remember Rowan is just new and shiny. You loved me first."

"I did."

The words flew out of her mouth, followed immediately by seizing worry. Was she capable of making this many confessions in a day? Albeit, loving your best friend was *very different* from the way she felt about Rowan. Queasiness still mounted as Claire considered the well of emotion surging through her veins. It had begun as a trickle this morning, but now Claire wondered if it would capsize her unstable footing at any moment.

"I know, bestie. I've known for years."

Meg blew out a breath, apparently at her emotional capacity too. "I'm home in four days. Give me two more to recover from living in a cramped space, and Knox and I will throw you a *'We were fake married, and now we're really married, but this isn't our wedding'* party next weekend."

The barking laugh leaving Claire's lips brought the attention of half of the tattoo shop. "How are you going to fit that party title on the invitation?"

Meg rolled her eyes through the screen. "No one sends invitations anymore. It'll easily fit in a text. You get to pick the theme. I've narrowed it down to toga, après-ski, or emo Elmo."

Claire tilted her head. "Après-ski would be way too hot."

Meg *hmm-hmmed*. "Agreed, but I liked the idea too much to discard it."

"Maybe for winter."

A derisive noise came over the video call. "Sure. I'll plan it during the two whole weeks of winter where we can actually wear something warm."

"It would be *hilarious* to see Erin in an emo and *Sesame Street* combo, but I have to go with toga." Claire paused. "It's practical and fun."

"What's practical and fun?" Rowan leaned down to kiss her temple before shifting himself into the video with an upward nod to Meg. The gauze bandage covering his ring finger matched the fresh one on hers.

"The toga theme for your marriage-but-not-a-wedding party next weekend."

Rowan's eyes quickly flicked down Claire's body, as if imagining her in nothing but a white sheet, before he tucked his bottom lip between his teeth.

"You two have to stop doing that. It's disturbing!"

He gave the screen an eyeroll. "I thought this was what you wanted, Meg-a-tron. Wasn't this the culmination of all your devious planning?"

"Don't make it sound like you're not deliriously happy about me scheming on your behalf."

Rowan gave a curt nod. "Oh, I absolutely am."

"*Fine.*"

"Fine."

Claire pinched her lips together to keep from chuckling at their sibling squabbling.

"Are you up to speed yet? I want to take my wife home." Out of the sight of the camera, Rowan wrapped his hand around Claire's waist and squeezed.

It was a fight to keep the response to his touch from showing on her face. He'd murmured those two words into the crook of her neck earlier, almost like a branding. *My wife.* Though she'd happily relinquished to his focused control as he'd worshiped her earlier, impatience was now making her restless. Her heel began to bounce against the polished concrete floor.

"Yes. Fine. I'll talk to you later." Meg huffed, though a smile slipped onto her lips again. "Claire, call me tomorrow."

Claire had barely said, "Will do," before Rowan ended the call for her. When she opened her mouth to protest, he leaned closer.

"Don't pretend you want to be on the phone in this shop when we both know where you'd rather be."

Her chin lifted to a defiant angle, but Rowan's lips only softened into a loving smile. "Come on, my love. Let's go home."

The way he could seamlessly transition from sending her spine-tingling heat back to the gentle, caring man she'd known her whole life was nothing short of astonishing. Claire wove her fingers gently around his bandaged hand, only realizing in that moment that the whole time she'd stayed with Rowan, she'd been casually calling his house *home*.

Not *your place*. Or *your house*. Home.

Claire waited for the fear to click down her spine as they broke into the late-afternoon heat and crossed the shoe-melting asphalt. It didn't come as the wind whipped her hair into a frenzy as it curled through the open windows, listening to Rowan hum along to the radio. It didn't slip between her teeth when the Jeep sailed down the two-lane road to Rowan's rural neighborhood.

When Rowan turned onto his short driveway, she clenched his forearm. "Let me out here."

The sun beat on her scalp as Rowan parked the car and slowly walked to join her. He didn't say a thing about the fact that she was standing in one-hundred-and-five-degree weather, holding herself and shivering. Rowan just waited beside her, facing the house. Two quick tears slipped past her lashes before she took a steadying breath.

"Thank you."

One hand framed her face, his thumb tracing over her quickly drying cheeks. "This has always been here for you. Will always be here for you. Even if it's not this house. Even if it's a tent in trees. I'll build whatever future you want, Claire. Just as long as we're together."

She nodded, another tear escaping.

His rock-scarred thumb soothed the wetness away.

"It's still so strange that I can say these things to you," Rowan said through a growing smile, smoothing his hands down her spine and banding them around her lower back. "I've thought them and kept them inside for so long." His soft chuckle rumbled against her. "Though, Meg says you scare easily, so I should probably pace myself."

"I think I loved you then." Claire watched Rowan's shoulders rise with a surprised inhale.

Honestly, she shocked herself with how easily that admission fell from her lips. It'd been the one thing Claire couldn't stop thinking about, wondering how she'd denied her feelings during the years she'd been away.

"I think I was confused because it was so tangled up in my grief over Gram and my belief that—" She swallowed, her throat impossibly tight. "That I don't deserve you."

The fractured look on Rowan's face almost made her lay her cheek against his chest and sob, but Claire summoned the strength she'd used to make it to the next trail bend and pushed through.

Her fingers traced up his arms, his steadiness making each word easier. "I was running from my grief. I was distracting myself with exertion and survival, but I was also trying to create as much distance between us as possible. I couldn't handle your affection, how I had felt a little less broken with my shoulder resting against yours or your fingers wrapping my wrist." She paused, wetting her lips.

Rowan—patient, beautiful Rowan—simply waited, allowing her to speak.

"And the night before I left, when I ruffled your hair . . . The devastated look in your eyes—" The tears broke then, unyielding, as her hands fisted the sleeves of his t-shirt. "I didn't want to hurt you like that, so I stayed away."

Rowan's arms tightened around her, a muscle in his jaw flexing.

"I figured—" Her words were wet and squeaky. "I figured, after all this time, your feelings for me would be gone. That you'd have forgotten about me."

One of his hands palmed her neck, bringing her closer. "I could never forget about you." He kissed one temple and then the other. "You . . ." His breath was heavy across her lips. "You're all I've ever wanted."

Claire closed the distance between their lips with a soft, tear-tinged kiss. "I love you. I'm going to try so hard to be good enough for you."

His thumb and forefinger tightened slightly as Rowan leaned back. "You already are. Right now. Messy." He kissed her cheek. "And human." His beard scruff rasped her other cheek as he set another kiss there. "And complicated." One last one on her forehead. "No one has it together. *No one.*"

Claire nodded, her tears still streaming. She'd done more crying this weekend than in her entire life. She'd probably just surpassed whatever tears she'd shed in her infancy.

"I also didn't realize, until I came back, how much I missed you as a friend."

That confession brought a smile to Rowan's full lips. "Don't tell Meg. I think she's already a little miffed that she has to share your attention now."

Leaning fully into him, Claire laid her head on his chest. "She'll be okay." The rhythmic beating of Rowan's heart quickly drowned out the flushed, rushing sound swarming her ears. "Besides, she has Knox to keep her busy."

The hand on her back became possessive as his fingers spread. "Can we stop talking about my sister?"

The rough edge to his words had Claire's breath quickening, but it wasn't until his fingertips slowly slid to pluck free one of her shoulder bows that Claire's heart revolted.

"That's one."

Her mouth parted with a shaky exhale. He'd said the same words earlier—one broad hand pinning her to the mattress—before fulfilling his promise of many more.

"Should we go inside?" Rowan asked over the shell of her ear.

Claire turned, breaking from his arms and sprinting toward the garage. Light exploded from her chest when Rowan's hearty laughter followed closely behind.

Chapter 28

"The floor is lava in three, two . . ."

That was the greeting Rowan received upon opening the door to the living room after finishing his late night of Monday appointments. One large vault and Rowan landed on the couch before Claire finished.

"One," she said, dimpled smile beaming from her cross-legged position atop his kitchen counter. "Hi."

"Hi, yourself." Rowan toed the shoes off his dangling feet, letting them clatter to the ground before kneeling backward on the couch to face her.

A James Arthur song murmured in the background, singing the praises of the domestic bliss Rowan was currently experiencing. Claire's hair was a bit wild around her face, meaning she'd driven home with the windows open even though it was a bazillion degrees outside. A to-go bag from his favorite taco truck rested on the counter between them. Rowan couldn't help the grin tugging on his lips.

"What?"

You have the rest of your life to tell her how amazing she is. Pace yourself.

The heel of his palm rubbed at the ache in his chest as Rowan let his smile turn roguish. "Did you put yourself all the way over there because you thought I couldn't reach you?"

Claire's eyes flashed. "Oh, I absolutely knew you could."

She'd wedged herself into the corner beside the sink. Jumping from the couch to the eat-in countertop was possible, but the impact might damage the ledge. The easiest option was to use a couch pillow to close the distance to the stools, but Rowan immediately dismissed it. Once he'd figured out his route, his hand rubbed his jaw to stifle his smirk.

"That good, huh?"

"You'll see." His finger's made quick work of unbuttoning his dress shirt.

An audible puff left Claire's mouth when he pulled it off his shoulders.

"What? I don't want to rip a seam." Rowan expected Claire to scoff at his gratuitous peacocking, but her hooked index finger just traced her lips as she watched, distracted.

He momentarily disappeared from her view, curling up and using the back of the couch for leverage. Then Rowan did a shoulder stand that ended in a slow, steady backbend over the couch edge until his bare feet reached a stool and knocked it toward him. His face was flushed by the time he'd returned upright since he'd made sure to pause when his body was fully extended, for his wife's benefit.

Claire tucked her knees into her chest, her fidgety fingers wrapping around her ankles. A chuckle left his lips as he balanced one foot on the fallen stool seat and then the other on the lowest rung, easily walking to the counter. Rowan had to stoop to make his way past the light over the sink before he sat beside her, close but not touching.

"I got tacos." Her gaze darted between his ribs, waist, and abs.

One gentle finger under Claire's chin brought her hazy eyes into focus. "Thank you."

Her mouth opened, pausing as a somberness washed over her cheekbones. She pressed her lips together and swallowed. "Sometimes this doesn't seem real."

A small smile tugged at his mouth. "I know."

She bit her bottom lip. "It makes me worry. What if something bad happens? What if . . ."

They still hadn't gotten the pathology results, and he knew it was wearing on her.

"You don't think I'm terrified? Literally all my dreams have come true. Things I've been wanting for years. You're here." Rowan couldn't help kissing her softly, framing her jaw in his fingertips. She fit so perfectly in his hands. "In the span of a month, my entire life changed. And assuming you're healthy and the pathology results come back normal, we haven't even done the hard work yet. I've been letting us live in this bubble, but eventually we need to figure out all the normal things."

Until four weeks ago, Claire's life centered around constant relocation. If she still wanted that, Rowan would need to figure out a solution. He'd already looked into licensure requirements to conduct his practice in other places, converting clients to virtual appointments. It'd mean he would have to take more traditional clients since the parolees he saw were required to attend in person. Since his contract with the state didn't expire until the new year, the next few months might mean long distance.

"Always so practical." She poked in that exact spot in the ribs that always made him jump.

This time, instead of elbowing her in the jaw, Rowan slid to stand between her dangling legs. Claire warned him about imminent death by fire on account of the fictional lava, but when he pulled her flush against his torso, her words slipped into incoherent murmurs.

"I like our bubble," she whispered after a long, satiating kiss.

Rowan smiled against her lips. "For now, we'll stay here. It's our honeymoon phase, after all."

Firm hands pushed his shoulders away. "It is. Isn't it?"

Her radiant eyes threatened to demolish what was left of his straining heart. "Yes." He leaned forward slowly to whisper the rest of his answer over the sensitive skin beneath her ear. "It is."

Before Rowan could pick her up to fully enjoy their honeymoon phase, his phone rang with Zane's call.

His friends still thought that he was suffering with Claire's presence. Rowan hadn't mentioned anything at the water park, since they'd been in a 'trial period.' This Friday, however, at opening night of Kevin and Kyle's 90s-inspired *Midsummer Night's Dream*, Rowan planned to set everyone straight.

"Let me just make sure everything's okay. Zane usually only calls if he needs something."

Impatience flickered in Claire's eyes, but she braced her hands on the edge of the countertop and nodded.

"Rowan, hey." Zane's usually joyful voice was tinged with worry.

"What is it?" Rowan quickly crossed to the couch, shrugging one arm into his discarded shirt while pressing the phone to his ear with his other shoulder.

"Ann's not feeling well."

The sound of retching in the background simultaneously triggered sympathy and an automatic gag reflex. Rowan stifled the latter.

"She's been throwing up for hours and . . ." Zane's voice dropped off.

"It's probably just norovirus or food poisoning." Rowan kept his tone reassuring and even.

"I know, but I want to take her to Urgent Care before they close. I need to make sure it's not anything . . . else." With Zane's history of loved ones battling cancer, needing that extra reassurance made sense. "But I have no one to watch Caroline. Tess and Isaac are out of town. So are the grandparents. Kevin and Kyle are living at the theater with the opening a—"

"I can watch Caroline." His fingers buttoned up his shirt, not bothering to tuck it back in.

Of all his friends, Rowan had watched Caroline the least. When they'd been in their early twenties, the 'dorm bros' used to babysit in teams to make it easier. Usually, he and Kevin had gone to Zane's apartment together. Kevin's exuberance and zeal for kids had made Rowan's presence essentially unnecessary.

"Why don't I come pick her up?"

"Really?" Zane sighed. "Oh, man, that would be so great."

Ending the call and pocketing his phone, Rowan turned to find Claire holding the dinner bag in one hand, Jeep keys in the other. "Tacos to go?"

"I love you." He gave her a quick kiss while grabbing for the keys.

"I love you too." She pulled on his lapels to steal a second kiss. "But I'm staying here to get this place sleepover ready."

The corner of his mouth quirked. "Do I want to know what that entails?"

"No. You do not." That firelight was burning in her irises as she playfully quipped her words.

Rowan shook his head, unable to stop himself from kissing Claire a third time before leaving.

Chapter 29

It took a while to find Rowan's spare rock-climbing gear since he kept his everyday equipment in the back of his Jeep. Once she figured out how to secure the climbing nuts into the hinges of the upper kitchen cabinets, it only took a few carabiners latched to the mounting frame behind the TV to get the base structure for what became a rope lattice stretching from one wall of the open-concept living space to the other. Above that, she'd strewn every extra blanket, towel, and bedsheet she could find.

Relocating the coffee table against the plate windows to the backyard and pushing the couch against the kitchen stools, Claire created a wide-open space for her small tent. The pièce de résistance was found while returning the unused rope to the garage. Tiny white Christmas lights draped below the network, making the happenstance of fabric above look like an ethereal canopy.

When the garage door opened, Claire had just finished unrolling her sleeping bag. She rocked back on her heels at the entrance to the tent.

Caroline practically flew to Claire's side. Her red pajama set looked like one an executive businesswoman would wear, not an eight-year-old girl. White piping traced the edges of the loose-fitting pants and long-sleeved collared top. Claire half expected to see the girl's initials monogrammed over the small breast pocket.

"Is this where I'm sleeping?" An elated smile overtook Caroline's small face.

"If you like." Claire casually lifted a shoulder. "You could always sleep in Rowan's bed, and he can take the fort."

As expected, Caroline looked appalled.

"No way." She chucked her backpack into the tent, narrowly missing Claire's left arm while calling dibs.

Claire laughed and glanced at Rowan. He hadn't moved from his position by the door, that deep groove etching between his brows. As his fingers sequentially tightened and then released around his Jeep keys, Claire's intestines twinned into knots. She'd warned him that she was getting his home ready for Caroline, but he probably didn't anticipate *this*.

Rowan shook his head and rubbed his jaw. "I'm so jealous. This is ten times better than the ones you and Meg made as kids."

She crossed to him before whispering, "I wanted to make leaving home last minute more enjoyable for Caroline, but we can leave it up and sleep here tomorrow if you'd like."

Tonight, they were to keep up the charade of her being Rowan's "roomie." She'd intentionally saved a blanket and pillow and set them on the floor at the foot of the bed in the bedroom to keep up appearances. When Rowan had called on his way to Zane's, explaining that he'd planned on telling his friends about their relationship next Friday and didn't want his niece to be the first to know, Claire had understood.

"No uncles allowed," Caroline quipped from inside the tent.

Rowan stalked over, peering down through the mesh roof with his hands on his hips. "You're in *my* house."

Claire smiled as Caroline simply rolled her eyes while rummaging through her bag. They'd done this playful teasing at the water park too.

"Where can I brush my teeth?" Caroline held up an electric toothbrush and an oversized tube of bubble gum toothpaste.

"I'll show you," Claire said, leading her to the half bathroom that she'd cleaned in anticipation.

Once Caroline had gone through a surprisingly rigorous bedtime routine, she asked, "How'd you both hurt the same finger?"

Claire caught Rowan's gaze. They should have planned how to handle their bandaged tattoos.

"Would you believe that we were bitten by a box turtle in the same spot?" Claire leaned on her elbow from her outstretched position, lying beside the entrance to the tent.

"No." Caroline's lips wobbled as she fought a smile.

"How about that your Uncle Rowan was attempting to save three kittens from being swept away in monsoon flood waters, and they ungratefully scratched us both?" She arched an eyebrow.

"Uncle Rowan doesn't like cats, only dogs." Caroline glared at him before crawling into the tent. "A major character flaw."

"He likes bobcats," Claire said as Rowan sat cross-legged beside her. "There's one that lives nearby that he gives water to every day. His name is Herbert."

"Uncle Ethan's middle name is Herbert." She picked at an invisible piece of lint on her sleeve, lips downturned as she flicked it away.

A surprised laugh came from Rowan before he ran his hand over his mouth, quieting. "I forgot about that."

"Having a bobcat live near you is pretty fun," Caroline said. "I've only seen ground squirrels and quail around Dad's house, but sometimes coyotes run through the wash behind Isaac's house. Mom hates how loud they yip."

The conversation diverged into everyone's favorite desert animal before Claire told a few of her animal-encounter stories from her years on the trail. Caroline's eyelids slowly drooped a fraction more with each tale. By the time Claire recounted the popular story of a moody moose refusing to vacate her campsite, Caroline was barely conscious. Claire gently pulled up the top of the sleeping bag over the girl's small shoulders and turned off the kitchen lights before joining Rowan in the bedroom.

Her husband was resting on the bed with one hand behind his head and the other on his chest, a peaceful expression softening his features. Forgoing the decoy bed on the ground, Claire nestled into the crook of his shoulder before softly whispering, "I love you."

"I love you." His lips met hers, sweetly but with a focused intensity that sent light sprinting to her toes. "I don't think I'll ever be able to tell you—to show you—how much."

His fingers stroked up and down her back as they snuggled in tranquil silence.

"I'm sorry if I changed too much tonight," Claire said after a long while.

"No." His breath was soothing over her temple. "It's perfect. We're going to sleep out there for a week."

"Good." Claire smiled. "I didn't want to upset you."

He'd been so much more flexible with her ideas the last few weeks, but Rowan still enjoyed his routines. Particularly at home. It was important to her that Rowan set the pace when they stayed in since she usually dictated their activities on the two nights they went out.

Rowan stilled as his thumb drummed duplicates on her shoulder blade.

"What is it?"

She lifted her gaze, but Rowan slid his hazel eyes to the ceiling. "Nothing."

It most definitely wasn't *nothing*, but Rowan had never pressed her to talk, with the exception of telling him about the mix-up with the pathology results weeks ago, so Claire let it go. Rowan had this communication thing down pat. When he was ready to tell her, she had no doubt he would.

◊◊◊

When Claire woke the next morning, Rowan was gone. She expected to find him cooking breakfast with Caroline, but the young girl was perched atop the coffee table, sketchbook in hand, surveying the desert beyond the glass windows.

"Hey," Claire said softly so as to not surprise her. "Where's Rowan?"

"He left." Caroline never took her gaze off the shifting shadows of the saguaros, making determined pencil marks on the page. "He was in one of his moods."

"One of his moods?" Her forehead wrinkled.

"Yeah, you know." Three more sharp slashes to the page. "When he gets all broody."

"Broody?" Claire's mind flashed to last night, to how it'd taken long moments for his body to relax beneath her before she'd drifted off to sleep in the crook of his shoulder.

"It means cranky or morose," Caroline stated matter-of-factly, glancing up. "He gets like that sometimes."

When Claire's eyes slipped to the sketch, Caroline quickly covered it with her forearm. "He said he needed to get something from the grocery store. I tried to call and ask if he could please get apple juice"—she lifted up her smartwatch-clad wrist—"but his phone is over there." Caroline pointed to the kitchen charger.

Claire sat on the ground beside the table, watching the mesquite trees wave in the early morning wind as her mind whirled. Rowan never forgot things. Her thumb found her wrist, tracing the heart outline.

Caroline set her sketchbook aside. "We could surprise him with an epic breakfast. That might help. Do you know how to make flapjacks? They're essentially pancakes, just with a fancy name."

A slow, long breath filled her lungs as Claire pushed away the dread tightening her shoulders.

"I think we can figure it out together," Claire said, standing and outstretching her hand.

Caroline's luminescent smile, as her soft fingers slid between Claire's, tugged at her belly.

Someday, a voice inside her whispered. That one word demolished the sadness that usually infiltrated her skin after thinking about children. Many of her teenage dreams had already materialized; perhaps this part could too. There were so many—*many*—things to discuss with Rowan, starting with what distracted him enough to leave without his phone. But the concept of parenthood being a possibility made effervescence shimmer through her bloodstream.

"My dad's been showing me how to make letters. We can spell Uncle Rowan's name."

Claire squeezed Caroline's fingers as they strode to the kitchen. "I think he'd like that."

Chapter 30

Rowan cradled his head in his hands, cursing himself for forgetting his phone on his kitchen counter. He only had another twenty minutes before he'd need to drive home in order to get ready for his first Tuesday client. The cool cement step beneath him should have been steadying, but the untethered sensation from last night persisted. It'd chased him like an unrelenting shadow, forbidding the mercy of sleep.

A woodpecker tapped against a nearby exhaust vent on one of the other townhouses, the sound grating against his temple. Rowan pushed to his feet to see Erin whiz around the corner, her purple cycling jersey bright against the tans and browns of her housing complex. Stopping in the narrow driveway, she unclipped her shoes from the pedals.

"Come inside. I've got a pot brewing."

He must look worse than expected if Erin was offering him coffee, knowing his preferences.

Erin was unhurried in pouring them each a cup, doctoring hers with French vanilla creamer and raw sugar. Only when she'd brought his black mug to where he stood leaning on the edge of the laminate counter did Erin finally speak.

"Did she leave?"

It took his exhausted brain a moment to understand that his sister meant Claire.

"No." The word scraped past the stone in his throat.

Claire had been incredible last night, making the end of his long workday joyful before constructing Caroline the best blanket fort he'd ever seen.

It'd been those six little words that had kept him up all night.

"I didn't want to upset you."

An innocuous sentence at its core, but it'd been the memory of hundreds of versions of those words from his early childhood that'd made his blood run cold.

"We have to clean up before Dad gets home, or he'll get upset."

"Remember, we don't want to upset Dad by talking during dinner."

"Let's leave the room before Dad gets upset."

Sometimes they were Erin's words, sometimes his mother's, always they were spoken with a ribbon of fear stitched between the consonants.

Rowan fully understood that Claire hadn't been frightened of him as she'd sighed into his shoulder and fell asleep, but her words brought up the memory of his actions at the bar in Trail Dust Town.

That had been the first and only time he'd lost control of himself, but there'd been a first time for his birth father too. What if each time after, the fuse grew shorter and shorter? What if this was the beginning to a predestined future?

What if it wasn't Claire's health that was going to tear them apart?

What if it was him?

"Row?"

He flinched at Erin's featherlight touch over his forearm.

Rowan's mouth fell open, but only silent air left it. His vocal cords refused to produce sound, to verbalize his worst fears. The memory of his behavior at the saloon felt like a rope dragging him underwater.

Erin's hazel eyes traced his face, concern etching the lines of her mouth. When she wrapped her arms around him, his knees buckled. His sister's grip didn't waver as Rowan slid against the edge of the counter, slumping onto the floor. Erin followed him, her warmth continuing to surround him.

"I'm— I'm trying not to, but—" The desperate drag of breath filling his lungs wasn't enough. "I think I'm turning into him."

A painful noise squeaked from Erin's throat as she tucked his head beneath her chin. Long moments passed before she asked, "What happened?"

It was slow and halting, but Rowan recounted that night—how he'd lost himself to the rage that warred within him.

"I'm sorry," he whispered as tears collected at the edges of his vision.

Erin took half a breath before hugging him tighter. "I know. I know you are."

Although he'd outgrown his eldest sister long ago, Rowan felt as small as he'd been at five as she held and rocked him—just as Erin had in the backseat of their mother's car as they drove two states away to safety.

"But I need you to understand something. You're not him. You might have lost control for one moment, one time, but you're not him." Her words were soft but strong. "You've done amazing things with your life, trying to help other people with situations like ours, trying to teach men how to use their minds instead of their fists to process their emotions."

Panic surged as if Rowan was losing his grip on a six-millimeter handhold, seconds from plummeting fifty feet to the earth below. "But I didn't control it. I was going to hurt him, Erin. Really hurt him."

His sister relinquished her grip to meet his gaze. "You made one mistake, but I don't believe for a second that you would have gone through with it. Claire helped, but had she not, I still believe you would have stopped yourself."

Tears streamed from his next blink.

Erin's hands were gentle on his shoulders. "You're not anything like him, Rowan. You are one of the best men I know."

He crumpled against her again, and Erin soothed a hand over his back. "That part of our lives is over. We're the adults now. *We* make the choices. We decide what gets to stay in our lives. There's no predetermined map we have to follow. We always get to choose. Every day, every second, we get to choose."

His sister's steady words slipped into the agitated part of his brain, soothing the worry that had been picking him apart.

Erin leaned back to press her hand to the center of his chest. "I have never, not once, thought that you were like him." His terrified heart clenched beneath the pressure of his sister's palm. "You are a good man."

Rowan collected his sister's hand in both of his as another sob tore from him. "Thank you," he whispered.

They were a tangle of awkward sibling limbs on the floor of her kitchen, holding each other for several minutes.

Erin rubbed at the corner of her eye, but Rowan knew she'd deny tears being there. "I know I have no right to advise on your relationship, but if it was me, and the woman I loved for so long finally got over herself enough to love me back, I'd tell her everything. About how much work you've done. About what happened when we were little. All of it."

"Yeah." He leaned away from Erin's comforting embrace. "I was planning to."

She surveyed him for a few heartbeats before nodding. "Good. Now get out of here. Don't your appointments start soon?"

The laugh bubbling up his throat brought a sliver of relief with it. Leave it to his oldest sister to be exactly what he needed and then boss him around in the next breath.

"They do." He stood, lifting her into a rib-squeezing hug. "Thanks, sis."

Rowan was two steps from the front door when he remembered the lie he'd told Caroline. "Do you have an unopened breakfast item I could borrow?"

◊◊◊

Claire's forehead wrinkled at the box of grits Rowan brought home before showing him what she and Caroline had been up to. Two large plates of pancakes rested on the kitchen island next to the sizzling griddle—one of misshapen rejects that Claire deemed still edible, and another of letters. He ate an *R* and *W* while Caroline enjoyed a plate-sized *C* before Zane called, shyly informing Rowan that Ann only had the stomach flu and that he was on his way over.

When Caroline ducked into the half-bath, Claire stopped him on the way to get changed for his first appointment.

"Just tell me we're okay." The way she'd whispered it while staring at the notch between his collarbones nearly broke him. "That I didn't ruin things last night."

"My love"—Rowan tilted her face up, catching the tension in her whiskey eyes—"you could never ruin things. It was me. I have something I need to share with you, but that will unfortunately have to wait until my lunch break since my first appointment starts in five minutes."

"So we're okay?" Her thumb was rubbing her heart tattoo.

Rowan collected her wrist in his fingers as his other hand palmed her head. He could only answer with a deep kiss, one that he hoped radiated his love for Claire straight from his soul.

When his wife's lips dropped from his and her eyes remained closed, just like they'd done at the courthouse, Rowan's heart felt too large for his chest. The door handle to the half-bath jiggled, causing them to step back to avoid being caught.

The next few moments were a flurry of him getting dressed and wishing Caroline goodbye. Claire would make sure Caroline had all her things before Zane arrived.

Helping his clients work through their issues all morning allowed Rowan to push his aside for a few hours. The weight of what he needed to tell Claire felt like his shoes were leaden, but Erin was right. This wasn't something that could be worked out later as they found a rhythm in their relationship.

"Hey." Her greeting was a wet hiccup when Rowan found Claire in her tent at his lunch break.

Half a second was all Rowan needed to crawl inside and gather her to his chest. "What is it?"

"Tele-therapy is hard." She rubbed her nose with the back of her hand. "And I only asked questions about how denial worked to understand how I suppressed my emotions for years. How am I going to manage talking about myself for an hour every week?"

Rowan kissed her temple. "Go slow. Sometimes I have clients who discuss football with me for most of their time before asking one pertinent question and then leaving. Not every session can be revelatory, but they all build on each other." Something clicked in his mind. "Like steps on a trail."

His wife nodded against him, and Rowan savored the sensation of her skin against his and her sweet sage scent.

"What did you want to tell me this morning?" Claire asked after a beat.

"It can wait." Rowan didn't want to add stress when her first therapy session had already been tough.

His wife pushed back, rubbing both her palms over her cheeks and taking a deep breath. "I'd like to know."

How strong she was being for him sent an ache radiating down his forearms. They should have discussed this after he'd lost control that night. Instead, he'd let himself be distracted by the mind-blowing fact that Claire had wanted him and the blissful weeks that followed.

"I have to keep boundaries and stay in control all of the time because if I don't, I might lose the ability to keep my anger in check, and I'll snap like I did at the saloon." Swallowing was excruciating. "My birth father was . . . a violent man. He never touched Mom or us, but he was in and out of jail for hurting others. At times—" His voice threatened to crack. "At times, I worry I'm too much like him."

Claire grabbed his hand, squeezing it while staying quiet to let him continue.

The sip of air he stole was insufficient. "There's this anger simmering all the time. It began when I was a teenager. I talked to Dad about it, and he helped me to work through it with breathing exercises and removing myself from stressful situations. He helped me learn to control it. With my degree, I learned additional techniques and decided to focus my practice on teaching other men."

His heartbeat thrummed in his ears.

"I should have told you this before . . ." His gaze fell to her unbandaged ring finger. "Before you inked my name on your body. I'm sorry."

Claire's fingertips brought his forehead to rock against hers. "You forget that I've known you since you were eight. I've seen you move through life with a purpose I'd always admired. I didn't understand the reasons behind your choices, but that doesn't change anything about us." She leaned back, her eyes so full of love and trust it stole his breath. "I know I'm safe with you. I've always been safe with you."

Though her words were the balm Rowan's tight muscles needed, confusion swept him as Claire's pearlescent laugh bounced off the bright-orange tent fabric.

"I'm sorry." She snorted, holding her hand over her mouth with a horrified expression. "I know I shouldn't be laughing right now, but I'm just so relieved."

His brow pinched. "Relieved?"

"I'm so messed up for thinking this, but I'm relieved that you're a little broken because"—she bit her lip—"maybe we can be broken together?" Another snort-laugh escaped, Claire's eyes widening. "I'm sorry. That's horrible."

"No." Rowan kissed her firmly, twining his arms around her. "That's perfect."

His wife giggled against his mouth, her fizzy energy washing away his tension. "I heard somewhere that no one has it all together."

"I love you." All the other words failed him, were insufficient in describing the way his entire existence felt aligned with hers.

"I love you." Claire gave him another long kiss, the tone of it shifting as her hands fisted the shirt over his abs. "How, um . . . How much time do you have before your next appointment?"

The corner of his mouth quirked before his lips traveled down her neck. "Just enough."

Chapter 31

Almost two weeks later, Claire was helping Meg unpack her things into Knox's house. Since it was a Monday and Rowan would be busy until eight, Claire had plenty of time to be Meg's design sounding board before heading home to her husband. Maybe she could even finagle a trip to Coneheads out of her best friend, especially now that they'd implemented her suggestion to provide gluten-free sugar cones.

"Knox doesn't mind you redecorating without him?" Claire asked, setting an overloaded milk-crate next to the king-sized bed. Meg had been living with Knox since they'd returned to Tucson, but most of her belongings were still in the garage.

Her best friend dropped the box she'd been carrying and wiped sweat from her brow. "I'm not fully redecorating. We agreed to blend our aesthetics."

Claire's gaze flicked over the red neon light bars tracing every corner, framed movie posters, and shelves packed with figurines. Meg's style had always leaned toward feminine-inspired Art Deco. How gamer boy and retro glamor girl were going to meet in the middle was beyond her.

Meg waved a hand before diving into the box. "Besides, he's back in work mode, and since I don't have a wedding until this weekend, it's time to tackle unpacking."

When Claire had said hello earlier, Knox had barely looked up from his graphic design drawing tablet as he'd murmured a greeting. His distracted state didn't bother Claire. Rowan got like that whenever he was deeply focused on writing client notes.

Since Claire spent a part of every day with Meg, she'd also gotten to know Knox. His sharp wit had almost immediately won Claire over, but it'd been how unbelievably happy he made her best friend that'd sealed the deal. A laugh bubbled up Claire's throat, noticing the parallel between their relationships.

Knox was the steady calm to Meg's chaos.

Much like Rowan was to hers.

The toga-themed marriage-but-not-a-wedding party Meg and Knox had thrown that first weekend had been a complete riot. Augie had fully embraced the theme, invoking Dionysus with a crown of grape leaves and gilded goblet. Not surprisingly, Kevin's and Kyle's costumes had also been top tier, but they'd admitted their red-rimmed robes were leftovers from a past *Julius Caesar* production.

Kevin had picked up Claire and spun her three times before announcing that he couldn't be happier that their *little arrangement* blossomed into something more. Zane had been equally joyous, but Kyle's reserved congratulations were given in a if-you-hurt-my-friend-I'll-kill-you kind of way that Claire respected. She had the rest of her life to prove to Rowan and everyone else that she wasn't going anywhere.

In addition to celebrating their unconventional union, their family and friends also celebrated Claire's negative pathology results. Other than her celiac diagnosis, everything else was—thankfully—normal. Then Knox had shocked the room by dropping to one knee and proposing to Meg, making it a triple celebration.

Claire smiled at Meg's sapphire solitaire as her friend ruthlessly tore into another box.

"I saw your post." A set of ethereal lavender drapes were tossed aside as Meg glanced up with a wry eyebrow bounce. "Did you notice a drop in followers now that you're officially off the market?"

Claire had announced her marriage with a photo of their tattooed hands and one of Rowan halfway up a Mt. Lemmon crag. When he'd asked her to go climbing with him yesterday, Claire had been excited to share in something he loved. When Rowan had taken off his shirt before climbing to anchor the top rope, Claire couldn't help sneaking a few pictures.

The comments today were double those for any normal post. While most were simple congratulations, a few made her chuckle.

@justawalkinggirl *Hot hubby alert! So happy for you.*

@kskiki2 *Dang, girl, I'll take that shot over trail ones any day. Keep 'em coming.*

@hikinggreta *Don't make rock hard jokes. Don't make rock hard jokes.*

@thezoesmith *Wedding ring tattoo, those muscles, and the man bun? Lord, I see what you've done for my friend Claire . . .*

Her plan was still to travel but to do so less often and to spend longer stretches living in Tucson. To fill the weeks between destinations, Claire had asked Erin if she'd be interested in an idea Claire had been thinking about since the Wholistic Health Fair. With Canyon Outdoor Supply Company's endorsement, she wanted to lead women-only camping sessions to help others become more comfortable outdoors. Claire was unsure if anyone would be interested, but she still wanted to give it a try.

As far as the rest of her OnlyApp content, Claire planned to finally venture onto the video side of the app with gear tutorials and travel tips. There were many things she could share, like how a dragonfly clip kept the bugs away almost as well as a mesh head-net, or that high-quality hiking socks were anatomically designed for the left and right foot. Claire would also keep her habit of her daily hike and post memorable images from those as well.

Meg tapping away at a tiny black remote as the colors of the rope lights switched from purple to teal to pink brought Claire back into the room.

"If anyone unfollows me after that post, they're probably the creepy types I don't want following me anyway."

"Good point." The lights settled on a sunny gold, and Meg let out an approving noise.

Claire sat cross-legged on the ground as Meg swapped out a movie poster for a black-framed bronze geometric print. Weirdly, it blended perfectly with the vintage *Star Wars* poster beside it. Meg tilted her head, pausing, and then was a flurry of action again. Three small figurines were replaced by a resplendent goddess statue.

"Should I ask about the T-word, or is it still banned from polite conversation?" Meg asked, repositioning the items on the shelf.

Claire made a dismissive—almost impertinent—noise. "It's banned. Why don't you tell me how blissful engaged life is instead?"

Therapy had been harder than most days on the toughest trails. Afterward, Claire would have to sit with a bowl of sour gummy worm popcorn and rewatch a few episodes of her comfort Turkish romance to recalibrate. Marching twelve miles in mid-day, one-hundred-and-ten-degree heat was not an option Claire had been willing to entertain—even with how much she loved the desert.

This week, her therapist had casually mentioned that those with a history of abandonment often push others away to avoid being left themselves. Dr. Day's comforting smile had followed that reality-shifting sentence, but it'd felt as if her therapist had just disemboweled Claire.

This week's homework consisted of three worthiness affirmations.

I am worthy of love and respect.

I am enough just as I am.

I am worthy of my own love and affection.

Though she'd never been good at homework, it was time to grow. That instinctive resistance still coursed through her veins, but Claire took the affirmation sticky note out of her pocket every hour and repeated them to herself. Rowan's abundant affection made that first affirmation palatable, though it would probably take years for Claire to wholly accept it.

Each day, Claire grew better at vocalizing her love for Rowan too. She still had mountains of work to do, but Claire was trying. It helped that she loved the way those three little words lit the green flecks in her husband's eyes.

Sometimes, when her emotions swirled like an intangible mist, Claire would resort to touch instead. When Rowan came out of his office, haggard from a mentally exhausting day, Claire could offer comfort without words. She could unbind his hair and drag her nails over his scalp until his chest heaved with peaceful, even breaths.

"I *could* go on and on about Knox, or . . ." Meg's wicked grin tipped her lips. "We can plan our Vegas bachelorette party."

"Fire dancing!" The idea burst from her.

Her best friend only laughed, sitting cross-legged in front of Claire. Their knees brushed just like they had so many times before. "You want to see fire dancing?"

"I want to *learn* how to do it." Claire raised her eyebrows.

"*Oh.*" Meg gave her an impressed nod. "That's much more fun. Should we learn trapeze while we're there?"

"Yes, and that fabric-hanging-from-the-ceiling thing."

"I think they're called aerial silks," Knox said, arms bracing the doorway.

"Row! Get out!" Meg clamped a hand over her mouth, chuckling. "Sorry, babe. Old habit."

Her fiancé only smiled, shaking his head. "You ladies want lunch? I was thinking Casa Molina."

"Heck yeah!" Both friends punched up from the floor.

◊◊◊

Later, Claire had stopped by Rowan's favorite taco stand before returning home. It had become their unspoken Monday night routine. The simple fact that Claire had a routine that wasn't related to the way she packed gear to optimally balance weight across her hips simultaneously made panic and joy twitch her muscles.

A heavy sigh left her lips as Claire set the greasy bag on the counter. "You're such a mess," she muttered to herself.

Her head bowed, heavy beneath the weight of her thoughts. Sometimes, even the affirmations couldn't keep her afloat.

"But you're *my* mess." She hadn't heard Rowan leave his office, but before Claire could turn around, his hands wove over her waist, hugging her from behind. "I love your mess." His breath warmed the delicate shell of her ear.

That pulled a snort from her. Rowan *did not* love mess. "No, you d—"

Before Claire could finish the rest of that protest, Rowan's firm hands spun her, his mouth finding hers in an unyielding kiss.

"I'll never get tired," he rasped against her mouth, his grip tightening over her hips. "I'll never get tired of coming out of that door and seeing you here."

There was no room to answer as her husband kissed her again, lifting her onto the kitchen counter to better align their heights.

Eventually, Rowan pulled back with a roguish smile. "Eat quick. I made a reservation for axe throwing at eight-forty."

"You?" She raised her brows at him.

"Me." He booped her on the nose before grabbing two water glasses. "*After* we drop by Goodwill." Rowan flashed her a mischievous wink.

That starburst sensation cascaded through her veins, her smile luminous.

This was certainly unexpected.

◊◊◊

Donned in a metallic mini-dress over plaid leggings, the puff sleeves of Claire's dress shuddered as she launched a hatchet toward the wooden bullseye. The sounds of steely blades striking their targets were swiftly followed by cheers. Her weapon, however, slammed sideways into the wood before clattering to the ground.

A frustrated noise escaped her throat.

"If only you'd let me purchase an appropriate shirt. Then I might have taken pity on you and offered help." Rowan's arms were still firmly crossed over his chest. He'd only released that position to take a sip from his condensing pint glass or throw his axe with Viking precision.

"It's worth the struggle." Claire couldn't help that the snug black tank was the perfect complement to the bright-red slacks she'd found for her husband.

He stalked over, lowering his voice. "How about we make a deal? I'll stop wearing a shirt around the house, if you promise to not show me off like a prized stallion when we're out in public again."

A rough swallow preceded her nod, her heart rate tripling in the span of a second.

Rowan always made her completely jumbled when he approached her with that energy. It was as strange as it was exhilarating.

"Good." The word slipped over her ear as his fingertips collected the axe from her hand. "Now step back and marvel at your husband's ability."

His out-of-character bravado snapped her back to reality. Claire shoved him in the shoulder, disregarding the way his laughter tickled up her spine as she walked away.

Once she was behind the safety line, sipping on her hard cider, Rowan paused. He quirked an eyebrow over his shoulder, picked up the second axe, and threw them both. One landed dead center in his bullseye, and the other in the second inner circle of hers.

"Come on!" She gestured with her free hand.

Rowan returned the weapons to their fasteners before collecting her waist in his hands. "Why are you fussing? I thought you'd like me spontaneously planning this activity for us." That obnoxious twist still tilted the corner of his mouth.

"I do." Claire set down her drink on the table, seconds from poking him in that ticklish spot, when Rowan's expression sobered.

"Good." The earnestness in his eyes made her heart squeeze. "Because you make me want to test all the boundaries." He took an unsteady breath. "There are some that have to stay in place, but others could be shifted. Loosened."

Her forehead wrinkled. "You don't need to change."

"I think we're constantly changing. No person is exactly who they were the day before. Life fluctuates, and we shift ourselves to accommodate it." The wholesome affection in Rowan's gaze stole her next breath. "I want to keep making these small changes with you. I want to grow with you."

The future ran wild over her vision. Them together, doing more fun activities like this, but also nurturing each other through simple everyday actions. Claire waited for that too-big sensation to tighten her skin, for her emotions to make her want to bolt for the door, but a steady pulsing fortified her next movements.

Sliding her hands to frame Rowan's face, Claire said, "I want to grow with you too."

The soft brush of his lips was a near duplicate of their tender courthouse kiss. Before Claire could relent to the fire igniting her belly and fully press into him, Rowan held her left wrist, bringing a settling kiss to the inside of her heart tattoo.

"It's your turn, my love." When her husband stepped back, the syncopated slamming of hatchets mixed with the scents of plywood and beer was almost overwhelming.

"Let's go home instead."

Rowan's knowing grin sent light shimmering to her toes. "Soon."

A second frustrated noise left her throat.

"Want me to show you how it's done?" Rowan crowded her like a bad rom-com lead, trying to show his date how to shoot a billiards combo.

Claire shouldered him off, ignoring his husky chuckle.

Stepping up to the throwing line, she muttered to herself, "You spent years living outside. There's nothing you can't do."

That last sentence made her pause. She'd always had confidence in her self-sufficiency, but now Claire wondered if that confidence in her physical abilities could blur into trust in other aspects of her life. Her emotional growth was going to be slow and probably frequented by backslides, but with diligent work, it was as achievable as all the trails she'd completed.

The hatchet poised over her head, Claire steadied her breathing, took a step forward, and flung the weapon. The hatchet sunk into the outer edge of the bullseye with a satisfying whack. It was her turn to wink over her shoulder.

Rowan's arms were crossed again, but his smile sparked something in Claire's soul.

So much of what laid ahead was unforeseen. Falling in love with her best friend's brother had been completely unexpected. But Claire now understood that this life—with him—was just another adventure.

Epilogue

Four years later

Rowan's hiking boot nearly slipped on a boulder's mossy patch. The trail around Jordan Pond in Acadia National Park began as a peaceful walk around the lake until Claire insisted they take this cutoff to get to the Island Explorer bus stop quicker. Little did they know, the cutoff ended in a steep landslide of table-sized boulders. Normally, that wouldn't be a problem, but . . .

Claire made a strained sound from behind him. Distracted, Rowan misstepped, the rock biting into his palms as he caught himself.

"What gone to do with you, Dada?" A tiny voice from the child-carrying pack on his back echoed the playful question he and Claire often asked each other.

Luna turned, her leg kicking him in the side. "Can Mama carry me?"

"No, sweets." Rowan held a hand out to Claire, helping her over the boulder. "Mama is carrying your brother."

Claire rubbed her rounded belly peeking from her unzipped windbreaker. "And your brother is a lot heavier than you were."

His hands gathered Claire to his chest, her seven-month belly between them. "Let's take a break. I'm worried about you falling."

Claire remained surefooted throughout Luna's pregnancy, but having an energetic three-year-old on top of the insomnia that came with this pregnancy often made Claire stumble while walking around the house.

His wife relinquished, sitting on a nearby rock and swinging her daypack onto the ground. "Snack time?"

Luna cheered and wiggled in a happy little dance. They'd had popovers and tea at the Jordan Pond House Restaurant an hour ago, but both of the ladies in his life loved to eat. The moisture in the air mingled with the sweat dotting his brow as Rowan carefully unhooked his pack and helped his daughter out. From this elevation, the large lake had been swallowed into the clouds, gray mist surrounding them.

Claire bit into a gluten-free raspberry fig bar and a cheese stick at the same time, sighing. After opening Luna's snack, Rowan positioned himself behind his wife, pressing his thumbs firmly into the base of her spine. A groan escaped Claire's lips as her head bowed forward.

"Thank you," she whispered.

"Of course, my love," Rowan said, knowing her back had been sorer this time around. "That's my giant child in there, after all."

"I really should have thought of that before going through this again." His wife's eyes were still closed, brow relaxed.

The teasing remark held no validity because Claire had been disappointed when the twenty-week ultrasound hadn't revealed twins. Both wanting three children, they knew this pregnancy would be followed by another. Rowan loved Claire whether she was covered in algae from a failed creek crossing or caked in dust from when they made the addition to the house for the kids' rooms, but nothing could have prepared him for the soul-satiating joy of seeing the woman he loved pregnant with his children.

"Good thing your stubborn husband insisted on a cabin, so there's a comfortable bed to nap in after this hike." He began kneading between her shoulder blades.

"He's so bossy," she quipped.

"You like when I'm bossy." The words were a husky whisper only she could hear.

Claire looked over her shoulder, those whiskey eyes flashing, but before she could respond, their daughter shot up from her spot, sitting in the dirt.

"All done." She meticulously tucked her granola wrapper into the snack bag that had held apple slices. "Pack it in. Pack it out."

Rowan crossed in front of Claire, sneaking a kiss. "Why don't I let her boulder a bit before we keep going? I don't think it's much farther."

His wife nodded, and Rowan made a game of chasing his daughter over the rocks. Luna was as steady as her unpregnant mother and loved their family hikes. They'd only brought the carrying pack along as a precaution in case Luna had tuckered out early. She was almost big enough to join them on rock-climbing trips too.

Yesterday, while both Claire and Luna napped, Rowan had joined a few climbers to ascend the coarse-grained pink granite sea cliffs. Though the multi-pitch route was challenging, Rowan had never experienced the tranquility of climbing over water. Sea spray had cooled his face as the Atlantic Ocean pounded at the base of the rock face. He'd returned to the cabin with pictures and a promise to bring Claire back someday.

Once Luna was tired of bouldering, Rowan tossed her on his back. Claire's face tilted toward the slight break in the clouds, the elusive sunlight bouncing off her cheekbones. Because of the expected cloud coverage, she'd forwent her hiking cap today. After snagging his phone from his pocket, Rowan snapped a few pictures of his gorgeous wife with the lake now shining beyond her.

Rowan showed Claire his phone screen as he used his other arm to lower Luna to the ground. "Maybe this one is post-worthy. Either way, I wanted it for myself."

He'd become an unofficial contributor to her OnlyApp travel page over the years, capturing trail shots and occasionally being the unknowing subject of a post. Luna—or rather, the back of their daughter—also graced many photos since she came on almost all of their trips. Twice a year, Claire took week-long trips without their daughter. One solo-trip, and one where they left Luna with overjoyed grandparents and took a long hiking trip together.

Claire's full-wattage smile warmed him more than the sunlight. "That's perfect. Thank you."

Subduing the prideful swell in his chest, Rowan saved the photo to his background. His lock screen was a photo of the three of them at Christmas. Pretty soon, it would change to one from the newborn photo session Meg already had scheduled a week after Claire's due date.

Thinking of his sister, a gratitude-filled chuckle left Rowan's lips. Had she not meddled in fantastic fashion all those years ago, he wouldn't have gotten this second chance with Claire.

"That reminds me," Claire said between heaving breaths once they were back on the trail upward. He'd insisted she climb first, so he could help if she stumbled. "I need you to get a shot of me doing a few yoga poses for Heather. Maybe after dinner at Agamont Park?"

Claire had rekindled her relationship with Gram's former business partner during Luna's pregnancy when she'd become a regular at Blissful Desert Yoga's prenatal yoga class. Since then, she'd helped Heather with the studio's social media campaigns.

"Sure."

"And I also need to email Erin about . . ." She paused, leaning her forearm on her knee.

"Claire"—he rested his hand on her lower back—"tell me all of this later. Let's just finish this trail."

Claire nodded, stepping upward again.

"Besides, your next WOW trip isn't until months after the baby is born. Whatever Erin wants can wait." Rowan caught her by the elbow when she lilted right. "Once we're done with this hike, I want you to relax."

Women Outdoor Workshops, or WOW, had begun with camping excursions up Mount Lemmon and had expanded to include weekend skill workshops hosted by the store. Her trips and classes had become so popular that Claire was training other Canyon Outdoor Supply Company employees to teach as well. Letters and photos of thanks from the women who'd been empowered by Claire crowded a corkboard in their kitchen.

Since it'd been a busy few years, the plan was for both of them to reduce their work hours when their son was born, allowing them to spend more family time together.

Claire spun so quickly that Rowan's heart hammered with worry, but then her cool fingers caught his jaw a second before her lips met his. Instinct had him deepening the kiss, tugging her as close as possible with one hand while weaving the other beneath her braid. Luna protested from her bird's-eye position behind him, but neither of them cared. Let their daughter see what a loving relationship looked like, what she should demand for herself once she was grown.

"I love you so much." Claire rocked her forehead against his.

Rowan memorized the beautiful arch of his wife's peaceful brows, the slight smile on her lips, the sweet scent of her hair as he kissed that unruly cowlick and tucked back the tendril blown loose by the breeze. "I love you."

Not to be left out, Luna added, "Love you, Mama. Love you, Dada."

Claire smiled at their daughter, both dimples shining as they chorused, "We love you, Luna."

When they arrived at the bus stop, Luna was asleep in the pack. Rowan carefully removed her from the carrier and cradled Luna over his shoulder. Moments later, they climbed aboard the free shuttle that would drop them within a short quarter-mile from their rented cabin.

Claire interlaced her fingers with his once they were seated on the aisle-facing seats. "I know we'd narrowed it down to Archer or Noah, but last night, when I couldn't sleep, I thought of a name I liked even more." Her hand clenched, and Rowan turned his head to catch the nervousness in her gaze.

Automatically, Rowan stretched his thumb to rub over her heart tattoo, soothing her. "What is it?" He made the question as soft as their daughter's sleeping cheek.

"If it's okay with you, I'd like to name him Augie—after the man who taught you to be such an incredible father."

There were times in their relationship when Claire's words knocked him sideways. Expressing herself verbally still came with effort, though she'd improved immensely from their early days. The fact that his wife wanted to name their son after his dad meant the world to Rowan.

When they'd become pregnant soon after their vow renewal, both of them had been shocked. Pregnancy wasn't always a guaranteed thing. After watching his friends, Kevin and Becca, struggle with infertility treatments before deciding to adopt, Rowan expected it would take time to start a family of their own.

He'd been wrong.

Rowan also hadn't anticipated how terrified he'd be after that first ultrasound. All his fears of being like his birth father resurfaced with scratching, poisoned claws. After a few weeks of scattered sleep, Rowan reconnected with his therapist. Many clinical psychologists also underwent therapy every now and then to help deal with the emotional rigors of working with clients. Talking with both his therapist and Augie helped him work through those fears before Luna arrived. He still asked his dad for advice since parenthood was ever-changing.

"Really?" Rowan couldn't help the breathy wonder in his voice.

Claire nodded, a smile growing as she set her palm on her belly. "Do you think Augie would like that?"

"Are you kidding?" A laugh punched out before he remembered Luna was slumbering atop him. "He'll be ecstatic," Rowan said, quieter.

His gorgeous wife simply beamed. He'd always loved Claire, but he was surprised how that love grew and changed over time, strengthening every minute.

Taking his steadying hand off their daughter's back, Rowan tilted Claire's chin upward for a kiss that never landed.

Instead, the bus suddenly lurched to a stop. Luna fell backward, nearly colliding with Claire's belly. Rowan reacted in time to guide their daughter sideways so she didn't crush her unborn brother. Luna burst into tears, her head lulling backward off their knees. Both packs, which had been stacked neatly, sprawled over the aisle when Luna went full flaily tantrum. Once Rowan had righted the packs, tucked Luna into his lap, and apologized to the other travelers, he glanced back up at his wife.

Claire subtly shook her head, her lips trembling with a suppressed smile. "What am I going to do with you?"

Ever since that day in the rain, the answer to this playful question remained the same.

Love me.

His grin was automatic. "You already know the answer to that."

Acknowledgements

So many wonderful people made this book possible. First, a loving thank you to my developmental editor Rachel Garber. She always has my back and points out when I've missed something. Thank you to my beta readers Lisa Wittrock and Louise Morris for reading this book and giving feedback while under a time crunch. A huge thank you to Jenn Lockwood for her immaculate Copy edit—working with her is a complete joy every time.

I'm grateful to Dr. Jacqueline Fulcher for helping me understand clinical psychology in order to write Rowan's profession. Enni Tuomisalo once again brought my characters to life by designing the cover. A big thank you to my incredible ARC team for reading, reviewing, and shouting out my books. Your enthusiasm is like a bright spark of starlight, and I'm so grateful for you.

Last year, we took our daughter to the children's hospital and walked out with a celiac diagnosis. Like Claire, our daughter didn't have any gastrointestinal symptoms and hadn't suffered bone loss yet. I've learned from other mamas of celiac kiddos that broken bones can often be the first symptom. When I asked my daughter if I could use her story in a book, she was ecstatic. I hope when she's old enough to read this, it'll make her smile. Thank you to the rest of my amazing family and my friends for your continued support. I couldn't do this without you.

To you, my reader, I'm so happy that you chose to spend your time with this book. I loved Rowan and Claire's story, and I truly hope you did too. Thank you for being here!

About the Author

Laura Langa is an award-winning sweet romance author. She strives to write stories that pull at her readers' heartstrings and create relatable characters you can't help but root for. Laura loves trees and all things green, hates flossing but forces herself to do it every night, drinks tea—not coffee, and believes that salt air can often cure a bad mood.

Visit her website at www.LauraLanga.com
Subscribe to her newsletter for the latest details at www.LauraLanga.com/Newsletter
Follow on Instagram and Facebook @LauraLangaWrites

www.ingramcontent.com/pod-product-compliance
Lightning Source LLC
Chambersburg PA
CBHW021235310726
48971CB00006B/1830